ECHOES ON THE ROCK

JANA J. DEARDEN

For my Waldensian ancestors.
May their echoes never die.

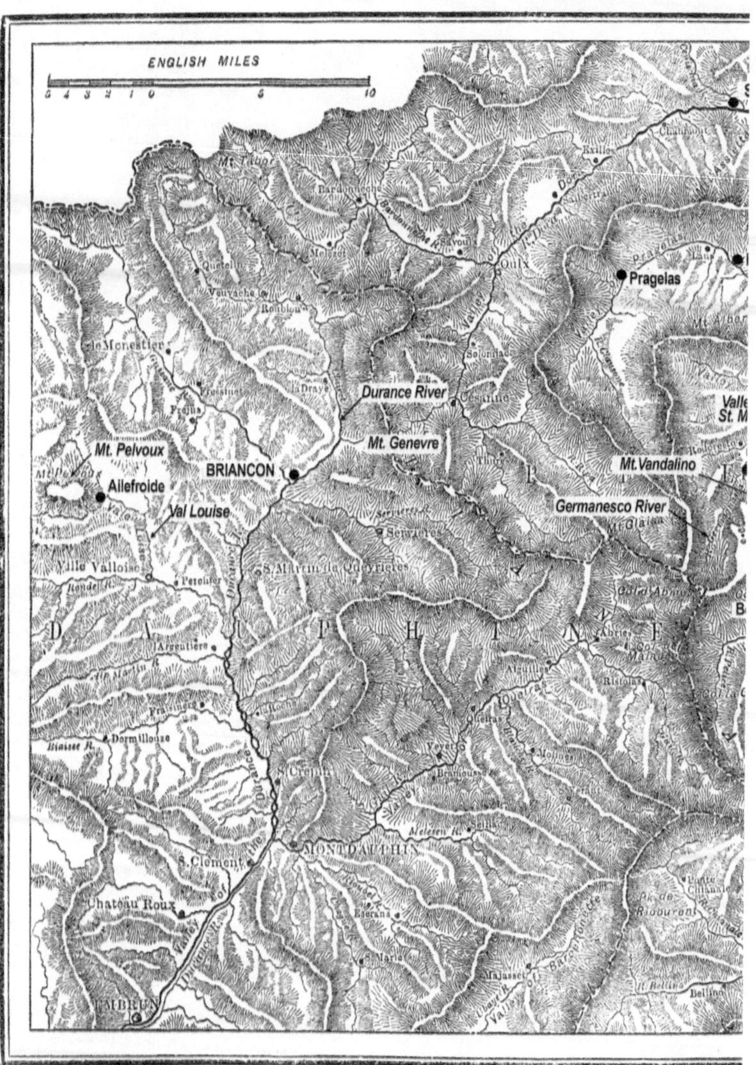

ENGLISH MILES
5 4 3 2 1 0   5   10
Mt. Pelvoux
Ailefroide
BRIANCON
Val Louise
Durance River
Mt. Genevre
Pragelas
Mt. Vandalino
Germanesco River
MONTDAUPHIN
EMBRUN

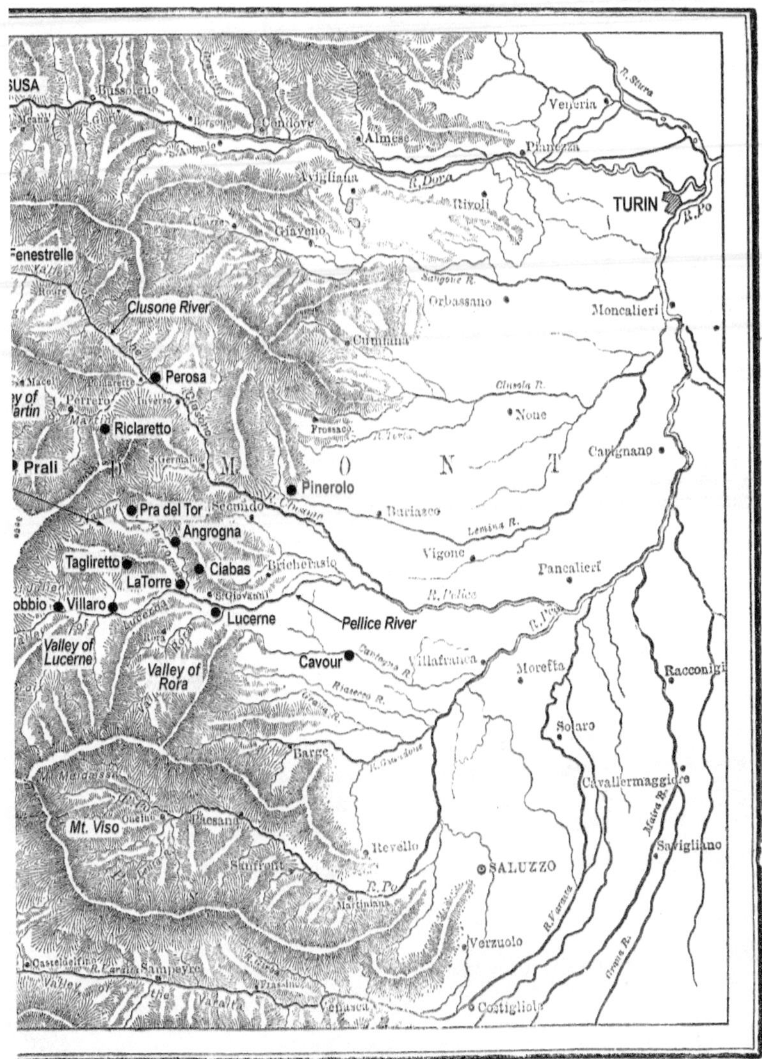

DENSIAN VALLEYS.

PART ONE

While night engulfed the cities of Europe, the brave Vaudois kept their lamps lit. The rock whispers the tales of those who passed, to those who have the ears to hear. Listen.

LENA

La Tour Pellice, Piedmont Valley,
Italy, June 1487

Tradition was strong in the valleys of Piedmont. The people clung to the stories of their fathers, as the chestnut tree clung to the chiseled rocks of the canyons. And it was a precarious hold indeed.

Madeleine's heart nearly beat through the walls of her chest as she huddled with her family in the dark cave, surrounded by the rocks that had protected their ancestors for generations. The villagers had spent the night pressed together like that in the cold darkness, hushing the children, rocking gently, and waiting. Madeleine couldn't help but doze a little. It had been such a long night when they ran for their lives from the army of the Pope's men. At seventeen, she felt responsible for keeping her younger siblings safe. This was not the first time they had hidden in the rocky caverns above their homes, but it was a tradition she would rather have left to her ancestors.

They always knew they were different, that they were special. The Lord's apostle himself had come through their valleys, had taught them in their homes, and they had not forgotten. The Vaudois would never forget.

A little light gleamed through a slit in the rock above, and she could make out her mother, grandmother, brother, and sister on the ground next to her. Only her grandmother was alert, and her eyes found Madeleines'. In those brown depths, she saw long-remembered pain, as much of her story was unspoken between them, too horrible to be uttered.

As the light grew brighter, those around her stirred. The horn sounded that all was safe, and the villagers exhaled together. There was no rushing to the entrance, no panic, the elders of the village exited first as was their due, and then the women and children who had sheltered there.

They returned to their rock and slate homes in La Tour Pellice. Madeleine hurried up the wooden steps to the second story, where her family had always gathered to eat and pray. Madeleine, or Lena, as her family and friends called her, just wanted a moment to catch her breath. She continued to the third-floor loft, where much of their food was dried and stored. Lena opened the thick wooden shutters at the north end of the house. There was a perfect view of the Cottian Alps and their neighbor's slate roof which was even with the wandering mountain path below.

The breeze was cool and ruffled her dark hair. She had large brown eyes like her grandmother, and high cheekbones like her mother. Lena was petite, only about five feet tall, but she was strong and could carry heavy loads up and down the mountain to their home.

She could see the deep valley cut through by the rushing mountain river, with Mont Genevre rising before her eyes and leading to France. Her people were the Vaudois or sometimes referred to as Waldensians. And in that moment, Lena wondered why they couldn't be left in peace. For as long as she could remember, they had worshipped God in secret. Secretly studying the scriptures with her family at home and on occasion, secretly meeting with the congregation in the same cave above her home where she had just found refuge.

Last week her family had even attended mass with her Catholic neighbors to avoid suspicion. Their beliefs were not sanctioned by the Roman Catholics, and so they were branded heretics by the pope.

Her quiet reflection was interrupted by excited voices downstairs, and she quickly went down to find her brother Peter, who was reporting on what happened when her father met with the Pope's representatives. He was out of breath from running up the mountain. His hair was sticking straight up because he always ran his fingers through it when he was nervous. At sixteen, he was taller than Lena and looked much like his father.

"Father and the other men have gone to Roccomaneat to defend the valley long enough for us to escape. I have come here to get you Lena, Joseph, Marie, mother, and Grandma Jaquet. We need to get to safety in Pra del Tor as soon as possible," he said, as he began gathering their weapons, bows, bucklers, and lances.

"What happened at the meeting?" asked her mother as she, too, began gathering food and utensils in cloth bags.

"Father and Brother Campos went out at dawn to meet with their leader. It was the papal legate Cattaneo himself!" Peter exclaimed in disbelief. "Father asked them not to condemn us without listening to our beliefs and assured them we are Christians and faithful subjects to the duke. He said it was a quest for power that was bringing them to our valleys. Brother Campos told them to beware of calling God's anger down upon themselves by persecuting us for no reason."

"How did they respond?" Lena asked, trying to imagine her father standing bravely in front of such a group of hostile men.

"Cattaneo shouted an oath, and his men began to laugh. Then father said, 'If it is God's will, all the forces you have assembled will avail you nothing.'

No more talking was needed. Grandma Jaquet brought her cooking pot. As they exited their house, they were joined by others from their village evacuating to the mountain retreat. Shortly, they reached the base of Roccomaneat, the high ridge where their men planned to make a stand.

"I will take Grandma and the children to the Pra del Tor, you two stay and help your father and the others," said her mother. Lena was surprised. She hoped to fight for her valley however she could but had not expected her mother to allow it. She hugged her family, assuring her mother that she would be careful and that all would be well. She wanted to be brave but never imagined in her wildest dreams that troops would come to her valley.

Lena had always heard that the lofty mountains surrounding the valleys on the Italian side of the mountains, where they lived, made them much harder to invade. While the valleys on the French side were more separate from one another, making them easier prey for the Pope's army.

Their village was at the intersection of her valley of Angrogna and Val Lucerne, which ran east to west along the Pellice River.

Directly north of Angrogna lay the Val Germanasca curving to the east and intersecting with Val Pragelas. East of that was Val Perosa and the town of Pinerolo. Her people knew the secret mountain passes by heart, allowing them to travel and communicate with one another.

Lena and Peter began the climb that would take them to the rocky knoll of Roccomaneat. She remembered happier days of chasing her brother up the trail and challenging him to a duel to be king of the rocks. Now they moved quickly up the path, united to defend their home. As they ascended the ridge, the valley laid out before them in all her glory. Lena loved this view, the glint of silver from the river below, the green valley nestled between wooded hills that climbed ever steeper. All looked peaceful from here. But today, things were not peaceful.

"Peter, Lena, come help us with these!" It was her father, he was a small, dark, wiry man. His face held some wrinkles from time and worry, but his brown eyes had always twinkled. Now he was serious, "stack as many rocks as you can here, next to this boulder," he instructed.

"Father, how are you?" Lena, who could barely contain her emotions, ran forward and embraced him. His tunic was streaked with dirt and sweat.

"I am fine, my dear; there is no need to worry," he said kindly, scanning her face, "but we haven't much time. Let's get to work." Lena swallowed the lump in her throat as she started collecting rocks. At least his tunic was not stained with blood yet, she thought.

They handed out breastplates covered with chestnut bark to all the men and boys on the front line. And as much as Lena wanted to believe in peace, it seemed they must fight. After the rocks were stacked, she joined some women and children who were clustered behind the front lines of archers. They had not had time to escape the path of the oncoming army.

Lena had always dreamed of doing heroic things like Esther in the Bible, standing up for her people against significant odds. But until today, her heroics had been small efforts to daily serve her family and quietly read her scriptures.

"We will be alright, Lena!" exclaimed her neighbor Sister Revelli as she squeezed her hand. "Our men have trained well, and our cause is just." Sister Revelli was an optimistic and prayerful woman. Several years ago, when Lena and her brother had been very sick, Sister Revelli had come to their house and promised they would all recover. While Lena appreciated her faith, she was afraid it might not be enough. The lump in her throat moved to her stomach as she saw Cattaneo's army coming toward them down in the valley.

"There are so many of them. They looked like locusts in the valley."

"Then, perhaps we will drown them in the Pellice River," said Sister Revelli with a little laugh. They didn't have to wait long for the locusts to come.

DANIEL

Lyon, France, June 1487

The crowd was quiet as Daniel took his mark and brought his bow forward. He could visualize the arrow going exactly where he wanted. A bit of side wind ruffled his hair, but it was a clean release.

"Hit!" The judge's voice rang out. Now he just had to wait for Johanne's shot. The crowd was a bit restless, anxious to crown a victor. Johanne took aim.

"Hit!" The two arrows stuck out of the target bird suspended from the clock tower. They were the only two left in the tournament that had lasted four long hours. So, there would be one more round. Daniel and Johanne were instructed to move forward forty steps. This shot was the most challenging. Now at only ten paces back from the tower, the target was literally towering above them. Daniel supposed this skill might someday be helpful in a battle situation.

As he took his stance, he realized this was the most important shot of his life, but he wouldn't let himself think that now. He must be calm and contain all his emotions, he was good at that. He took aim, willing the arrow upward.

"Hit!" called the judge. Hearing that, Daniel finally exhaled, and the crowd cheered. Now it came down to Johanne's shot. As he took his mark, Daniel didn't want to watch, but it was his future after all, so he faced it drinking in the crowd, the clear blue sky, the heat, and the arrow streaking upward.

"Miss!" The crowd went wild, cheering, jumping, and tossing hats into the air. Johanne clapped him on the back, and others surrounded him, lifting him up and carrying him forward to get his trophy and the prize money of 50 francs! He had never seen that much money. This had been his dream for all of his eighteen years, or at least as long as he could remember. And it felt as good as he had imagined.

The festival continued in the streets for hours, with vendors selling all manner of food and crafts. Daniel was carried along in the wave of people dancing in a long line through the streets and haggling over prices. The pungent smells of sweat, smoke, and slowly souring meat hung in the air. Daniel and his new-found friends celebrated well into the night. He finally fell onto his straw mattress as the first light bloomed on the horizon. He allowed himself a moment to think of his father and hoped that he would have been proud.

His father, Louis Reynaud, had served in the first Free Archers militia, supplementing the family income with the four francs per month for his service. Daniel had been proud to see his father dressed in his coat of mail, jerkin, and helmet heading off to fight for France. The pride was all that sustained him when his father failed to return home. He had been twelve then. By the time he was fifteen, his mother and sister were gone. They had died when the devastating sickness hit his hamlet.

He arrived in Lyon a few months ago and spent some of the last of his money on a meat pie from a local vendor. Johanne sold him the food and noticing him eating greedily. He asked if he needed work.

"My father needs someone reliable to open his shop and deal with early customers while he bakes. Are you interested?"

"Definitely!" he replied. So now Daniel slept above the shop in the third-floor attic with Johanne, happy to have a friend who shared his passion for shooting.

That night, his eyes lingered on the bow as he put it under his mattress. His family was gone. He wished things were different, but today he had made his mark in the world, and hopefully, his fortune was just around the corner.

The new day dawned even brighter, clothed in his recent glory. Out in the courtyard, he poured a jug of water over his head, rinsing dirt and sweat from his face and curly brown hair. Anything seemed possible to Daniel as he walked down the narrow, cobbled streets, joking with Johanne and eating a fresh pear from the market. Eventually, they ended up in the main square and approached the cathedral, where a small crowd had gathered to see the latest papal bull attached to the door. Jostled a bit, he found himself at the front of the group where the priest was reading the notice.

All Catholics of Savoy, France, and Italy were invited to take up the cross and fight against the "malicious and abominable sect of malignants," the Vaudois heretics in the Piedmont valleys. All who answered the call to fight this pernicious heresy were "absolved from all ecclesiastical pains and penalties, general and particular."

Daniel thought for a moment, the "Vaudois," where had he heard that name before? Then he remembered something his mother had said once about meeting Vaudois missionaries at a neighbor's chalet.

The Pope's message also promised a remission of all sins to anyone who should kill a heretic. He said if the Vaudois refused to recant, they would be "crushed like venomous snakes." The bull went on further to "annul all contracts made in favor of the Vaudois and forbade all persons to give them any aid whatsoever, empowering all persons to take possession of their property." The notice was signed and sealed by Pope Innocent VIII of Rome.

"This is just what we were looking for!" exclaimed Johanne, pulling Daniel away from the crowd.

"What do you mean?"

"A chance to prove ourselves and make a good wage, not to mention the adventure of a war," Johanne could hardly contain his excitement. "You heard it. There will also be property to be divided among the victors! What could be better?"

Daniel could feel his friend's excitement and the intensity of the crowd. He had dreamed of fame and fortune and never being hungry again. Was this what he had been waiting for? Or was there more to his dream?

MATTEO

Pinerolo, Italy, June 1487

"This is my brother, reporting for duty, Sir." The captain looked him over. Although he was only fifteen, he was stocky and strong and looked older.

"He should work out," said the captain. It had been his brother's idea to join Albert Cattaneo, appointed by the Pope to lead the fight against the Vaudois. He was already training with the army. Now Matteo Gerard was waiting to be outfitted for his new position as the standard bearer for the Piedmont troops. His brother Lorenzo was the one who usually got all the attention. He was smart and talented, as his parents always told him. That left Matteo to assume he wasn't smart or talented.

Cattaneo had spent the past two years as the official inquisitor for their district. Matteo was familiar with his work but needed help understanding the problem. As they walked back to his brother's tent, he hoped Lorenzo could answer his questions.

"Don't the Waldensians claim they have followed their fathers' religious traditions for centuries?" asked Matteo.

"I don't know anything about their beliefs. But I am honored to be chosen to combat this heresy in whatever way I can, and I hope I can count on you?"

"Of course," said Matteo, who only wanted to make his family proud. Apparently, his brother believed they could do much more to get the Waldensians to return to the church.

"It's time to increase the penalties for their actions."

"I've seen offenders of the faith in the town square wearing a yellow cross on the front and back of their clothing," said Matteo.

"Yes, but more must be done to send the message that we will not tolerate these heresies," said Lorenzo, obviously exasperated. The brothers did not spend much time together, so Matteo held to every word his brother shared with him. Most importantly, he would do almost anything to be like him.

"Maybe they should be thrown in prison at the first offense to discourage the others," offered Matteo.

"That would be a good start!" replied his brother. Matteo glowed with the belief that his brother liked his suggestion. "The independent ideas of that Priest Bonelli caused most of the problems. When he rejected the supremacy of Rome and the force of papal decrees."

"He taught that to his congregation?" Matteo was shocked.

"Yes, he was eventually silenced, but that is the sort of thing that encourages these heretics to speak out," he paused. "But now that military intervention is authorized, we have nothing to worry about."

Matteo, his brother, and the rest of the soldiers made camp with Cattaneo in the south at Pinerolo, Italy. Hugo de la Palu was appointed the commanding officer of the French troops to the north. Their goal was to attack from these two opposite points and advance until meeting in the centrally located valley of Angrogna, and there deal the final blow to the insidious heretics of the valleys.

DANIEL

Lyon, France, June 1487

Daniel and Johanne had successfully joined the free archers, thus securing a military wage. They had been assigned to their company and had been encouraged to attend mass before marching with the army in the morning.

Daniel, Johanne, and a few others from their company pushed through the massive wooden doors and entered the dark confines of the cathedral. They moved hesitantly forward as none were used to this environment, and the light from outside had made them temporarily blind. Johanne took charge and steered them toward an open pew. Most of the crowd was silent, with a few hushed whispers. Daniel peered through the tall screen separating the priest's domain from the crowd in the nave. Two large candles were resting on the altar, and a life-size statue of the Virgin Mary was above and behind the altar. The priest began reading from the Bible. It was in Latin, so none of the congregation could understand what he read. Daniel looked up at the massive arches, which were overwhelming in their grandeur. He estimated the ceiling must be 30 meters high. He felt small and insignificant.

Daniel's mind began wandering. He remembered his last time in the church vividly. He had come to see the priest to request the burial of his mother and sisters. He had taken most of his mother's savings from under the hearthstone at his home. And in case that wasn't enough, he had also brought her holy relic of straw from the manger of Jesus. The priest took the money and the relic in exchange for the burial, although chastising him for relinquishing such a holy relic.

He and others in his village were not impressed with the example of the priests and clerks, who taught chastity, but were not chaste. He had also seen priests who were forbidden to have but one mass per day repeat the Introit and split a mass into six, collecting an oblation for each. Daniel himself could not take the Eucharist as he had no offering of bread or wine to pay for the privilege.

The church bells ringing brought him back to the present as the congregation prayed together. The priest and some deacons received the Holy Eucharist, the bread and wine literally transformed to become the blood and body of Christ. Most parishioners received it only on the holiest days, as they did not consider themselves worthy at other times. The congregation who had stood returned to their pews and the priest blessed Daniel and his fellows in their crusade against the heretics.

MATTEO

Roccomaneat, Italy, June 1487

Matteo knew the plump, pale-faced Cattaneo didn't care much for battle. He preferred to stay in the background and have his commanders do the dirty work. Commander Mondovi, a large muscular man with a dark, swarthy face, led his contingent. A career soldier unconcerned with the apparent superior position of the Waldensians on the mountain. Matteo did his best to stay out of the fray of the battle. But he also had a great view of the action.

The Piedmontese archers fired the first volley. A few arrows landed behind the Vaudois, who sent their own wave of arrows. As Cattaneo's troops tried to gain ground, the Vaudois men sent some rocks rolling down the hill. The men lost their footing, forcing them back a bit. The path up the mountain was too steep and narrow for the horses. After a few attempts, the Piedmontese soldiers were forced to use the infantry. Barricades of rock and timbers slowed the troops, and the battle went back and forth for some time. Matteo's troops would gain some ground upon the mountain and then be driven back by rocks and arrows. There was intense fighting as the women and children cowered behind the rocks.

Suddenly, some of Cattaneo's men fighting with swords broke over the ridge. They had managed to get a ladder up against the hillside, where they pushed back a group of the Vaudois men. Then, hand-to-hand combat broke out between those who had climbed over the ridge and the Vaudois. Some Vaudois were fending off the swords with large, sharpened sticks or poles. The clamor of the fighting men mixed with the sounds of women screaming and children crying. A middle-aged woman fell to her knees, "Oh, Father, do not forsake us!" she cried. The rest of the women and children also fell to their knees and cried together.

"Oh Lord, help them. Please save us!"

The troops at the base of the high ridge heard their pleas echo on the rock. Commander Mondovi, mounted upon his horse, led the laughter of ridicule that rippled through their ranks.

"Did you hear that?" they all cried. Mondovi raised the visor of his helmet and lifted his face toward that God to whom the prayers were directed.

"By my word, you shall be saved with a vengeance!" he yelled. Just as the words escaped his mouth, an arrow shot from the ridge pierced the center of his forehead, embedded in his brain, and he fell with a great crash from his mount.

Matteo stared in disbelief. Some soldiers ran to his aid, but most stood stunned. Was this some form of sorcery? Had the Vaudois somehow bewitched the arrow? Those who were closest to the commander turned and fled in terror. Others were confused by the terror on their comrades' faces but were unwilling to stick around to find out why.

At that very moment, a volley of arrows rained down on the confusion, and the Vaudois chose to descend from their high ground. They rushed forward, and Matteo and the rest of the soldiers fled as one body.

LENA

La Tour Pellice, Italy, June 1487

As news of the rout of Cattaneo's troops at Roccomaneat spread up and down the valley, Lena's family returned to their home. A large bonfire was built that night as the villagers celebrated together in the center of town. Rough wooden plank tables were laden with chestnut cakes, apple hand pies, cheese, fruit, and bread to share together and rejoice in the kindness of their Heavenly Father in hearing their prayers. They knew that only through His strength would they be able to conquer their enemies and live in peace.

Lena joined a group of friends most she had known her whole life, except for Martha Peyronel, whose family had recently moved to La Tour. They regaled each other concerning the events of the day and their part in the fight.

"Pierre Revel is the man who killed their commander," Lena shared with the group.

"I knew if anyone could make that shot, it would be him!" exclaimed Thomas Malan, "people say they've never seen anyone with talent like that since "Old Bear" Bertoch.

"What happened to Old Bear?" asked Lena's friend Catherine.

"He hasn't been seen for a while now," replied Thomas. "It used to be my mother would put out a bit of cheese and bread up near that cave he was said to sleep in."

"I guess what happened made him lose his mind," commented Catherine.

"He wasn't crazy," said Lena firmly, "although what he lived through would account for it. He was my uncle."

"What happened?" asked Martha, who had only lived in the village the past year.

"Well, Uncle Bertoch and his wife had been married just five years when the so-called 'purge' of the heretics commenced from Turin. They came to the village when Bertoch was on the mountain hunting. They carried off his four-year-old daughter along with five other children from Pramollo. They said they would be raised by Catholic families and saved from a heretic life."

"His poor wife Lydia," said Lena, continuing the story, "when Uncle Bertoch came off the mountain from his hunting and found out there was nothing he could do, she was inconsolable. He found her wandering the village many nights, looking for her lost child. He would bring her home and put her to bed."

"One day, she wandered off, and they found her drowned in the lake," added Thomas. Her friends had all grown quiet. They all knew, of course, the history of their people, the countless sufferings, imprisonment, and deaths by burning, all because of their faith, because they were different. Lena remembered her mother saying what a beautiful singing voice Lydia had and how the community had lost an angel that day.

"Bertoch was never the same," said Thomas. "He left the church, went up the mountain, and found his cave. I don't know if he ever found peace."

As Lena sat gazing into the flickering fire surrounded by her family and friends, she felt a serene peace and wished Uncle Bertoch would someday feel that same peace again.

DANIEL

Val Louise, Dauphine Alps, August
1487

The morning mist clung to the mountains as Daniel and his troops marched through Briancon. It melted with the touch of the sun and revealed the limestone cliffs behind. He heard the Durance River gnashing its way through the gorge. They passed fertile green fields as they headed south and made their way to Val Louise.

The village was deserted; all had escaped before them. Daniel had seen the dust of traveling carts and the heretics as they rushed to their mountain caves. Their lookouts had reported lines of people on the narrow cliff path loaded with parcels and carrying their young children. They had been given every opportunity to recant or surrender, yet they remained on their steep path. Daniel could not understand it. What could make them act so foolishly in the face of such a great army?

The army continued toward the Ailefroide. Walnut trees shadowed the path. They moved along the foot of a prominent ridge toward the junction of the streams descending from the mountain glaciers. As Daniel ascended the hill, he saw the Grand Pelvoux mountain. The peaks looked like six or seven thousand feet of rock cliffs reaching toward the sky. The main army camped at the base of the rocky trail. Their commander, Hugo de la Palu, ordered one-hundred troops up the steep slope.

As the afternoon wore on, Daniel ate some bread and cheese that he had scavenged from the village. Suddenly a cracking noise like thunder erupted in the canyon. Rocks and boulders of all sizes were raining down from the heights above. Daniel lunged under a wooden cart, narrowly missing a rock as big as his head. His heart was pounding as he listened to rocks rolling and bouncing off the mountain, hitting their targets with a thud or a scream. As he crawled out from under the cart, he saw boulders of all sizes scattered around the camp. He heard the commander's orders ringing through the canyon,

"Pull back, pull back!" Only half of the troops returned down the path, some carrying their hobbling or bloodied comrades with them. There was a man near Daniel who was shouting for help. One of the boulders had pinned his leg. Daniel found a stout branch and levered it under the rock; as he pushed down another soldier pulled him free. From the look of things, it seemed impossible to overcome the superior position of the heretics. That night a war council was held in Palu's tent.

Daniel and his comrades tried to sleep nearby in the rocky glen.

"Are you asleep, Daniel?" asked Johanne.

"No, I was wondering what we can do to fight these people?"

"If you ask me, they are crazy, and deserve to die! They would listen to the bishops if they knew what was good for them."

Daniel thought about his own struggle to listen to the bishops and his belief in his own strength.

"They must think they are stronger," he responded.

"Stronger than the French army?" Johanne was disgusted, "then that is their mistake if they believe in the strength of this cave." Daniel watched the shadows of the officers in the light of the lanterns on the tent wall. He was having a hard time forgetting the recent shadows of flame on the houses at Val Fressineres, the valley they had just come from. Some of the people there would not recant their religion, at least not until Palu set fire to their houses, some with the families still inside.

As he tried to sleep, he kept remembering the feel of the torch in his hand, and the order he had received to set fire to the cottage. He heard the crackling sound as the fire took hold and the voices of the family frantically yelling through the smoke, "We recant, we recant!"

The soldiers awoke early. The tent was still in the darkness of the mountain. Palu had summoned Johanne and two other leaders to his tent. As Daniel and the rest of his unit dressed quickly, they did not have to wait long for their orders.

"I am to lead a group up the side of the rock, away from the trail, and we'll approach the cave from above," Johanne reported. "Palu believes they will never expect an attack from above their position." The men murmured their questions about the feasibility of such a plan.

"I will take fifty of you, and mountain climbing experience would be a plus," he added. Daniel was one of the first ten to volunteer, this was the kind of challenge he enjoyed. Thirty others were recruited from their unit, along with ten additional troops. Daniel had a few supplies, rope, and his dagger, as they quickly began their ascent of the mountain through the boulders and crevices.

The contingent worked their way climbing carefully from rock to rock. Daniel was able to chip some handholds with his axe. It was quiet except for the sound of rushing water in the stream now perilously far below. The sweat dripped into his eye, but he didn't dare change his hold on the rock. It seemed like hours had passed. Finally, there was a yell up ahead as Johanne reached the top. Daniel focused on the rock in front of him, his fingers held onto the ledge, and with one last push, he swung his legs up to collapse at the top. How many hours had it been? The sun was high in the sky now. The good news was they were above the cave.

"Did they really think they could hide from Palu?" one of the soldiers muttered as he passed Daniel.

"It won't be long now!" exclaimed Johanne.

"Secure the rope, Daniel; we can descend from here," ordered Johanne. Daniel grabbed the end of the rope and knotted it to a large tree and, for good measure, to a large boulder that didn't look like it was going anywhere soon. "We'll have to go silently one at a time."

Daniel was the last to descend the rock face, hand over hand, on the rope. They were on a ledge just above the cave now. The plan was working. Daniel could see Palu moving in from below, from his perch just above the cave entrance. Many troops scattered along the switchback trail below, using the boulders put in place to stop them as shields. Daniel saw they had slowly gained more ground and were waiting for the signal that all was ready from above.

"Good, let's secure five ropes up here, and we'll send five of you down at once. When you're free of the rope, we'll send down the next group," explained Johanne. "Have your knives ready!" he hissed. "Daniel, we can use your strength to help lower the men." He took up his position at the rope. Johanne gave the signal to Palu, and the men jumped over the edge of the rock. He believed Palu was right, and the peasants would never expect an attack from above over the formidable rock face.

There was screaming and yelling below. The Waldenses stationed at the cave entrance were surprised and then panicked. Daniel watched from above incredulously as some tried to flee and fell to their deaths on the rocks below. Johanne and the other men made short work with their knives of those still fighting. Within fifteen minutes, the troops from below had made their way up the path to secure the cave entrance. Those not killed had retreated inside the cave.

"Let's end this now!" yelled Palu, "gather some wood!" Daniel and those at the top of the ropes gathered wood or cut branches of new growth on the trees clinging to the rocks nearby. They tied the bundles together. Daniel looped some of them across his body and descended to the cave mouth. Soldiers pulled the bundles from his body and feverishly stacked the wood piles at the cave entrance.

"What are we doing?" Daniel asked Johanne, "Is there to be no surrender?"

"They have had time to surrender," replied Johanne. "Palu said we are to end this!" Daniel moved off to the side of the cave as other soldiers pushed forward with torches.

"The Heretics will learn their lesson today!" he heard among the yells of triumph. He was feeling no victory. There had been no battle. The wood caught fire, the smoke was dark and dense as it filled the large opening of the cave, and the fire licked toward the dark recesses inside of the cave as the smoke preceded it. He watched in horror as the smoke did its work.

Suddenly, from the depths of the cave, a teenage boy came running toward them. He held a hatchet with both hands above his head. He was screaming, "The light that shineth in darkness!" As he emerged from the smoke coughing, Palu extended his foot in front of the staggering boy and succeeded in tripping him. As he fell to the rocks below, the men laughed. Daniel felt sick; this was no fair fight. He retreated from the cave as the smoke continued its work.

Later that evening, bonfires blazed in the camp at the foot of the great mountain, and good wine flowed.

"The smoke killed every heretic in the cave!" said Johanne as he met Daniel at the bonfire. "Palu said almost 3,000, including children."

"We don't have to worry about their pollution in this valley again," chimed in another soldier, "and they had enough supplies to feed our army for months." The two went off, arm in arm, to join the party. Daniel retired to his tent. He was alone and had never felt more alone than he did at this moment. His mind raced along with his pulse. He had not signed up for this. Fighting men in battle was one thing; murdering women and children in cold blood was another. The commander seemed less interested in his skills as an archer and more interested in his skills with a torch! What was he going to do?

BERTOCH

Val Louise, Dauphine Alps, August 1487

Paul "Old Bear" Bertoch heard the soldiers before he saw them. He was out hunting in the high country where he had killed a chamois and laid it across his shoulders. As he made his way through the forest to the path, he heard talking and stopped abruptly.

"This is a waste of time," he heard one man say, "if they weren't in the cave, I'm sure they've got the message loud and clear!" he laughed derisively.

"We have our orders," this came from an older man, "and we'll burn the rest of them out if we have to."

Bertoch retreated carefully back up the ridge. From that vantage point, he could see a dark column of smoke piercing the sky from the direction of Ailefroide. So, he thought, the Pope's men were back in the valley again, bringing death and destruction. He hoped to live the remainder of his life in solitude, separated from his kinsmen, the Vaudois, the Piedmontese, the French, and the Catholics, who were all his enemies. He just wanted to be left alone, and now he stumbled upon this!

He felt anger bubbling inside. He knew he could easily get past the scouting party and back to his cave undetected. He had spent his life being undetected. He had mastered the art of invisibility, and he liked it. But what of the other villages to the south? Did they know of the impending danger? And what of his birthplace La Tour? He still had some family members there. Surely, they would be safe, as many mountains separated them from the cave of Ailefroide. As his mind dwelt on these thoughts, his feet took over, leading him toward his cave, which was in the same direction as La Tour.

Arriving home, he quickly cut up the meat he was carrying. Even in his hurry, he would not waste food. He cut it into thin strips and layered them in salt before closing the barrel. He grabbed a bag of chestnuts and some dried fruit for his journey. There was one man he could speak with in La Tour, and he would do his best to find him alone. He did not want to talk any more than necessary.

As he prepared to leave the cave, his mind would not stop. The Popes continue to persecute them, he thought. It wasn't enough that they kidnaped and disinherited their children, confiscated their goods, condemned innocents, imprisoning and executing them as well. All this he had experienced. But the wound still fresh in his mind was the memory of the burial of his beloved Lydia. The Catholics had forbidden him to bury her in the churchyard. So, he had found his own special place in the corner of a meadow near two chestnut trees whose branches had intertwined. You could not tell where one ended and the other began. This had pleased him.

After they had taken his daughter and he lost his wife to her grieving mind, he could not live with his kindred Vaudois. He did not believe in a God that would allow such pain. But he also could not join with the Catholic persecutors, they might be his neighbors, but never his friends. So, he lived apart, answering his own conscience.

LENA

La Tour, Italy, August 1487

The villagers of La Tour knew the danger wasn't over, but they had bought some additional time. Before any more preparations for battle, they yearned to come together on the Sabbath to commune with God. Lena and her family dressed in their best clothes, and Lena removed her ever-present apron. The apron used for collecting berries in the summer and ripe chestnuts and firewood in the fall. She took a little more care with her long dark hair, carefully braiding and smoothing it under her clean white cap.

They waited until night enclosed the valley and they kept lights burning in their homes. Then, small groups climbed the mountain to the cave above the village. They left their houses at different times, a pattern followed at several places along the valley, with some meeting together in their homes. Lena's family gathered around the entrance to the cave. Lena's friend Susanne greeted her warmly.

"I heard what your father did. He was very brave!" she exclaimed.

"I know," said Lena hugging Susanne, "He thinks he didn't do anything that anyone else would have done." Susanne was several inches taller than Lena. They had been friends since they were young and had many adventures exploring their mountain together.

"Come on, girls, it's time for the meeting," called Madame Jaquet.

Some torches had been lit and placed in holders along the wall. At the front of the cavern room was a simple wooden table, laid with two large wooden cups of sacramental wine and thinly sliced bread, all covered with a cloth of white linen. Lena and Susanne sat on the women's side of the room while her father and brothers sat on the other. Their bishop, or as they called him Barbe or Uncle Malan, stood and addressed the crowd.

"As we have been greatly blessed this past week," he said, "let us now pray together." He bowed his head, as did all those gathered in the church, "Our Father which art in heaven, we beseech thee, that according to the promises which thou hast made, thou wilt be among those who are gathered in thy name. Since we are about to read, hear and meditate upon the Holy Scriptures, enlighten our minds, and purify our hearts, so that we may understand and receive the things therein. We say these things in the name of our Savior Jesus Christ, Amen."

Lena felt grateful the Lord had heard their prayers and protected her father and her family. Barbe Malan then read the first three chapters of Paul's epistle to the Ephesians, concluding with Mathew 21:22; *"And all things whatsoever ye shall ask in prayer, believing, ye shall receive."*

The congregation nodded to themselves. Most of them, including the children, had memorized the book of Mathew, and many other Bible texts. Lena decided she would study Mathew more during her reading time that week. She was anxious to know what else the Lord had planned for her. One of her two closest friends had married last year, and Susanne was anxiously awaiting the return of Lena's brother Michel from his mission to Germany. Lena thought she would like to teach others to read and write, as she was taught, but also had learned a great deal about healing with local herbs, and her father said perhaps she would be a healer like her aunt. She noticed her little brother Joseph lying under her father's bench. He wasn't wiggling about, so she assumed he had gone to sleep.

The group began quietly singing a hymn, and the Barbe read from 1 Corinthians concerning the sacrament. They took the bread in remembrance of Christ's body, which was broken, and the wine in memory of his blood, which was shed. The Barbe admonished them not to take the sacrament if they found themselves unworthy, then the group came forward two by two to partake. The congregation sang one last hymn, and their voices blended in perfect harmony. They were united in their love of the pure gospel of Jesus Christ and in the belief that their God knew them and would assist them during this trial. Barbe Malan then addressed them and offered a closing prayer. As Lena left the cave, she thought of the words that inspired her people: Lux lucet in tenebris, "The light shineth in darkness." Please, God, she thought, let your light lead us through this dark time.

DANIEL

Near Fenestrelle, Dauphine Alps,
August 1487

The plan had formed as Daniel lay sleepless in his tent. He decided the best thing to do was fake his own death. In the morning, Daniel was joining a small contingent that Palu had ordered over the Alps to continue the raiding and burning of all the Vaudois villages in their path. The raging torrent of the Chisolm River would provide the perfect excuse. He would volunteer for sentry duty, and during the long night, as he went to fill his canteen, he would lose his footing in the dark and fall into the river. No one would be surprised to never see him again after that.

He would follow the riverbed for a time and then move upward on the mountain. He was counting on the fact that his comrades loved drinking and celebrating at night, and he should have several hours head start as they broke camp. He also supposed he could move quicker alone when not hampered by mules carrying supplies. Part of him wanted to tell Johanne of his plan, to save him from any pain his actions might cause. But he felt that their minds and hearts were already separated. Johanne gloried in the soldier's actions, while Daniel had nightmares.

A hundred troops set out the following morning, and by the time they reached their camp that night, Daniel was fairly confident in his plan. He succeeded in securing the night duty on the river side of the camp. The crashing of the water and rolling of boulders in the torrent would have surely drowned out any call for help that he may have uttered during the night. Daniel layered his shirts and added a few extra provisions to his shoulder pack. He left his helmet at the river's edge and crept back into the brush along the bank, making his way quietly away from the camp. He planned to go in a different direction than his former comrades hoping to alert some villagers in time to avert disaster.

His course took him over towering cliffs that looked down on verdant valleys dotted with cattle. There were times he stayed on the path, which wandered next to a river, and other times he veered off over the mountain hidden by the pine forests. The stars in their vast array were more stunning than the cathedral ceiling.

As morning came, he let himself feel a wave of relief for his successful escape. He had just shouldered his pack and rounded a bend of the river when he came face to face with two Vaudois working in the cornfield.

"Halt!" The command came from the older of the two men. "Why have you entered our valley?" Daniel quickly put his hands in the air to show he intended them no harm.

"Are you a scout for the French? Asked the other, who Daniel could now see was a bit younger than himself and had stepped forward as though to protect the older man. Daniel had never wanted to scare them.

"I have left my troops and am here to warn you. I want no part in their actions!" exclaimed Daniel.

"How are we to believe you?" asked the older man. Daniel thought he must look quite a sight being dirty and exhausted from the climb to their valley and coming upon them so abruptly. He thought his only chance with them was to be as honest as possible.

"Even now, the forces of the Pope's army are descending on your valleys, hoping to surprise you and attack from the north and the south. I did arrive here with the French contingent from the north, but I hope to exit in a far different manner. I can only hope there is some better use of my skills here in your village, and perhaps I can ease my conscience and forget the horrors I have witnessed by helping save your families." There was a long moment when the two men eyed him carefully. What would happen if they didn't believe him? Then, finally, they looked at each other and seemed to take him at his word. The older man nodded.

"Alright then, let's take you to the Barbe and see if we can find a way to secure our hamlet."

Bertoch

Near Villar Pellice, Piedmont, August 1487

Bertoch chose the path of least resistance. He crossed to the east side of the Durance River, planning to stay away from the French troops. He headed south, traveling mainly at night. He made his way through the mountain pass at Colle de la Croix and followed a trail that would take him to the Pellice Valley. He reached Bobbio, and to his amazement, the streets and houses were empty. Nothing was burned, so he assumed he was ahead of the army. He continued toward Villar Pellice but had only gone half the distance when he heard the sounds of a great concourse of men. Leaving the path, he climbed a steep embankment, finding refuge high above where he could observe the progress of the marching army. They marched six abreast row after row, until he stopped counting. They passed him at twilight, and he quietly made his way along the mountain using brush and trees as cover.

Approaching Villar Pellice from the east, he noticed a few inhabitants huddled together near the center of town. There was smoke coming from a barn. As he stepped into the failing light, the group looked at him in terror.

"I come in peace," he said, holding his hands open to show no weapon. "I was trying to warn the villagers," he continued.

"We have been warned," said an old woman who had just joined the group.

"Are you Vaudois?" he asked.

"No, we are Catholic, but it did not matter to those fiends," she said. "When they found the Vaudois had left their homes, and still others had traveled through here, they molested and plundered all those who were left, saying we had allowed the Vaudois to sleep here."

A young boy added, "My father told them we had done nothing to help them, but they would not believe us."

"They discovered five Vaudois hiding in some brush on the hillside, and they carried them off for trial, but even that was not enough to satisfy them," said a man who seemed to be the boy's father.

Bertoch looked at the disorder around him, "Let me help." Some were gathering scattered possessions that were of no value to the mercenaries. Others were staring into space. He searched the nearest house and found a stool and a piece of wood which he hastily fashioned into a bench. He then helped the older woman to sit down, as well as several others who seemed lost in shock. It was dark now, and some men were building a fire.

The young boy joined him as he began to search the houses for food or anything that might be helpful. As he entered the second house, he heard sobbing coming from a darkened corner. Asking the boy to find some water, he entered alone. There was a broken lantern near the door, but he managed to light the candle. He called out, "I am Paul Bertoch. Who is there? Do you need help?"

The shadows stretched out from the candle piercing the darkness and illuminating a young girl. Her clothes were ripped, and there was a nasty gash on her cheek. Her eyes looked at him with fear, relief, and then shame.

"There is no helping me. I am lost forever!" She exclaimed. She seemed worn out from sobbing. He cast his eyes around the cottage and saw a blanket under a bed. He retrieved the blanket setting the candle on the floor. He wrapped the quilt around her shoulders.

"Please let me help you," Bertoch spoke quietly as he did not want to frighten her anymore. "The men who have done this are gone. I will protect you."

The girl's wide eyes looked up at him, and he wondered what he must look like. It had been years since he had seen his appearance in a piece of polished silver. His beard was bushy, and so was his hair, mostly covered by a cap. He was tall and broad, which might be intimidating, but he had washed his clothes yesterday, so he hoped he looked a little less frightening.

She drew her bare knees into her chest, hugging them to her. She also pulled the blanket tightly around her as though to ward off the images in her mind.

"Are you sure they are gone?" she asked quietly.

"Yes, I saw the whole column marching away right in front of me," he said convincingly. Just then, an older woman came to the door in a panic.

"Francesca!" she exclaimed as she saw the girl in the shadows.

"Grandmother, Oh Grandmother," the girl began to cry again. The woman moved quickly to her side.

"I have been looking for you everywhere!" she exclaimed. "What has happened?" Her eyes searched Francesca's face as her wrinkled hand smoothed her dark hair.

"They came in, two men; they wouldn't let me go," at this, her voice broke. Her grandmother held her, Bertoch waited.

"Can you get us some water?" she asked. He went to the door just as the young man returned with a flask of water and a dipper.

"This is all I could find," he said.

Bertoch brought the water to the women, "We will be okay for a moment while we wash," said the grandma.

"I will be guarding outside the door," he assured them.

DANIEL

Prali, Piedmont, August 1487

The two men took Daniel immediately to see the Barbe of the village. They introduced themselves as Monsieur Philippe Monnet and his son Louis. He felt they weren't entirely convinced by his story and wanted another opinion. The Barbe greeted the men cordially and listened to Daniel's story.

He realized he would have to open up to these people more than he was comfortable. Comfortable would not lead them to trust him. Only truth could do that.

"The truth is I came with the Pope's army from France. I was part of the initial attack on the heret—he stopped—on your people. I regret more than you'll ever know that my hand held a torch that threatened and killed defenseless people," he paused, hoping they would accept him. "I now offer my hand and bow in any way they may be useful to help your people survive."

"What can we do to avoid the horrible fate of our brothers?" asked the Barbe.

"I don't think they will be expecting a fight. Now the element of surprise is on your side, you know this valley, and you know which direction they will come. Maybe that can be your advantage."

"Then let's get ready!" he replied. For two days the villagers gathered stones for their slingshots and sharpened their arrows and spears. Daniel worked with the people as they planned to ambush the troops. That night he sat around the fire that burned brightly in the grate of Philippe Monnet and his family. Daniel asked to know more about the Waldensian people, and Philippe seemed pleased to share their history.

"Some believe our church began with Peter Waldo, a merchant of Lyon, who had his own journey to God. He sold all he owned and gave to the poor. He and his followers taught the gospel as missionaries. At the end of the twelfth century, the inquisition drove them out of Lyon. Many came to our mountains and joined us. Our current missionary efforts are a direct result of what they shared about their missionary work."

"I have heard of the 'Poor Men of Lyon,'" said Daniel. "They dressed simply and traveled extensively to share their message."

"That is true; however, our beginnings are much earlier than Waldo," continued Phillipe. "Christ's disciples crossed the Alps through the Montgenevre pass on their way to Gaul in the first century. They were the first to teach the people in Piedmont. Then in the fourth century, we were taught by the priest Vigilantius, who was born in Gaul and was initially a contemporary of the Christian scholar Jerome. Vigilantius based his beliefs on the scriptures and attacked the notion that celibacy is the duty of the clergy. He ridiculed the blind reverence paid to the relics or the bones of martyrs and prophets. He suggested that burning candles, like the Pagans, before their shrines would lead to transgression."

"Many of our people can trace their beliefs back to Claude, the Catholic bishop of Turin in the Ninth Century," said Louis, "He maintained that Christ is the only head of the church."

"Yes," agreed Philippe. "He was a beloved leader. At his death many of his followers were persecuted by popes and princes and driven into the mountains. Their beliefs were preserved from generation to generation down to the present time, passed from father to son and mother to daughter. This church in the valleys of the Cottian Alps has held true to the Bible in faith and practice. These are those who are known as the Vaudois, or 'Those who dwell in the Valleys.'"

MATTEO
Valley of Lucerne, Piedmont,
September 1487

After the disaster at Roccomaneat, Albert Cattaneo split up his army of about 9,000 men, sending soldiers to all the southern valleys at once. Matteo and his banner rode with Cattaneo as he led the largest contingent up to the Val Lucerna. He had hoped he would be assigned with his brother, but Lorenzo was sent to Val Germanesca. Their group met little resistance as all the inhabitants had evacuated to the mountain's higher elevations. They circled the base of the Castelluza, then started up the valley. To the right, a torrent of water poured through a jagged cleft in the rock to join the Pellice River. The thunder of the water made the army quicken its pace. Their steps matched Matteo's beating heart. They marched through soft fields of corn decorated with garlands of grapes. The flat green valley stood in stark contrast to the towering unruly piles and pinnacles of rock jutting from the mountains above. The abundance of mountain springs made the valley glitter like an emerald in the sun.

Matteo was stunned by the beauty, but he was pretty sure Cattaneo noticed none of it. His long face, with his heavy-lidded eyes, seemed to indicate sleepiness. Finally, Matteo and the soldiers arrived at the village of Bobbio, having traversed the intervening miles and finding only stray cattle and poultry.

"What is the report?" Cattaneo asked his lieutenant commander, somewhat peevishly.

"Like the other villages, we've found a few old people who swear on the cross that they are true Catholics."

"Well, I guess we shall see," he replied, a sadistic smile forming at his lips.

Matteo had heard of Bobbio, the small village at the base of a gigantic cliff and the towering Col Le Croix mountains, whose summit led to France. As he lowered his gaze from the cliffs, the lieutenant commander addressed him.

"You there, you're to come with us over the mountains. We want our banner flying as we conquer the valley of Prali." Thus, Matteo was chosen to accompany the 700-foot soldiers led by the lieutenant. Cattaneo sent them north of Bobbio over the highest slopes of the mountain. Matteo felt special. He knew his brother would be proud when he heard Matteo led the troops to victory. He could almost hear the people of the village where he grew up cheering for him as he returned victorious, a hero to the cause.

Looking upward, all Matteo could see was a crowd of immense rocks, one upon another, with no visible means through. But the soldiers started up on the footpath worn by decades of herdsmen tending their flocks. They passed apple, cherry, and chestnut trees but no sign of the inhabitants, only vacant rock houses. No sooner had they ascended one long winding pass than they would face another, steeper and more precarious than the last. The Pellice River was now a torrent of rushing water squeezed between the narrow rock formations. A constant reminder that one misstep on the trail could have them rolling like boulders in the river. Matteo looked toward the horizon, where they saw a cascade of endless snow-capped mountain peaks.

He gasped for breath as they climbed the last hundred yards on hands and knees. Together the soldiers scrambled over a steep grassy knoll, where they, at last, gained the summit and looked down upon Prali. Across the plain were scattered numerous hamlets. The lieutenant and his seven hundred soldiers rushed down upon the mountain plain. The men of Prali were ready to meet them.

LENA

Between La Tour and the Pra del Tor,
Piedmont, September 1487

This time the residents of La Tour headed to Pra del Tor, the safest place they knew, together and united. Lena and her neighbors crossed the Angrogna River and, turning left, proceeded up the valley. They traveled a half-mile through a meadow with fields of corn on either hand, some not yet harvested. Then the path began to get steeper as it rose above the river. Rock cliffs cast shadows along the trail, and a few houses peered out from the foliage. Finally, after about an hour and a half, they reached the pass's summit leading over the hill. Here they stopped, letting Grandma Jaquet and others have a brief rest.

"I am so sorry dear Grandma, that you must make this climb in such a hurry," said Lena, her eyes filled with concern for her beloved Grandma.

"I am a tough old bird," said Grandma, "It will take more than Cattaneo to stop me!" Lena laughed along with her brother and sister.

"Oh, Grandma, I think Cattaneo will be sorry if he ever meets you along this path!"

Lena was so glad her family was climbing together to the Pra del Tor. She had always felt comforted by the nearness of the rock and the strength of the mountain. After their break, they took the winding path among the smaller mountains until they reached the great peak at the head of the Angrogna. There was nothing but sheer rock ahead, with only the narrow gorge cut through from which the river continued its journey. The walking path was now cut into the rock, with the mountain rising perpendicular on the right and the river thundering down on the left.

The company began quietly singing together. Their voices sounded bigger when echoed back to them from the canyon walls,

> *"For the strength of the hills we bless thee, Our God, our father's God;*
> *Thou hast made thy children mighty, By the touch of the mountain sod.*
> *Thou hast led thy chosen Israel to freedom's last abode;*
> *For the strength of the hills, we bless thee, Our God, our father's God."*

The sound of the hymn gave Lena courage as she was again reminded of all her forefathers had sacrificed. She knew the place she was headed on this dangerous winding path was protected and preserved by God. She reached out her hand and touched the cliff wall. It was cold and patterned with dark shadows, but here and there, sunlight pierced through from the top of the canyon, and the diffusion of light lit the particles of air before her face. Opposite her, a small stream cascaded down the chiseled cliff to strengthen the Angrogna. Moving from shadows to sunshine the scene changed until they arrived at a point where the mountain on her right angled into the path, and a massive rock fixed into the side of the river leaned to meet it.

This was the "gate" of the Pra and the only entrance; it was so narrow it would only allow one horse or two men. Lena reached out and helped her younger sister through the gate of rock. She always felt as though she was entering a sacred place. The path opened into a long, green meadow within a majestic ring of snow-capped granite peaks. Standing in the cathedral of their God, they had reached the Pra del Tor or Meadow of the Tower.

There were a few cottages scattered about, some at the base of the mountains. The temple, their largest building, stood to the left of the river. This was where they held the School of the Prophets and instructed the missionaries. Their barbe directed them where to go; some shared the houses, and some pitched tents. Lena's family went to a corner in the temple building.

Lena had been in the building once before. Three years ago, there had been a congregational meeting there just before the missionaries, including her brother, had been sent out. She remembered the hope and joy she had felt there, as Michel and his companion Brother Muston had willingly chosen to go forth and preach the "gospel of the kingdom...in all the world," as it said in Mathew 24:14. Brother Muston was older as there was always an elder missionary teamed with a younger one to help teach and guide them on the journey. Again, she remembered Brother Muston's kindness to her. Once, when Lena was sick, he had stopped by their cottage offering some medicine from his mother, who was good with herbs. She was grateful, as she immediately felt better.

As Lena stood on the wooden balcony of the temple building, she looked out on the secluded valley and somehow felt safe. The stars were beginning to appear, hovering near her face and making the snow glitter before her eyes. She took comfort in knowing that somewhere Brother Muston was leading her brother home.

Daniel

Prali, Piedmont, September 1487

Letting the soldiers think there was no resistance, Daniel and the people of Prali allowed the soldiers to move through the first and second hamlets. They stationed themselves behind their dwellings, rock corrals, and outcroppings. They were armed with their bows, hatchets, swords, slings, and the assurance that their cause was a noble one, fighting for their lives, their homes, and their God. They met the Piedmontese army with righteous anger.

The soldiers seemed stunned, exhausted from their strenuous climb to the valley. Initially hit with a wave of arrows from the archers. Those lucky enough to survive the first attack met with the swords, hatchets and slings of those who knew the terrain over which they were fighting and found every rock precious.

"For Prali, Prali!" came the calls left and right, repeating off the rocks and resounding in the ears of the attackers. The last sounds they would ever hear.

MATTEO

Prali, Piedmont, September 1487

Matteo had become a little more comfortable with the sound of battle, the yelling, clanging, grunting, and screams that swirled around him.

He had charged down the verdant green pasture along with his fellows and held the banner high. The wind tried as it might to pull him and his flag back up the mountain, but he fought to keep it high above the heads of his comrades. And then those beside him began to fall at an alarming rate. His friend Bertran was first with a sword slash to his side. There was nothing Matteo could do. He just kept moving. This fight was unlike any he had experienced before. The attackers did not march toward them and were not assembled in an order that Matteo could make out. Rather, as his men marched toward the village, the rocks and trees came to life and began attacking them! The rocks hurled stones, and the trees shot arrows from all sides. It was hard to know just where to attack.

After the initial onslaught, the villagers emerged through the dust like a vision. Matteo broke off to the right side with a small group, still holding his flag high.

"Stay strong, fight the heretics!" the comrade at his near left yelled and then fell silent. Matteo hazarded a quick look and saw he was down, pierced with an arrow.

The group he was with ran toward the river. The sound of the water drowned the shouts of the men around him as their pursuers overtook them. That was the moment Matteo dropped his flag and ran to the boulders strewn along the bank. His heart was beating so hard he could not tell the difference between his heart and the sound of the tumbling water. And then he was tumbling, half jumping, half falling into the current. It carried him downstream about a quarter mile. He saw a small outcrop of dirt and snow ahead, and he half swam, half walked, and crouched beneath it with the icy water up to his thighs. And then he waited.

DANIEL

Prali, Piedmont, September 1487

As the dust settled, the villagers were jubilant. They fell to their knees as one, praising God and thanking him for his deliverance. Daniel's arm was sore from clasping handshakes with many people who praised and blessed him. These people were so sincere Daniel hardly knew what to think. They had trusted him, brought him to their fireside, and listened to his ideas to secure their hamlet. Suddenly, he had more friends than he could imagine.

He helped his new friends as they began the grim task of removing 700 bodies. Some near the river were rolled in and carried away; others were gathered and burned together, taking the better part of two days. They also held burials for the handful of men they had lost. Then, on the third day, as they prepared to feast together in the valley, the scouts spotted a soldier staggering toward them from the river. Daniel moved toward the man.

"Halt! What is your business here?" He saw the soldier was unarmed, wet from the waist down, and shivering.

"I have come to turn myself in. I've been hiding near the river," said the man raising his hands above his head as his teeth began to chatter. "I need help...," he managed the last words before collapsing. Daniel called out, and soon several men were carrying the man, who was just a boy, to the nearest house.

Pierre Chatelain and his wife ushered them in as they stripped the wet clothes from the boy and wrapped him in layers of blankets. Madame Chatelain roused him enough to spoon some hot broth down his throat. The couple tended to him all through the night. He was sleeping peacefully in the morning when Daniel, and Philippe Monnet, came early to the door to inquire about the soldier.

"He has not been awake enough to find out any information," said Monsieur Chatelain.

"I wonder if he knows he is the only survivor of his troop?" said Daniel.

"I think not," answered Madame Chatelain, "who would ever believe such a thing if they had not seen it with their own eyes?" The boy, roused from his sleep, looked up at them.

"Are you saying there is no one left but me?"

"Yes, that's right, you are alone," replied Daniel.

"I can't believe it!"

"Yes, it is hard to believe," agreed Daniel.

"You are welcome to stay here among us if you are done fighting," offered Monsieur Monnet. Daniel wasn't surprised at that, after how they treated him.

"No, I need to get back," he replied. "I need to find my brother; he will know what to do."

"What is your name?" asked Daniel.

"Matteo, Matteo Gerrard."

"Well, Matteo, perhaps you can tell the story to your comrades. Maybe then they will leave our valleys in peace," said Monnet.

The boy's strength returned, and the village sent the lone man back to Bobbio on the long path he had recently climbed with his comrades. The message they sent with him was: "If your men return to Prali, they will die!"

BERTOCH

Villar Pellice, Piedmont, Italy,
September 1487

Paul Bertoch stood guard at the cottage, he had been too late to make much difference, but he was determined to do what he could. The girl, Francesca, came to the door of the cottage, she wore a clean dress, and her hair had been freshly braided. The older woman stepped forward.

"Thank you for helping us," said the woman, "My name is Madame Russo, and this is my granddaughter Francesca.

"I am happy to meet you both," said Bertoch. "I wish I could have done more." Saying those words, he remembered other times of sorrow when he had felt equally useless.

"Are the silkworms alright?" asked Francesca. She hurried to a grove of trees behind the cottage, where the others followed her.

"This is out of the way of the destruction; I think the bushes hid the mats," offered Bertoch. They were standing among the trees, which stood about 40 feet tall. The larvae mats were stacked vertically on a wooden structure. Francesca moved forward to examine them and ensure no harm had been done. She walked to a nearby mulberry tree where she picked a handful of leaves and began shredding them.

"May I help you," asked Bertoch, hoping to do anything positive for the girl.

"Yes, they have missed several feedings, so we will have to see they are now well supplied with leaves." He worked alongside her spreading the leaves close to the worms. He had heard that the breeding of silkworms was helping support many farming families in the area.

"Francesca is one of the best spinners in the village," said Madame Russo. "We sell her silk thread to merchants in Turin for a good price."

After finishing their task, they walked to the center of town, most of the cleanup was finished. The soldiers had taken whatever foodstuff they could find, even things, from their pantry shelves. Together, they gathered what was left and prepared a meal for everyone over the fire in the square. Bertoch joined them and explained that he planned to travel to the Pra del Tor and see if there was more he could do to help his kinsmen.

Francesca looked down at the crackling embers of the fire, "Would you take me with you?" she asked.

Madame Russo gasped, then she looked at Francesca.

"For years, I have been stubborn," she said slowly, "several times when the soldiers have come to our valleys, my Catholic neighbors have sent their daughters away with the Vaudois to their safe valley for protection."

"Nona, it is not your fault," protested Francesca. Madame Russo raised her palm silently, asking her granddaughter to let her continue.

"I always believed that the army of the Pope would never harm our Catholic children," she continued, "And I did not want to be separated from my Francesca. Unfortunately, I was wrong, and my stubborn belief has now hurt her far more than any separation could." As she finished, she looked sadly at the girl who had come to her side. She smoothed her dark hair softly with her wrinkled hand.

"Please forgive me, Francesca, for failing to protect you as I always swore to do," tears now rolled down her cheeks.

"Grandma, I don't blame you. I wanted to stay."

"Will you take her to the Pra?" The woman turned her face toward Bertoch beseechingly, "I know she will be safe there with some of the other women and children of the village."

Bertoch looked at the women; he knew for himself the brutalities of the Pope's army. If she were his daughter, he would never hesitate to send her to the Pra. But he had lived alone for so long he wasn't much for companionship, and traveling by himself, he could move much faster. Yet, looking at her sad and haunted eyes, he knew he could not refuse. Perhaps he may find some redemption in protecting this child as he could not protect his own.

MATTEO

La Tour, Piedmont, September 1487

Matteo Gerard returned to Bobbio after a long and lonely descent on the narrow path he had climbed just a week earlier with his fellow soldiers. The guards at the Bobbio outpost welcomed him but were alarmed at hearing the message that he brought.

Matteo could tell that they didn't quite believe him about the death of all the soldiers. He rested a fortnight to regain his strength and then joined most of the troops heading back to Lucerna. He had just reunited with his brother when they heard the latest news that Hugo de la Palu and the French forces had pardoned hundreds of heretics in the north. They had seen the error of their ways after a great fire killed over 3,000 people.

"Just last night, we captured one of their missionaries trying to go up the Angrogne valley," exclaimed Lorenzo, who camped along with Matteo. "They look like normal tradesmen, but what they're trading is dangerous! They usually travel in twos, but I guess somehow, they became separated in the dark. I think we got the leader, though he seemed old enough to know better." Matteo wanted to tell his brother about what had happened to him, but Lorenzo was too excited about the captured missionary to listen.

Lorenzo was assigned to help escort the prisoner to his court appearance. He asked Matteo if he wanted to come along. "You spent some time with these people. Maybe you can tell when they're lying."

The prisoner was a slight man of about fifty years, his hair was greying, and he had a beard. Matteo noticed he was dressed rather shabbily and wore leather sandals on his feet. The inquisitors were all seated around a circular table when they brought the prisoner in and placed him on a small wooden stool in the center. The Popish Court of Ecclesiastical Justice consisted of ten men of rank, bishops, counts, nobles, four priests, and the chief inquisitor.

"Please state your name for the court," the secretary asked, who was busy scribbling notes.

"Jean Louis Muston," said the man.

The head inquisitor, the Bishop of Turin, stood and spoke to Muston. "You are brought here on serious allegations, we have been instructed to ascertain your guilt," the inquisitor paused as though to let the word "guilt" sink into those present and then continued. "The witnesses against you have said that you were caught teaching contrary to the faith of Christ. Therefore, we will question you on certain points of doctrine." The bishop seemed anxious to get on with the business at hand. He resumed his seat and began his questioning.

"First, concerning the body and blood of the Lord, is it better consecrated by a good man or a bad man?

"He who receives it worthily is saved, but he who receives it unworthily gains damnation," answered Muston. "The consecration is performed not more effectually by a good Priest than by an evil one."

"Is it true that you receive neither the Law of Moses, the Prophets, the Psalms, nor the Old Testament?" asked the bishop.

"We receive Moses, the Prophets, the Psalms, and the Old Testament, only so far as the several books of the entire volume have been respectively attested by Jesus and the Apostles."

Louis Muston continued, "In addition we reject every doctrine not founded upon them, or which contains anything contrary to them. We condemn all the ceremonies, traditions and ordinances of the Roman Church."

The secretary was scribbling intensely as the bishop continued his questioning.

"Do you agree that through the process of Transubstantiation, the bread and wine from the Lord's sacrament are converted to the actual body and blood of Christ?"

"We do believe that our Lord Jesus Christ ordained the sacrament of the Supper, which is the giving of thanks and the remembrance of the death and passion of Jesus Christ, to be celebrated in the Assembly of God's people. The bread and wine are distributed and taken as visible signs and representations of holy things. That is, the body and blood of Jesus Christ offered upon the cross for the remission of our sins and the reconciliation of mankind with God.

We do not believe the opinion of some, that the true and natural body of Christ, exists or is hidden in the bread of the Supper, or that any transmutation of the one into the other is affected. This opinion is repugnant to the work of God, and contrary to the articles of our faith. The Lord Jesus Christ is present in the sacrament of the Supper, by the power, and presence of his Spirit in the hearts of his elect and faithful." There were loud murmurings now among the judges as he finished his answer. The Chief inquisitor stopped for a moment as one of the judges handed him a piece of parchment.

Matteo was surprised at the quiet confidence of Louis Muston as he lifted his head and met the eyes of his accusers. Matteo himself was trembling at the words that Muston had spoken. They seemed to pierce his soul, and although the room was cold and drafty, he felt a warmth within his breast. What courage this man showed. He seemed like the soldiers going to battle he had recently served under.

"Do you deny that you have conversed with evil spirits?"

"I profoundly deny that and would like to see evidence of such a charge," answered Muston in a strained voice. One of the judges passed another parchment to the bishop.

"Are you willing to swear to the truth of your statements?"

Muston looked thoughtful, "I cannot swear, as my conscience will not allow me to do such." Mateo remembered a conversation at the hearth of the Vaudois when he had overheard a Monsieur Cardon say that judges were using the Vaudois' reluctance for any swearing against them at the trials. The judges consulted together, ignoring the prisoner and the others in the room. Then, after about twenty minutes, they returned to their seats.

The head inquisitor now addressed the prisoner, "However misguided you have been, we are willing to spare your life if you will recant your faith and join us for a celebration of the Holy Mass."

At that, Muston rose from his wooden stool, "there are no conditions on which I will recant my faith," replied Muston.

The inquisitor looked disgusted, "Then you leave us no choice, but on these counts of the indictment, we pronounce you heretic, and you hereby are sentenced to be burned at the stake forthwith."

Matteo gasped. He had been treated kindly by these people of the mountains. Although they were his enemy in the battle, they had bandaged his wounds and fed him at their hearth. He had seen no signs of Satan within their midst. But the council had made their decision, surely, they could not be wrong? Lorenzo stood, and Matteo followed; as they reached Muston, he turned to those who would take him to the jail and the stake.

"I believe in God, the Father, the Son, and the Holy Ghost. I believe there is a resurrection of the blessed of God, to possess the kingdom of Heaven forever, and a resurrection of the cursed of God, to perpetual fire and torment. It is an honor for me to die in the ministry of my Lord Jesus Christ who sent me upon His errand amongst the people. I am but a humble teacher and follower of my Lord," with that, he turned and walked out of the chamber, and his guards followed him.

BERTOCH

Lucerne Valley, Piedmont, October
1487

Bertoch had been taking care of himself and only himself for so long that he was a little afraid of his new traveling companion. However, he couldn't see any way to refuse Francesca and Madame Russo's request, especially considering he had arrived too late to aid anyone in the village. He felt this was one thing he could actually do, and as Bertoch had once been a man of action, he must act.

Madame Russo had quickly helped Francesca pack a small bag of clothing and personal items. She had also found a bottle of grape juice, some cheese and fruit.

"Monsieur Bertoch, you promise to deliver my granddaughter safely to the Pra?" She peered into his face, her brown eyes looking into his character, his commitment to his charge.

"On my honor and in remembrance of my dear wife, I shall keep her safe," he replied. Francesca clung to her grandmother, who whispered some comforting words in her ear.

"This will be only a short time; soon, we will be together again," she promised.

As they headed west out of the village toward Lucerne, Francesca called back, "Watch over the silkworms, Nonna!" Dusk was approaching, and Bertoch wanted to cross just on the outskirts of Lucerne in case any guards were posted. They would then turn to the northwest and head up the valley of Angrogna while the troops were busy in Bobbio and elsewhere.

Francesca followed him quietly. There wasn't much of an opportunity for talking, which suited Bertoch. The girl was well-behaved. He guessed she was fifteen or sixteen years, she did not complain about the pace he was taking, and he tried to remember to take more breaks than he usually planned. At dusk, they waited for darkness to help guard their steps past Lucerne. They took off their packs and leaned against a large rock shaded by some brush. Francesca took the fruit from her pack and offered some to Bertoch, which he found he was eager to consume. They ate in silence, which was normal for Bertoch. But he wanted to put the girl at ease. So he asked, "Where are your parents?"

"I believe they are dead," said Francesca, "at least that is what they told me at the convent." Bertoch thought she seemed somewhat detached from the story.

"Oh, you lived at the convent near Turin?"

"Yes, until Nonna Russo brought me with her to Villar Pellice."

"How long ago was that?" asked Bertoch.

"About three years."

"How long did you live at the convent?"

"As long as I can remember, I was five or six, and I remember waking in the night and crying for my parents. Nonna Russo was one of several nuns who cared for me. She was by far the nicest." Bertoch felt sorrier for the girl than he had before.

"You were mistreated there?"

"Just endless hours of study and prayers, there were a few other children I took lessons with as I got older, some older and some younger. The boys and girls were taught together for a while," she continued. "I argued with Sister Grassi, who always said, 'my tongue would lead me to Satan!' I had many questions about things but received few answers."

"Yes, that has been my experience with the Church of Rome," said Bertoch softly. "I, too, have received few answers."

Darkness had settled around them as they spoke. They shouldered their packs together and, skirting the lights of Lucerne, traveled northwest up the Angrogna valley without meeting anyone.

LENA
Pra del Tor, Piedmont, Italy, October
1487

Everyone had been hoping for news of the battle. Waiting anxiously for messengers, and then suddenly, there came six men from Prali. The scouts first spotted their group coming from the northern mountains to the stronghold of Del Tor. It seemed like a special occasion. Lena stood next to her father as the men came closer. One man walked a little ahead of the group. He seemed confident in his stride and anxious to speak to the elders. Another man stepped forward, and her father seemed to know him.

"How are you, Monsieur Monnet?" he said as they shook hands.

"I am well. I am well. Partly because of this young man who saved Prali from certain destruction!" He stepped back and gestured the man forward. "This is Daniel Reynaud. He came to our village as a stranger to warn us of our peril," said Monnet, "I introduce him now as a friend." Daniel shook her father's hand, and then his eyes found Lena's. They were light brown, with flecks of light dancing in them; he seemed to look right into her heart, and for a moment, Lena almost forgot to breathe.

"This is my daughter Madeleine," her father gestured as Daniel bowed to her. He had a bag slung across his broad shoulders, a large bow, and a bag of arrows tied at his waist. He looked up again, and for a brief minute, it was just the two of them on that bright, windy day. It must have been only a moment, Lena thought later, but it just seemed longer.

Later that night, Daniel and his group told the story of the battle of Prali to many people gathered around a bonfire to hear it. Lena watched Daniel as he spoke about helping the people prepare for the surprise attack. He didn't seem boastful but also didn't show too much emotion. He stated the facts as he saw them unfold. The story was unbelievable, how they had killed the seven hundred soldiers who had come to slaughter them. It was like the stories her Grandmother Jaquet told, but before, they had just been stories from the past, and now, they were real. It seemed like Daniel had looked right at her when he explained how he got to the valley and expressed sorrow for the unwarranted attack on the people, but she wasn't exactly sure.

Over the next few weeks, they prepared for the winter snow. Word had reached them that Cattaneo had fallen back and secured most of his troops at the head of Lena's valley at Lucerne. His soldiers drove wooden pikes into the ground surrounding the camp and secured their guardhouses and advanced posts; it seemed he would not proceed in the season of snow.

Daniel proved very useful to the many families gathering corn and chestnuts for the winter. On one such expedition, Lena found herself working side by side with Daniel under a large chestnut tree.

"Your people are different from any I have met," he said.

"Do we have horns, as you have been told? Lena joked. Daniel blushed, and she was sure he had heard the stories before about the heretic people of the Alps.

"I don't think I ever believed that! Please don't judge me by what I was." His eyes pleaded with her, and as his hand grasped the basket Lena was carrying, his fingers brushed hers. Her heart grew light, and she was afraid she was blushing too.

"I guess you know better now," she replied.

"Tell me why you are different?" he asked, "why has everyone accepted me at my word?"

"We try to be true disciples of Christ and we live by the words of the gospel and the apostles," Lena explained. "We have studied their words and actions our whole lives. Our ancestors wrote down much of the New Testament. Those manuscripts have gotten smaller and smaller so that we could hide them easily from those who condemn us."

"That part, I think, is so amazing," he said. "I think it would be so wonderful to study the scriptures for myself, to learn what they say to me!"

"Why don't you borrow our family scriptures? Then you will know for yourself what they teach," Lena offered.

There was a long pause before Daniel answered, which made her wonder if she had been too bold.

"I can't read much," he admitted, "except for the signs in the market advertising food!" They laughed.

"Oh, I'm sorry," she paused a moment. "I would be happy to teach you if you're interested, you could come by after dinner tomorrow."

"Nothing would make me happier," said Daniel with a little bow. But, although he said it would make him happy, he looked pretty worried to Lena.

"I am afraid if you know all that I have seen and done, you won't want to talk with me," he continued getting very quiet, "you won't judge me worthy."

"It is not my place to judge you, but I believe what I see for myself." Lena spoke frankly now, "You have left those who would do evil, and I hope you see that we have done nothing worthy of death?"

DANIEL

Pra del Tor, Piedmont, October 1487

The next evening, Daniel and Lena sat close together on the wooden bench by the fire. Daniel was tentatively voicing the words from the symbols on the page as directed by Lena. They had been studying together for about an hour when they took a break. Lena's mother brought them some bread and goat's milk, and Monsieur Jaquet put another log on the fire as he sat down to join them.

"Do you have more questions about our faith?" he asked.

"Yes, actually, I was wondering how the pope figures in all of this?"

"Well, we believe the only successors of the apostles are those who imitate their lives. Those who seek out the riches of the world above all else do not follow the lives of the apostles and are not the true guides of the church."

"I see, and somehow you don't believe in the worship of images. Or that owning a sacred relic from Christ's life will make you closer to him."

"No, we do not venerate images or objects. Following that line of thinking, men might venerate swaddling clothes, mangers, or donkeys because they were associated with Christ. We believe the priests contrived the practice for the sake of lucre."

"It is surprising to hear you say that, as I had always thought it was a strange practice and seemed to be wrong to take money from poor people to buy such souvenirs." Daniel was thinking of his poor mother.

"It is easier to fool those who have not read the scriptures for themselves," said Monsieur Jaquet looking serious.

"We take pleasure in poverty and innocence, which have been a source of strength for us," said Lena. "Well, at least it has kept us humble!" she quipped, and they all laughed.

"But true Christians would not persecute and imprison good people," said her father, "as it says in the *Noble Lesson*; 'By this, we may know that they are not good shepherds: For they love not the sheep, except for their fleeces.'" He paused, "I am impressed with your willingness to do hard things to find out the truth for yourself." Daniel realized he had always had questions. To find out that the answers to these questions really did matter to him.

"Merci, you and your family have shown me great kindness. I hope that someday soon I will know for myself, as you say." Daniel smiled, and Lena smiled with him.

LENA

Pra del Tor, Piedmont, October 1487

Twilight was stretching colorful fingers across the sky, and Lena was helping prepare dinner when she heard a commotion outside. Drying her hands, she ran to the window. Looking out she saw a small group gathered and could make out her father among them. She unknotted her apron and went quickly to the door.

"Lena, it is Michel; he has returned!" shouted her father. She ran forward. Her mother was there, embracing the tall, dark-haired man, who was familiar but different. Her mother stepped back, tears flowing down her cheeks.

"Look, how grown-up you are!" she exclaimed. "I would have hardly known you on the street."

Lena ran forward, and her brother caught her up in a bear hug. She pressed her cheek next to his cloak; how she had missed him.

"Come, come, all of you must come inside and hear his story," said her father as he gestured to the crowd of perhaps fifteen neighbors. Daniel was among the group, having just got off guard duty at the entrance to the valley. Family and neighbors retreated into the college building that housed several families. Dinner was forgotten as they gathered around the fire to hear from Brother Michel.

"I tried to get here as quickly as possible, but it was no easy matter with troops spread throughout all the southern valleys," Michel apologized.

"I am sure you have done your best, but we must ask, are the stories we have heard true about Brother Muston?" asked his father.

"I am so sorry, but they are true," he said, at this some groans and whispers were heard among the group. "We separated just outside of Lucerne, as we had information that someone had informed the local priest of our presence in the village. Brother Muston felt he should go forward as planned but instructed me to go west toward Rora but veer north over the mountain and make my way here. He insisted that I go, we had just parted, and I was one hundred feet up the mountain into the forest when I saw men with lanterns and shouting down below where Brother Muston had been heading." His voice was quiet, a single tear escaped his eye and slid down his cheek, "he saved my life." The men in the room simultaneously removed their hats, and Daniel followed the others.

"Let us bow our heads in remembrance of our noble brother, Jean Louis Muston, a man of faith, who died serving our Lord Jesus Christ." All those present bowed their heads and said "Amen" together.

Michel continued his mission report of the strength of the Vaudois in the towns of Nuremberg, Germany, and Fribourg, Switzerland. The two men had traveled by night and secured refuge by day with those who followed their beliefs.

"In Nuremberg, a group of thirty came to hear us preach at the Reiser home. We told them of our struggles here and offered up prayers on their behalf. Brother Muston prayed for their sins to be forgiven and the peace of God to be with them." He continued, "Sister Frena Wegner thanked us for bringing the Christian truth to her family. She said we had changed their lives for good." Michel was silent for a moment, then said, "she asked Brother Muston to thank his family for letting him come and share this message with her."

"That is a great testament to Brother Muston. I'm sure his mother would love to have you visit her tomorrow," said Lena's mother.

"I also have important news," he reached into his nearby satchel and pulled out a handful of pamphlets. "Our friends in Germany have had these printed up to help spread the good word of the gospel." He passed out a few folios of paper. They were about nine inches wide by twelve inches long. Across the top were the words, "The Light Shineth in Darkness." Everyone was amazed. As Lena rubbed her finger across the black print, each character was crisp and clear, with even lines across the page.

"This is a new method of printing that uses special oil-based ink and small movable metal type. These are printed at a shop in Nuremberg that has been open about fifteen years."

Lena's father took the pamphlet and read out loud:

> *"O Brethren, attend to this excellent lesson:*
> *Daily we see the signs of the increase of evil and decrease*

of good.
These are the perils, which the Scriptures mention:
and the same recorded in the gospels and confirmed in
St. Paul's writings.
No man living can know the hour of his death:
therefore, we ought to fear the more because we are not
sure whether we shall die today or tomorrow.
But when the Day of Judgment comes,
everyone will receive his full payment:
both those that have done evil and those that have done
good.
But whoever wishes to do well must begin with the love
of God.
He should likewise call on his glorious Son, the dear
child of the blessed virgin Mary;
And on the Holy Spirit, who shows us the right way...,"

Her father paused and looked up at the group.

"Ahh, words from the Noble Lesson," said her mother, "that is a good thing to share with others." Lena noticed her father looking at Daniel in the crowd as he elaborated. "This is a poem written by our ancestors almost 300 years ago. The poem has seven sections dealing with the history of the Bible, Jesus' life, the way of true repentance, and the persecution of corrupt papists." Daniel nodded his head.

"It speaks of the many lessons we can learn from the mistakes that various people in the Bible made," continued Lena, "it teaches us about true faith and repentance."

"Please continue," said Daniel, "I would like to hear more."

Her father looked down at the parchment as the group followed along with their copies reading:

> *"Yet the Apostles were so strong in fear of the Lord, and*
> *likewise the men, and women, who were with them,*
> *That they did not leave off speaking and doing for all*
> *that,*
> *Whatever might come of it, so that they might win*
> *Jesus Christ.*
> *Great were their torments, according to what is*
> *written;*
> *And only because they taught the doctrine of Jesus*
> *Christ."*

There was silence as he finished this part of the document. All were thinking of Brother Muston and the price he had paid for speaking his truth of Jesus Christ.

"Is that the end of the writing?" asked Monsieur Valla.

"No, there is some more at the end, from the epistle we sent on our beliefs to the Savoyards," said Monsieur Jaquet. "Here, see for yourselves he said as he passed a few folios out to the group."

"This is wonderful," exclaimed Lena, "and you say they are distributing these in Bavaria and other places?"

"Yes, wherever possible, and still ensure the safety of the missionaries," said Michel.

The crowd dispersed, with a few people lingering to talk and others returning to their temporary homes a few at a time, as they were used to doing so as not to attract attention.

Lena was alone when Daniel approached her to talk.

"I am so happy for your brother's safe return," he said. "I know many wicked things have happened to your people, yet you do not teach your children to hate or despise the Catholics who have done these things?"

"We want them to believe in the good in others, and since we must live as neighbors, it is better not to hate," answered Lena.

"Living among you, I see that your people only want peace and the right to worship in the way you believe is right. These ideas seem good to me, I like being free to think and read the scriptures for myself."

"You seem happier than when you first came here," said Lena. She smiled as she looked up at him and again felt the now familiar flutter in her stomach.

"I am, maybe, happier than I've been in a long time," he replied.

LENA

Pra del Tor, Piedmont, November
1487

Lena and Daniel had managed to squeeze in another reading lesson among all the other tasks they were assigned. They sat together at a table in the corner of the temple building. An oil lamp illuminated their faces and the text in front of them.

"The Lord is my shep...," Daniel paused.

"That's right, just divide it up in your mind into two short words."

"herd...shepherd," Daniel continued, "I shall not want. He maketh me to lie down in green pastures; he lead...," he paused.

"Yes, just sound out the letters," encouraged Lena.

"He leadeth me beside the still waters; he restoreth my soul."

"Good, good," exclaimed Lena. "I must say I am pretty proud of my student. You must be practicing on your own?

"Yes, all of my spare time," he admitted.

"Well, it shows. You should be proud."

"Mostly, I'm thankful. I had no idea how beautiful the written word could be. King David brings our yearning hearts closer to God in his psalms."

"Yes, if I tried to describe it, I would say that the words flow into my mind like a musical stream. Each word lilting upon the next. Winding in a slow eddy and then suddenly breaking forth and cascading over the rocks," said Lena, filled with her love of the scriptures.

"Perhaps considering what we will soon face, we should read Psalm 23:4?" said Daniel, who began;

"Yea, though I walk through the
Valley of the shadow of death.
I will fear no evil: for thou art with me:
Thy rod and thy staff, they comfort me."

"I believe God will comfort and sustain us through this difficult time," said Lena.

"As I read these words for myself, I feel their power. I actually feel God is speaking to me through David," explained Daniel.

"Yes, that is the joy of reading the scriptures for ourselves."

"I can't believe this simple act is forbidden to so many. What a great blessing you have amongst your people."

"Thank you for reminding me," said Lena, "I don't think you'll need many more lessons." They stared into one another's eyes. The lamp cast their shadows on the light plaster wall behind them. The shadows caught the moment Daniel placed his hand over Lena's on the table. Suddenly, Lena felt an electric warmth through her fingers up her arm and into her heart.

"I don't think I want the lessons to end," said Daniel. Lena gulped.

"Well, maybe we could work on past and present tenses," she whispered, not knowing where her voice had gone.

"That sounds perfect," he said as he brought her palm to his lips and kissed it.

MATTEO

Near Angrogna Valley, Piedmont, November 1487

The months were long and cold in the tent camp. Matteo thought longingly of his home with a fireplace in every room. Soon would be the time of the festival. His mother would serve wonderful things to eat. He tried to imagine the loaded banquet table as he ate the dried meat and bread for dinner. He was finishing a letter to his parents:

...there has been a lot of gambling and drinking in camp. A few fights have broken out, but Lorenzo and I are safe. Spring will come, and hopefully we will see an end to this affair.

Sincerely,

Your Son, Matteo

His winter dreams were haunted by the gaunt face of Brother Muston. He seemed more of a goodly man, than those who surrounded him now. But he didn't want to disappoint his brother by appearing weak, so he kept his thoughts to himself.

The two played chess with an old set that Lorenzo had brought.

"Remember when you wanted to be a troubadour?" Asked his brother.

"Yes," he still secretly wished it would come true.

"I guess you were just excited by the singing and dancing at the festivals."

"Mostly, I like the stories they told of the brave knights going off to battle."

"I guess the reality is a little different," said Lorenzo.

"Yes, a real battle is different from the stories," he silently remembered all his fallen comrades. That night he dreamed he was a troubadour. He sang and told stories of the incredible feats he had done. The bonfires were burning bright at the festival. And his parents smiled at him proudly from the audience.

DANIEL

Pra del Tor, Piedmont, November
1487

Daniel felt a bit overwhelmed with all that had happened in a few short months. Here he was in this mountain valley which was truly a sanctuary from the world. Above him was the vastness of the sky; endless peaks surrounded him, whose tops were covered in clouds. He had plenty of time to ponder his life and his purpose. When Daniel left the soldiers, he knew he would never be able to go back to his past life. But he also knew he didn't believe in what they were doing and wanted to be better.

The sun was barely peeking above the high clouds. He sat on a rock by the stream, staring into the watery depths. Suddenly he saw the colorful glint of a fish swimming just under the surface. He became so preoccupied with the fish that he didn't notice Monsieur Jaquet coming toward him until he was next to him.

"Good morning, Daniel!" said Monsieur Jaquet, "how good to see you out this fine morning."

"Good morning to you," replied Daniel.

"May I sit with you a moment?" he asked.

"Yes, please do."

"You have had quite a journey," observed Jaquet.

"That is true. From Lyon to La Pra, it is quite a distance."

"No, I mean the journey of your soul."

"Yes, that is even more true, more than you know," Daniel watched the fish, which for some reason was swimming against the current now.

"Sometimes we have to leave things we love for something we love more," said Jaquet as he turned toward Daniel.

"Yes, I have enjoyed living in the city, where there is always something happening," he stood as though even the towering mountains could not contain him. "I have loved perfecting my skill with the bow with my friends. But I believe I am ready to trade in some of these things for something I love more."

"Is it for a person or a belief?" Jaquet asked. Daniel sunk down onto the boulder, now facing Jaquet.

"That is what I have been contemplating. Has my heart been changed? Do I believe the things you have been teaching me?"

"And what have you decided?"

"I guess I am still pondering what I love most," he replied. Daniel was thinking of his old dreams. He wasn't famous for being the best archer, but the Waldensians cared about him because he had helped save their lives. Somehow that meant more. He also realized that his biggest dream of being part of a family was close to coming true. But with that realization came his fear of losing everything again, and he wasn't sure he could do that.

Bertoch

Pra del Tor, November 1487

Shortly before the winter snows, Paul Bertoch and Francesca Russo arrived at The Pra. Bertoch could not help but notice the surprise on the villagers' faces. He had seen no one for almost twelve years. That, and his unusual traveling companion, surely caused a stir. However, they welcomed him warmly into their midst, and the Jaquet family offered to care for the girl.

They had been in the village for two weeks. When Bertoch approached the door of the temple building, a man transformed. He had shaved his great grey beard and trimmed his brown hair, which had a hint of grey at the temple. He looked much closer to his age of forty-two and was hardly recognizable as the man who had entered the village two weeks before. Lena opened the door and invited him in as he had been asked to dinner.

Francesca came forward, her dark hair hanging down around her face, as she came to greet him. Lena and Francesca had prepared dinner together. As they sat down, Lena shared a story about when her father had made a small sled out of tree bark.

"Father would tie the rope around his waist, and then he could pull me up the path to the village while he also carried wood home."

"That sounds fun," said Francesca.

"Do you have any childhood memories?" asked Lena.

"Not too many, but I do remember once, after a snowstorm, my father made a snow bear next to our house. It was about as tall as a bear cub, and I could ride on top. I had many happy days playing with my snow cub."

Everyone smiled. Bertoch felt all the blood drain from his face.

"What is wrong, Uncle?" exclaimed Lena, who looked at him with concern. He spoke slowly. "I once made a bear cub out of snow for my little girl."

Francesca had closed her eyes as though trying to remember a long-ago dream. Lena got up and rushed to her side just as Bertoch knelt beside her. Her eyes suddenly flew open, and as she gazed at him, a knowledge passed between them. His eyes filled with tears. She was his beloved daughter, and he was her long-lost father. She leaped forward, almost knocking him over, as they embraced one another.

"Is it you, Christine? My dear girl!" Bertoch mumbled over and over.

"Papa, Papa!" cried Francesca.

"Is it true?" He stared in disbelief. His heart was pounding as tears ran down his face. Was he dreaming?

"Yes, it is me I have returned."

Suddenly, there was a great tumult, or so it seemed, as everyone in the room started talking at once. "Where have you been?" "How did he find you?" "God be praised," it was happy confusion.

Finally, it quieted enough that Francesca could be heard, "What did you call me?"

"Your given name, Christine," answered Bertoch.

"I don't really remember that name. I only remember my mother combing my hair by the fire and my father," she paused and gestured, "You, telling a story with the firelight on your face."

"The pope's men took you from the village and said you were to be raised Catholic."

"I remember a large house where there was arguing, and then they took me to the convent," said Francesca.

"I searched and searched for you. I went to the convent once, maybe before you were there," said Bertoch. "They said my only hope was to renounce my religion, and then perhaps God would hear my prayers." He could not help remembering how helpless he felt. How angry he had been at God for allowing this to happen.

"I did not like life at the convent. I longed to be free to roam the mountains that I so loved. Grandmother Russo was a nun at the convent, she joined the nuns after she was widowed, and with no children of her own, she always looked out for me. When she saw how unhappy I was becoming, that it was making me ill, she made plans to leave the service. She had some connections in Turin during her marriage. She had them prepare papers that showed a family relationship between us and then was able to take me with her." Bertoch's tears began to wash away the pain as he held his daughter close. Maybe God had not forgotten him?

"Praise God, she is back in her rightful place," said Monsieur Jaquet. "The Pope's men came to our valleys and stole from us, now they have come again, and one of our daughters has returned."

LENA
Pra del Tor, January 1488

It was early one wintry morning six weeks later when Daniel appeared at Lena's front door. There had been a week of steady snowfall, but now the sunlight was sparkling off the white drifts and the promising blue sky. Daniel asked if she could speak with him for a moment on the balcony. She had grabbed her cloak and scarf and stepped out onto the wooden balcony from which they had a view of the valley and the slate rooftops of other cottages below.

"I'm sorry to disturb you so early," he apologized.

"I was already up attending to Grandma Jaquet. The cold is harder for her these days," said Lena.

"I wanted you to know that I am going to accompany those who are returning to Prali. I feel it my duty to help them return and check on their families before it is too late because of the snow."

"Doesn't father think it is already too late?" asked Lena.

"Yes, well, some have voiced that opinion. But the men are anxious to see their loved ones, not knowing exactly where the Pope's men are, they feel impressed to return now," said Daniel.

"And you are going with them," Lena whispered to herself. She knew this moment would come one day, as she doubted Daniel would want to spend his life in the valleys. But now that it was here, she wasn't sure she could face it.

"Please thank your family for all they have done for me."

"Of course, you have done so much to help us."

"And you, Lena, you have brought me the written word. I can never repay you."

"I don't need any payment," she looked down, as it was too hard to meet his eyes.

"I will return, Lena," he spoke quietly, and he removed his leather glove and took her hand.

"Make sure that is what you want," she said. She looked up then and met his gaze.

"I think my heart will lead me home," he reached out and touched her cheek, pushing back a stray lock of dark hair.

"Please be careful." Then he was gone melting into the frosty air like the morning mist on the mountains.

DANIEL

Alpine mountains above Pra del Tor, January 1488

Daniel headed out into the frigid morning with hope but also frustration. Hopefully, a mountain hike would clear his head, and he would see his way forward. Daniel was frustrated that he hadn't been open with Lena about his feelings. Why was it so hard for him to admit that he loved her? There was so much suffering and pain associated with those he loved. Could he risk that again? And it was complicated. He would only stay if he could embrace her faith.

Daniel felt his place now was with Philippe Monnet and the group who had welcomed him to their community and brought so many possibilities into his life. He was determined to help them return to Prali, and then if this God of theirs were willing, he would come back.

The travel group included Monnet, his son Louis, "Tuck" Aydetti, and three other men who had initially accompanied them from the Pra. They packed their gear quickly to take advantage of the break in the weather, then set out to the northwest. The others had boots like his, with fur skins wrapped around their feet. After a few hours of intense hiking, they had taken their last look at the Pra, now hidden by mountains and trees. It was a tedious climb, and the snow just kept getting deeper. At a few points the snow was soft, and they broke through down to their waists. They were starting down a path on the side of a narrow gorge when Tuck, who was breaking the trail, paused.

"This doesn't look good this way; see where the snow has deteriorated," he explained. "I recommend we take the higher trail up on the ridgeline."

There was murmuring among the group, with somewhat divided opinions.

"That will add hours to the trek, and it will be long past dark going that route," said Louis. The majority of the group concurred. They were too excited to rejoin their families in Prali to listen to Tuck's reasoning. As they started down the trail again, Daniel was now in front with Tuck, the five others in a single file behind.

It was so quiet, as only a snowy mountain can be. The quiet seemed to press on Daniels' ears, creating a sound of nothingness, while his feet kept trudging forward. No one dared speak now for fear of causing the snow to slide. Suddenly, a gust of freezing air blew over them, "Oh no!" shouted Tuck. He shoved Daniel under a rock cleft as a wall of snow came between them. The roar of the snow descended upon them like a vast white wave of power. Daniel crouched against the rock. It seemed like an hour, but it was probably only a few minutes. The thunder of the mountain ended, and it was silent once more, except for the sound of his thumping heart.

As he stood in the silence of the mountain, the ice crystals made a frosty mist around him. He looked through the haze, hoping his dear friends would be on the other side. At that moment, Daniel knew he didn't want to waste one more second separated from those he had come to love. He raised his head as the cloud of white powder settled. There was a smooth slope of mountain from above where the path had been and down the steep ravine. He looked back down the way he had come. What would he do if there was no one there?

Suddenly, he noticed some movement at the other end of the expanse of snow.

"Daniel, are you okay? It was Philippe Monnet, waving both arms. His son Louis was there along with another man. There was no one else in sight.

"I'm okay!" he called back. He looked down the slope thirty feet and saw a gloved hand sticking out of the top of the snow. A rush of adrenaline moved him forward. He thought that could have easily been his glove sticking out of the snowdrift.

"Philippe, hurry, bring the shovel. Let's see if we can save him!" Louis had hurt his arm, but the other three scrambled over the snow toward the outstretched hand. They knew time was the enemy now. Philippe used the small shovel from his pack, and the others dug down with their hands scooping snow as fast as possible. They touched a shoulder, then scraped the snow carefully away from Tuck's face. They hadn't known whose glove it was.

Daniel took a pulse, "he's alive!" With that, they worked harder, even though the snow was hard as clay. But they now had him uncovered except for his legs. While the others were feverishly digging, Daniel tried to revive him, but the force of the snow had knocked him out. Slowly he was coming around, spitting snow from his mouth, and coughing. Daniel gave him a drink from his canteen just as the others freed his legs.

"Is anything broken?" asked Daniel, with concern, as Tuck looked at him gratefully.

"I don't think so. Thank you, you saved my life."

"And you saved mine," said Daniel.

"Perhaps, but I feel like a wagon of boulders ran me over," exclaimed Tuck.

"Can you stand?" Daniel asked Tuck.

"Yes, with some help." The men helped raise Tuck and stood together, looking down the ravine. There were no signs of the other two men. The group made their way to the edge of the debris field from the avalanche.

"I knew it was coming, I felt the gust of air, but there was nothing I could do," explained Tuck. Leaving him in the care of Louis, the three men carefully walked further down the ravine, looking for any signs of the other two in their group. The canyon was eerily quiet now. It was hard to believe everything could change so suddenly and with such force. Two of them broke dead limbs from a nearby pine tree while Philippe used his stout walking stick as they fanned out along the debris field. Careful not to set any more snow in motion, they poked their sticks into the snow. After thirty minutes of a fruitless search, they were exhausted and forced to admit defeat. The gully below them was full of twenty feet of snow.

Feeling helpless to do more, they climbed back to their comrades, where they rested and ate some dried meat and fruit. They gathered around the small fire they had built to help dry their clothes and then discussed what to do next. Did they go on to the village of Prali or back the way they had come? They must get help to traverse the ravine and recover the rest of their party. Unfortunately, they did not have the tools or men to do it themselves.

Since they were closer to Prali, they decided to proceed to the safer path on the ridgeline, where there was rock and hard wind-packed snow. Before leaving the area, Daniel climbed a tree and tied a red scarf to a barren branch. This would mark the place if there were more snowfall before they could return.

After nightfall, the sad little party made their way from the mountaintops into the valley of Prali.

Daniel
Prali, January 1488

Shouts went up as Daniel, and the travelers from Pra del Tor entered the village of Prali. Any contact was welcome between church members who now seemed more separated than usual. The local Barbe came out to greet them and others close by on the street. Madame Monnet ran swiftly to the waiting arms of her husband and son. News of the loss of life in the avalanche spread quickly through the village. Some broke into tears, and others ran to notify the families of the fallen men.

Daniel was exhausted from the journey and sorry about the lost men. The travelers went to the closest cottage, fed, and warmed at the hearth, before being asked to tell their story.

"Let us immediately send out a request for volunteers to search the avalanche site," insisted Monnet. Daniel was sure they would have more help than they needed. It would take several days to organize and pack provisions, and they closely monitored the weather, as no one wanted to risk another life in the process. Daniel was staying with Monnet and his family. In the middle of all the preparations, he came to Monnet, anxious to talk with him.

"I cannot wait one more day to return to the Pra. I have scarcely slept a moment since we arrived, and I don't expect that to change until I can, at last, see Lena and tell her what I know now!" He was pacing back and forth and felt as if he might burst.

"I see," said Monnet thoughtfully, "do you want to tell me?" Daniel started to laugh because the things he was thinking of saying would sound silly to Monnet.

"I was young once," he said as he sat down on the nearest boulder.

"Yes, there are some things I can say. I've been thinking about what matters most in my life," he continued. "As I stood in the snow after the avalanche, I realized none of us know the future. There is no guarantee that our loved ones will be safe. We can only hold them close in the moments that we have. At some point I just had faith that God knew me and knew what I needed."

"Sometimes our path is not what we imagined it would be," said Monnet.

"I never could have imagined mine. But I know I want to be an example for good, and the things I have been learning help me see that I can choose my path. The past doesn't matter if I make better choices going forward."

"Well, it sounds like we better get you home," said Monnet as he clasped his friend by the arm and pulled him into a hug. Daniel had joined the rescue party working on the mountain for a week. Then four of Prali's best marksmen returned with him to La Pra to help in the coming battle.

LENA

Pra del Tor, Piedmont, February 1488

Lena heard that Daniel had returned to the valley. Her family invited him for dinner at the temple building. That afternoon there was a knock on the door. There stood Daniel, who was slightly out of breath and asked if he might speak with Lena outside. She was happy to see him and glad that he had survived the journey. But she steeled herself, not knowing what he was going to say. They started walking together.

"You came back," she said simply.

"I came back."

"What does that mean?"

"It means that I, Daniel Reynaud, believe that freedom is worth fighting for, and I want to be part of it, not an outsider," he stopped walking and turned to her. "I want this to be my life from now on!"

"I am so glad," said Lena, unable to contain her excitement.

"But wait, there is more," he continued.

"Oh no, I don't think I can handle anymore tonight," Lena quipped as she walked away further down the path leading to the stream.

"I must say it now while I'm feeling brave," Daniel rushed after her and turned her toward him. "And this new life of mine, it must include you!"

"Me! You don't need me. You have plenty of others willing to help and guide you on your journey."

Daniel's eyes searched hers pleadingly, "Please tell me you are joking! Surely, you know what I mean," he paused. "I mean, I love you, Lena. Please tell me you feel the same?" Lena smiled, and suddenly she couldn't tease him anymore since he looked a little frightened, waiting for her answer.

"Yes, my dear Daniel, I love you too," she said, clasping his hands.

"You mean it?"

She laughed outright now, "Well, I'm not taking it back!" He pulled her to him and kissed her softly. She held him tight. He was something she had never planned on, but now it seemed they had known each other forever.

At dinner that night, the family celebrated Daniel and Lena and the fact that God had led them to each other.

***

A few hours later, Lena found a quiet moment to speak to her Grandma Jaquet.

"Are you happy about Daniel and me?" she asked as she tucked a blanket around her.

"Yes, my dear. You know I had my concerns. I was afraid it was just your beauty he was attracted to."

"Oh, grandma!" Lena blushed as she sat on a wooden stool opposite Grandma's bed.

"But I have observed him carefully and feel he is indeed sincere. He has had a change of heart from what originally brought him to our valleys. We know all things are possible with God," she smiled.

"Thank you, Grandma," said Lena as she reached out and clasped her grandma's knarled brown hand. "All my life, I have hoped to do some great work that would stand out and be noticed by others. But now I think the small acts we continue to do will be enough."

"It is your small acts of prayer, faith, and service that have made you a true follower of Jesus Christ," said Grandma, nodding.

"Maybe if I just save one soul?"

"Daniel?" asked Grandma, peering at her.

"Yes, possibly Daniel. But maybe those we will influence together."

"Nothing can be better than that," agreed Grandma as she reached forward and kissed the top of Lena's head.

MATTEO

Piedmont valleys, March 1488

The snow was melting, and Alberto Cattaneo was now ready to turn his attention to the Valley of Angrogna, adjacent to where his main camp was entrenched. Matteo knew that Cattaneo expected to surprise the people gathered in their last stronghold, the Pra del Tor, or Meadow of the Tower. This was one of the most sacred spots of the Vaudois. It was here they had their college for tutoring young missionaries, and here also where their Barbes met in council. Their plan to attack the Vaudois north in the Dauphine Alps and south in the Cottian Alps was moving forward.

"Lorenzo, I hope that if one of us makes it home, it is you!" Matteo blurted out the night before the battle.

"Why would you say that?"

"Well, I don't think I would be missed very much. But you, it would break mother's heart." Lorenzo stared at him for a long moment. It seemed he was having trouble speaking.

"Matteo, I would miss you! Don't ever forget that." The next morning, Matteo hugged his brother before they went to their separate garrisons.

There were now nearly 3,000 troops anxious to move into the Angrogna. Some were on horseback, including Matteo carrying their banner. They crossed the river and turned left along the bank as it ascended the valley. The way became steeper until they reached the grassy plateau of the village of La Serre, where they decided to leave some of the horses. The inhabitants were long gone, leaving them little to do there. With every step down from La Serre, a view of the mountains began to open. A large wall of rock could be seen ahead, with peak after peak assembled behind it, like a giant stone regiment. They continued to worm their way around the smaller mountains until the Rocciaglia rose before them. Matteo had heard of the mountain, of course, but even Cattaneo paused when looking up at the fortress before him. This was a mountain spur of sheer towering rock. The only way forward was through the chasm the river had cut at the southern end. All the soldiers were on foot now. Cattaneo turned and addressed the soldiers:

"I intend to make good on my promise to rid the valleys of this continued pestilence. As such, Captain, I want you to lead your troops onward and do not return until every one of the heretics understands what it means to defy us!" said Cattaneo. "We will tear down this place stone by stone if necessary."

"Understood," said the captain, "I will not fail you. This river shall soon run red with the blood of heretics!"

The men moved forward, sensing the blood of battle and anxious for it. There had been too much talking and retreating; now, they could at last move forward and complete their mission. Matteo felt the weight of the wooden pole in his hands as he carried their banner. As they entered the dark canyon, he took one look back. The sheer walls blocked out most of the light and formed a narrow "V" through which he could see others climbing. He balanced the pole as best he could while climbing the steep path. As Matteo turned forward and marched ahead, he wasn't at all sure this would be easy after his experience at Prali.

BERTOCH

Pra del Tor, Piedmontese Alps, March
1488

The Vaudois had prepared for months to fight. Their scouts knew the exact location of the army and kept track of all their movements. Even to those most peaceful in the community, it was apparent that it was either fight for your people and your freedoms or die. So, they had chosen to fight. This time Bertoch would be fighting with them.

Earlier that morning, Bertoch and his beloved daughter met with the congregation in the meadow. Barbe Paschale had lifted their spirits with his words of courage.

"We, pastors, and all officers promise to unite ourselves with one another before the living God, and on the life of our souls, while God shall preserve us, even if we are but three or four. That we may maintain the kingdom of the gospel in these valleys, even unto death."

The congregation then read Psalm 74: *"For God is my King of old, working salvation in the midst of the earth... Remember this, that the enemy hath reproached, O Lord, and that the foolish people have blasphemed thy name. O deliver not the soul of thy turtledove unto the multitude of the wicked: forget not the congregation of thy poor forever."*

Barbe Paschale recalled the many times that God had remembered his people in their times of need. If there was ever a time of need, this was it, thought Bertoch. So he prayed quietly for the people's success and publicly in the palm of this mountain cathedral, which was open to the heavens.

Monsieur Jaquet and Bertoch were leaders in the battle preparations. Since Daniel's return just a few weeks ago, he had done all in his power to help the Vaudois. Rocks as large as melons had been gathered at the edges of the canyon for days now. Others had been busy making as many arrows as possible. All had brought their swords and daggers with them, and many had wooden breastplates, shirts of mail or pieces of armor taken from their enemies.

Bertoch assigned those who would man the top of the canyon with rocks and archers. He stationed others at the opening to the meadow with swords, hatchets, and war hammers to battle those who made it through the ravine. There was another line of archers behind them. Bertoch assigned Monsieur Jaquet to this group, who also carried their swords for close fighting. And Daniel Reynaud was with a small contingent inside the canyon just past the "gate" of stone. He and his fellow archers had found hiding places behind brush and boulders and would shoot at any who managed to make it through the gate.

"Please be careful, father," Francesca said as she gave Bertoch a big hug and kissed his cheek.

"I have not waited all these years to find you, to be separated again!" he exclaimed and then added quietly, "I do hope the Lord will grant us that blessing."

He heard the horn blow, the signal that the army was nearby. There would be another when the army had begun the climb. Bertoch watched as Francesca joined a group of women and children that hurried into the cottages farthest away from the threatening soldiers and back among the rocks and streams.

MATTEO

Pra del Tor, Piedmont, March 1488

The path toward the battle was on the right, the river, its companion, on the left. This river was no longer a stream flowing merrily through green meadows but a thundering torrent of icy water that plunged from rock to rock. The clanging of metal armor, pikes, and swords in the tight space added to the dread Matteo was beginning to feel as the company closed ranks and was forced to climb in some places only two abreast on the narrow path. The scene was streaked with light and shadow. It had already been five miles of rugged terrain to reach the mouth of the canyon. And now, this perilous climb through boulders teetering on the edge of the foaming river seemed unbelievably difficult to Matteo. He was unable to keep pace with the head of the group and found himself struggling back in the middle of the pack. He stopped for a moment to catch his breath against the vertical wall to his right. And as he looked up, he noticed a strange dark cloud overhead descending quickly into the canyon.

DANIEL

Pra del Tor, Piedmont, March 1488

Daniel waited motionless, along with his companions, after hearing the second signal. The enemy was approaching through the canyon, and now it was only a matter of time. He looked upward, where he could see others waiting on the cliffs. But then, right above them, he noticed a strange dark cloud. It was moving fast for a storm cloud, and he saw it come over the cliff and straight down into the canyon. The light from above dimmed and then went out. The dark mist made it so he could only see a few feet ahead. As if on cue, he heard the crashing of boulders from above. He heard screams, and men started running toward him through the gate. Daniel and his comrades used their swords to stop the soldiers from going any further toward the Pra. As some fell, others would take their places. Although the dark cloud impaired Daniel's vision, his opponents were worse off, especially those with helmets who had limited vision already. Most seemed anxious to escape the chaos behind them, but some engaged them in combat. Although his arrows were not much use here, he circled his opponent, attacking him from behind and bringing him to the ground with a swift stroke of his blade. He noticed a movement to the right from the corner of his eye. He turned just in time to see

Monsieur Jaquet leap from the darkness and land a blow with his large hammer on a man who had lurched toward him. There was hand-to-hand fighting as visibility changed within the mist.

MATTEO

Pra del Tor, Piedmont, March 1488

As the cloud descended into the canyon, Matteo pressed against the rock wall and found he could see only a few feet in either direction. Then, just as he was contemplating this strange event and wondering if the Vaudois had concocted this smoke, a large boulder crashed into the river, and others of all sizes followed it, one crushing a soldier next to him. His comrades panicked. Soldiers pushed toward him, coming down the path, shoving some over the precipice and into the raging river below.

Matteo was knocked off his feet. He lay sideways on the path, every time he tried to push himself up, someone knocked him down again. He was being trampled. His head was close to the river's edge, he pulled himself with his free arm over the edge of the path, where he toppled head over heels into the river. The shock of the cold water made it difficult to breathe. Swept along in the current, he thought perhaps he would escape this canyon prison after all. Suddenly, a fully armored man toppled into the river on top of him, pinning him down. His head hit the metal breastplate, and thankfully, that was the end of his mortal memories.

BERTOCH

Pra del Tor, Piedmont, March 1488

From above, Bertoch continued to send the rock missiles below. It was impossible to tell if they were hitting their targets but based on the yelling that echoed from the canyon walls, all hell was breaking loose below. After about a half hour, the cloud began to disperse, and they began to see the violence that had occurred in the canyon. Piles of soldiers lay dead along the path, some crushed by stones, but many trampled by their fellow soldiers in a rush to get away. There were hundreds of others in the river, having been knocked from the path or jumped. The river was not kind to those who ended there. As the cloud evaporated, Bertoch could see just a few stragglers who had managed to shelter under the dead or behind rocks, making their way out of the canyon. It seemed the battle was over, and miraculously the Vaudois had won. This time he had come prepared to die for what he had once espoused, and it had not been necessary. He called out the order to stop the hail of stones and fell to his knees.

DANIEL

Pra del Tor, Piedmont, March 1488

As the vapor dispersed, Daniel looked around at the carnage, he moved to his right looking for Monsieur Jaquet. On the ground lay a bloody rancoon, a long weapon with curved blades at the end, and two men dead next to it. Just ten feet away, he found Monsieur Jaquet awake but with a grievous injury to his side.

He knelt beside him, loosening his breastplate.

"It was just at the last moment before they fled. I saw the desperation in his eyes. I thought he was finished and turned away. I judged wrong, he lunged at me, and I got his blade in my side," with that, he coughed, and a bit of blood drizzled down his chin.

"Hold on, I will get some help!" exclaimed Daniel.

"I fear it is too late, my dear boy. Please tell my wife and children how very much I love them. It was not in vain, the Lord has his own purposes, but our freedom is not in vain."

Daniel held his hand, "I will tell them."

"And you, Daniel, stay to the path you have begun, and you will be safe. Take care of my Lena."

Tears streamed down Daniel's face, "Thank you for your trust, sir. May God be with you," he held on until Bartholemew Jaquet fell limp where he had stood guarding the gate of the Pra.

BERTOCH

Pra del Tor, Piedmont, March 1488

Bertoch hurried to the cottage to make sure that Francesca was safe. Now that the battle had ended, he could look forward to the future he hoped for with his daughter.

He found her celebrating with the other women and children.

"Oh, father, you are safe!" she exclaimed as he clasped her in a warm hug.

"Yes, I believe we may have peace again," he paused. "At least for a while." He knew well that the powerful could break peace treaties with the ebb and flow of politics, especially for the Waldensians.

"Papa, do you think that you can forgive them?"

"The army that attacked us?"

"No, those who took me away from you and mama?" They had walked away from the revelers and sat down near a mountain stream.

"I don't think..." he paused, "I don't know if that is possible."

"Papa, I want us to be able to live together in peace. I want Nonna to be part of my life. How can that happen if you cannot forgive the Catholics?"

"That is a good question. Of course, I want you to be happy, and I am glad Madame Russo took such good care of you."

"Papa, Jesus taught that we must love our enemies and pray for those who despitefully use and persecute us. I think the longer we let these horrible men control our thoughts and actions, the more power they have over us," she had dropped her head and spoke quietly, looking down at her hands in her lap. "If we help each other forgive them for everything they have done to our family and me, maybe we can at last move forward." She lifted her head and looked at him.

Tears ran down Bertoch's cheeks. "Can you forgive them?" he asked.

"I want to try," said Francesca. The look on her face reminded Bertoch of his beloved wife when she was determined to do something difficult.

"Then, I will try with you," he said.

DANIEL
Pinerolo, Piedmont, Italy, March
1488

The rout of the army at the Pra brought a quick end to the campaign against the Vaudois. Daniel assumed the commanders did not want to waste any more of their good men. Also, he felt the problems with rebellious nobles within his lands made Charles I, the Duke of Savoy, less enthusiastic about continuing the crusade against a small group of heretics in the mountains.

"I am sure their soldiers have more important things to attend to," stated Daniel, discussing the planned peace meeting.

"We have agreed to send a group of twelve men to do homage to the duke at his castle in Pinerolo," explained Phillipe Monnet to Daniel and the valley representatives sent to confer together. "I will represent Prali and the valley of Germanesca." They also sent Daniel to stand in for Lena's father and Val Angrogna.

"This sign of goodwill between us will hopefully end the crusade," said Monsieur Arnaud.

Daniel and the other men were escorted into a large hall where chairs were set up for them. Daniel had never seen such opulence, the polished inlaid tile floors, the ornate and beautiful paintings, even the carved wooden chairs that they sat in.

The duke entered accompanied by three men. He was only twenty years of age, and Daniel couldn't help but feel that he didn't have much more experience than himself. Although, he seemed genuinely curious about the mountain people. He asked the Vaudois to introduce themselves and, during their conversation, excused himself for having tolerated such a cruel war upon them.

"Your Grace, we wish to affirm our continued loyalty," replied Monsieur Monnet. Based on their conversation Daniel and the men had reason to believe they would have some liberty to practice their religion.

"I must ask, is it true that your children are born with a black throat, covered in hair, and one eye in the middle of their forehead?" the duke said incredulously.

"That is not true," said Monsieur Monnet, "and if there is any doubt in your mind, let us bring some of our children to meet you," he continued, "some of our wives and children even now are waiting for us in your garden."

"But of course, please bring them immediately," said the duke. So two men excused themselves as they went to get their wives and children.

"This is good; I will finally know for myself," said the duke.

The two men hurried back into the hall accompanied by their wives and four small children. The children looked curiously around them. Daniel imagined they had never seen such tapestries as those that hung upon the walls or a fireplace as tall as their parents. Their fathers urged them forward, the two girls curtsied, and the three-year-old boy bowed. The baby looked on from his mother's arms.

The duke came forward to greet them, crouched in front of them, and looked into their eyes.

"How old are you?" he asked. The three children all held out fingers to signify their ages. "Do you like my house?" he continued as they looked around. Finally, the oldest of the three, Mary Monnet, who was seven, spoke up, "It is the tallest building I have ever seen, and I like all the pictures on the wall!" she exclaimed.

"I like the pictures too. This one over here is the forest at Altessano and a hunting trip with my father," he exclaimed.

"I like the horses," said Mary. The duke placed his hand upon her head, "I see no fault here." Then, he turned to the rest of the group, including his assistants.

"Those who have slandered against them should be punished. They have influenced us with lies, yet there are no signs of Satan among them." The duke then called his servants forward and had them bring a basket of sweets to send home with the children.

"I hope we may now have peace," said Daniel as they departed the castle.

"God has indeed touched the Prince's heart," said Monsieur Malan.

The group returned home as news of their meeting with the Duke of Savoy spread quickly throughout the valleys. The people kindled bonfires on the tops of the mountains as a sign of their great rejoicing.

LENA
La Tour, Piedmont, March 1488

Sorrow filled Lena's heart as she and her family climbed the hill to the burial plot. Friends and family gathered together, and Lena began singing:

> *"We are watchers of a beacon, whose light must never die,*
> *We are guardians of an altar midst the silence of the sky."*

Her song drifted upward, echoing off the mountains, as other voices joined her:

> *"Here, the rocks yield founts of courage, struck forth as by thy rod.*
> *For the strength of the hills, we bless thee, Our God, our fathers' God."*

There was no doubt her father had been courageous until the end. He had fought for the freedom of worship that the Duke now granted. Now, he had passed the torch to Lena and her siblings.

They must teach the pure gospel to their children and continue in the faith as her father would wish. The Barbe spoke of Monsieur Jaquet's good works, his ability to negotiate, and his wish to have peace in the valleys.

Daniel put his arm around Lena, offering his shoulder for comfort. Lena knew he wished he had been able to spare them this grief. As the final prayer was given, she embraced her mother, who stood erect next to the grave. "You are not alone," she whispered.

After the funeral, Lena and Daniel walked away together with a united purpose. They veered off the path and continued until they reached the cave above the village. The afternoon sun lit up the entrance, and they had enough light to venture into the cavern. Daniel took out his knife, "Is this a good place?" he asked, gesturing to an area on the wall.

"I think that looks perfect," replied Lena. And so, he carefully carved their names into the rock wall, as others had done before them. He entwined the letters at the end of their names and then stood back to examine his work.

"We were here," he said.

"Yes, we will make our mark here on the rock and here in the village," echoed Lena. "Perhaps time will not forget what we have done here in these mountains."

PART TWO

"The Lord is my rock and my fortress, and my deliverer; my God, my strength, in whom I will trust; my buckler, and the horn of my salvation, and my high tower." –Psalm 18:2

MARIANNE

Riclaretto, Valley of St. Martin, Piedmont, Savoy, Italy, April 1560

Marianne was dreaming she was in Turin, the largest city she had ever known. She seemed to be lost among the buildings, and just as she reached the end of the street where she hoped to be in the hills that she loved, she would find another row of houses and shops. Then Marianne heard loud voices coming from down an alleyway, they were shouting, and she heard what sounded like the pounding of hooves. She forced herself to wake up. The pounding continued, and it was coming from her front door. As she sat up, she could see her parents peering through the wooden shutter. The only light came flickering from outside.

Suddenly the door was broken open, and a gust of cold air exploded into the room along with three men. They all had muskets; one had his knife drawn, dirty cloth covered the lower part of their faces, and their eyes glowed with feverish joy. Her mother screamed, and her younger brother and sister sat up in the bed next to her. One of the men dragged her father from the house. Her mother grabbed her little sister. Marianne reached for her brother as they were herded roughly from their house at the point of the muskets. Gunshots rang out in the frosty air.

Marianne could not believe her eyes. She shook her head as though she was still dreaming. "This can't be real," she whispered. She looked to the right and the left at the cluster of homes in her village. There were many men with torches, some on horseback. They were prodding the people out into the snowy street. She searched for her father, and just as she saw him in the crowd, another gunshot rang out. She turned back in time to see her neighbor, Monsieur Michelini, fall to the ground. The men were laughing now. They seemed to be enjoying themselves.

"Where is your God now?" one man shouted.

"Can he save you?" Taunted another, drawing his sword and plunging it through the nearest person. Marianne turned her brother's face into her nightgown. They were driven together, all in nightclothes, many with bare feet. Marianne said a silent prayer of thanksgiving that she always had cold feet and had worn her wool socks to bed. She had the clothes on her back, her parents, and her brother and sister. That was enough for now.

The marauders went into the empty homes, threw logs on the fireplaces, then stole anything of value. They raided the pantries, congratulating themselves on their good fortune. They stayed in the warm houses as they drank wine and yelled obscenities to the families shivering in the snow.

"You can come back to your homes if you promise to attend Mass!" they taunted.

"Hurry, follow me, and stay together," it was Marianne's father, Monsieur Peyronel. As he gathered the group, they hurried down the path, following each other as closely as possible. Marianne did not look back. She had believed they were all going to die! Shivering in the cold, and thinking that she had been useless in stopping the mob. She was afraid she might burst into tears, but the thought of her brave Grandma Francesca Peyronel kept her from doing so.

The temperature was still below freezing as the survivors headed down the valley of St. Martin and then turned and followed the Chisone River to the next village. They were searching for someone to help them along the way.

JOHN
Tagliaretto, Valley of Pellice,
Piedmont, April 1560

The plow had hit another rock, and John Reynaud took the extra time it took to dig it out with his shovel before guiding the ox down the row of dark soil. Almost finished, he wouldn't let a few rocks stop his work. He promised his father he would complete the lower field today.

All was peaceful on the mountain. Frothy bits of cloud laced the blue sky, and the sun warmed his back as he stooped over the plow. This was his favorite time of year. The ice and snow were finally gone, and the daisies and butterflies spotted the fields with their colors. At seventeen, John was becoming a man of the mountain like his father; like his father, he had learned that their master was the mountain. The alpine peaks in which they were nestled dictated the rhythms of their lives; its seasons and whims became their own. And it was only through hard work that a man could survive there.

They were fed by the mountain for just a few months a year, and their productivity in those months dictated how they would live for the rest. His people, the Vaudois, or Waldenses as they were now called, had carved out their lives in these rugged alpine slopes. Battling the stones, the poverty, and the weather, he was determined not to be the weak link in the family chain.

He finished plowing and led the ox back to the barn, which was actually under the main floor of his stone house. After feeding and brushing the ox, he joined his family for their evening meal.

"How did the plowing go today?" asked his father, Daniel Reynaud, Jr.

"There were a few more rocks than normal."

"I'm not surprised with the water running off the mountain this year," said his father as he took another portion of bread.

"And how was the meeting with the elders?" his mother asked as she poured grape juice into his father's mug.

"Barbe Mancini is surprised by the actions in Riclaretto. The ministers from Geneva encourage us to remain peaceful and to do nothing to antagonize the Roman Catholics or the noblemen any further."

"Father, you were right. We should have never joined with the Protestant group," declared John.

"It does seem we've had nothing but trouble since we openly declared our faith, especially since we built the temples," said his father.

"Do you agree, Grandpa?" asked John, turning to the old man who sat silently eating his meal.

Grandpa Daniel Reynaud looked up from his dinner. A few wisps of curly grey hair stuck out from under his woolen cap. His eyes still twinkled, and he still had a firm handshake. At ninety-two he used a cane now, but his memory was perfect.

Grandma Reynaud had died ten years ago, so now he split his time living with his children.

"I guess it depends on your point of view," he said. "In 1532, the Waldensian elders gathered in the largest group anyone could remember. All members of the faith were encouraged to attend the meeting, which was held in a large open field. The reformers were astounded at the gospel knowledge of this poor mountain people." John wanted to keep grandpa talking. He didn't often talk about the past, but when he did, James always learned something new about his family's history.

"Was William Farel a firebrand, as he's been described?" John asked.

"Well, he was there as the champion for the new Lutheran ideas. He wasn't a big man. He had a bushy red beard and a booming voice, if that's what you mean. He said it was time for us to take our place in the world, to come out of the shadows, and be a light to this dark nation. Bern, Switzerland, had chosen the Reformed faith, and he urged us to join with them and France."

"Did everyone agree with the idea?"

"Some wished for longer discussions. Others did not wish to give up the sanctioned sacraments of marriage, ordination by the laying on of hands, and oral confession. But the majority wanted to work toward the vision of authentic Christianity. So, we voted to join with the Reformed Protestants."

"We've lived among the Catholics for centuries and have always found a way to continue our faith. But there is no going back," added John's father. He paused as though collecting his thoughts.

"Some reports I've received of Calvin punishing those who argue against his doctrine have been disturbing to me."

"Are you thinking about Michael Servetus, the Spaniard?" asked Grandpa.

"Well, yes, he was convinced that the Bible contains no support for the doctrine of the Trinity, and he also condemned infant baptism," replied his father.

Stories of Servetus had come over the mountains from Geneva. He had opposed Calvin's views and secretly published several books. Unfortunately, he was arrested and condemned to death as a heretic just seven years ago. Many were unhappy over his death, although Calvin defended his actions as a move to suppress false doctrine. Decades of oppression for their beliefs by the Roman Catholics had made John sensitive to Calvin's activities.

"I can't believe our Protestant leaders are burning heretics!" exclaimed John.

"Father, you have taught us that 'peace cannot be found with hate' and that we must teach through our actions of sacrifice and love towards all," said John's younger sister, Mary.

"Right you are, my dear, and I hope we can continue practicing our beliefs in peace," With that, he opened his small hand-written book of the gospels and began to read in John 20:19; "*Then the same day at evening, being the first day of the week, when the doors were shut where the disciples were assembled for fear of the Jews, came Jesus and stood in the midst, and saith unto them. Peace be unto you.*" John hoped his father was right and that peace would prevail.

TACHARD

Valley of Pragelas, Piedmont, Territory of France, April 1560

News of the events in the valley of St. Martin had just reached the French Waldensians in Val Pragelas. Local pastor Martin Tachard was seething. He studied under Calvin in Geneva, then was assigned to his parish in Piedmont. He was tired of quietly accepting the abuses of the Catholic church. The monks of Pignerol continued to torment the Reformed churches around them. Not content with ransacking the churches, they took prisoners of men, women, and children, harassing them until they returned to mass, sending them to the galleys or the flames. They had all heard the story of James Baridari, who had his head blown off after his assailants filled his mouth with gunpowder.

Tachard thought of all the injustices they had suffered as he stood and addressed the people gathered at the church.

"Can we forget John Carignano, one of our own congregation picked up by monks as he went to market at Pignerol. On his way to the market, my friends! And after a week in prison, he was burned at the stake for heresy. Then there are the marauders, this gang with no authority that takes any opportunity to torment, torture, and murder members of our faith!" He paused a moment, letting it sink in as the people remembered the terrors they had been subjected to.

"A few months ago, I led some of you as we smashed the statues that had been put up in the churches of Pragelas and Fenestrelle, cleansing them of the pagan symbols. But now it is time for us to do more, now is the time to stand up for our rights!" he told his congregation. "We must come to the aid of our brethren. They must not be left to fight alone."

This time he led 150 volunteers across the border between France and Piedmont, Italy. The local villagers came to their doors to see the armed band. Others working in their fields stood still at the sight.

Tachard led them onward to the Val Martino, where they attacked the Catholic landowners, dragging them from their homes and burning one house to the ground. Some villagers helped them in their quest by pointing out several homes the Catholic invaders possessed. Fifteen men went to each house, forcing all occupants onto the street.

The marauders looked shocked, obviously never expecting any retaliation from the peace-loving Vaudois. Tachard drove the entire group down the path toward Turin. They told them they would face certain death if they dared to return,

Truchietti

Valley of St. Martin, Piedmont, Italy,
May 1560

"How dare the Vaudois cross an international border?" said Lord Charles Truchietti to his brother. The two were prominent landowners in the Valley of St. Martin. And it was Charles who had assembled the group of marauders and given them their orders to attack Riclaretto. His boots clicked across the tile floor as he headed toward the terrace. His father's death two years previous had only propelled him forward. As the oldest son, he had inherited lands and titles. And at eighteen, he felt it important to show strong leadership. His brother supported him in every way, and together they wielded great power in the area. His only wish was to fulfill the mission of The Duke of Savoy.

"We have been forced to watch the Vaudois become more and more brazen," said his brother, who had followed him.

"Yes, as if building six temples in five years proves they are somehow better?"

"It makes me sick to watch them creep out onto the plain of Piedmont and take some of our best farmland."

"This is the moment we have been waiting for. The war is finally over, and our Duke has returned to govern his people!" exclaimed Truchietti as he looked out upon his adjacent vineyard.

"I have heard that the peace terms with Spain include an agreement to put down the Reformation and the heretics," said his brother.

"I think with this new edict prohibiting all subjects from listening to non-Catholic preachers, we may be able to put these terrible times behind us," Truchietti said as he lifted his goblet, and the two men toasted the Duke of Savoy. The brothers agreed that the heresies of the Waldensians must stop, and between them, they decided to force the Duke's hand by giving him more information.

They led a group of fellow landowners from their valley to meet with the Duke at his castle in Pinnerolo. At the meeting, Charles Truchietti aired the grievances of the landlords.

"Most honored Duke, the Waldenses are busy constructing fortresses wherein they are preparing to fight against you!" exclaimed Truchietti.

"Can this be verified?" asked the Duke.

"Oh yes, we have brought papers detailing their activities for the past year," he stated. "We also have it on good authority that they are arming a garrison, with which I wouldn't be surprised if they intend to drive all the Roman Catholics from their lands."

"This is very disturbing news," remarked the Duke. After talking with his advisors for almost an hour, he returned to the group of Lords and told them he was authorizing the re-building of the Germanesco fortress that had previously lain in ruins, and he would tax the Waldensians to pay for it.

The Lords of the Valley of St. Martin thanked the Duke for his permission to act in their defense. As they returned home, a great thunderstorm overtook the party with howling winds and crashing thunder. They huddled under an outcropping of rock as fierce lightning flashed around them. Just as Charles Truchetti was joking that a suit of wet clothes was worth the eventual annihilation of the heretics, a thunderbolt hit a nearby tree. The sky flashed brightly on the terrified faces of his comrades as several of their horses bolted into the night.

"Perhaps we are wrong about this," stammered his brother, who knew the charges they had brought to the Duke of Savoy were false.

"I am never wrong!" exclaimed Charles Truchietti.

MARIANNE

Angrogna, Piedmont, Italy

Marianne Peyronel and her family had found refuge with their uncle David Ribetto in the village of Angrogna. She had such happy memories of Angrogna. Several years ago, her extended family had met there together sharing food, stories, and playing games. She had met John Reynaud, who was her second cousin or something like that. She had been about ten, and he was older and smarter. They each had led a battle against the other, armed with wooden swords made from sticks. The two of them were the last kids standing.

As they fought, Marianne was impressed with how he used the rocky terrain to his advantage, dodging and jumping over rocks. As for her, she was quicker and smaller and managed to land some blows and run away. Marianne ultimately won, but she was pretty sure John let her. He was the kind of boy who didn't need to prove he was the toughest. Or maybe he was just getting rid of a pesky kid. Either way, it was a great memory and helped take her mind off the recent attack on her home and family.

They were safe for now and able to return to their village all because of Pastor Tachard. But before they left, they wanted to meet at the temple to offer thanks for their safety. Authorities in

Geneva had made it clear that all violent activity must cease to preserve the peace of the valleys. So, they asked Tachard to address the congregation, which included many of his followers from Valle Pragelas.

"We must act in good conscience," he began, "as our Pastor Calvin has taught us, 'when we see our brethren afflicted for the cause of God, we must join with them and assist them in their affliction.' Let us not doubt that God will continue to display his power toward us so that we may have victory over Satan and our enemies."

Marianne was thrilled that there was a pastor who would stand up to those who would persecute them. She hung on every word of his sermon and hoped to learn more of his plans to stand against tyranny. Her Grandfather Bertoch had fought for freedom in 1488, and she wanted to be just like him. Although she was just sixteen years old, she was strong and, being the oldest, had convinced her father to teach her to shoot with the bow.

After the meeting, she sought out Pastor Tachard.

"I just wanted to thank you for all you have done for our village!" she said.

"I could not let them get away with no answer to their actions," replied Tachard.

"We have turned the other cheek many times. I want you to know that I will fight with you whenever I receive the call," Marianne stood tall, and her brown eyes did not blink as she looked at Tachard. She could tell by his expression that he was surprised by her words and maybe shocked that they were coming from a mere girl.

"Well, thank you. When the time comes, we will need all the help we can get!"

Her father had invited Tachard to stay with their Uncle Ribetto while he was in Angrogna. The next night, her family sat near the fire along with Tachard.

"I understand you were friends with our beloved Pastor Varaglia," said her father.

"Yes indeed, we met at the Academy at Geneva," he paused, "Varaglia certainly had an interesting story. He was a Franciscan monk for the Catholic church sent to save the heretics. But as he learned more about their doctrine, he became convinced that their teachings were correct. He then became a pastor for the Reformed faith."

"We were lucky to have him here in Angrogna," said her Uncle Ribetto, "even for such a short time."

"Yes, that was awful what happened," agreed Tachard. They all quietly bowed their heads, remembering his arrest in Turin and subsequent burning as a heretic two years earlier. "Once he made me promise that I would continue to study the gospel and all sacred texts so that we would know what was right for ourselves."

"That has saved us from error many times," agreed her father.

"We heard that he was happy to die serving his God and the Waldensian Reformed Church?" said Marianne, who had always wanted to know if that was true.

"Yes indeed, my dear girl, in fact, he wrote me a letter right before his death. I carry it with me always," and with that, he reached into the breast of his tunic and pulled out a worn parchment from which he began to read:

Dear Martin,

Some of my flock were planning to rescue me from my current state, but I have asked them to leave me in the hands of God. I received a letter from Calvin instructing me to 'let the glory which sustained St. Paul also inspire me with courage. For though I am captive, the word of God is not captive, and I can render testimony of it to many who will spread abroad the seed of life they have received from my lips.' I am content with whatever the Lord has declared for me. They will sooner want wood wherewith to burn us than ministers to burn. From day to day, we multiply, and the work of God endureth forever. Your brother in the faith.

Marianne was astonished by the story; what incredible faith he had! She didn't know what God would ask her to do, but she hoped she would be equal to the task.

TACHARD

Angrogna, Piedmont, Italy

The next day Tachard set out to find Lord Ranconis. He had noticed him in the crowd at the temple meeting. A cousin of Duke Emmanuel Philibert, he felt that if anyone could help them, it might be him. After several inquiries, he found where he was staying in Angrogna and asked for an audience with him.

"Lord Ranconis, I hope you will hear me out?" asked Pastor Tachard, hoping for the best.

"Yes, of course," said Ranconis, nodding. He led him to a garden bench where they could have some privacy.

"I am most interested in how we may appease the Duke and diffuse the situation here." said Tachard, "We plan to send a petition asking for the right to be heard before they condemn us."

"I think that would be most prudent," replied Ranconis, "there are those who suggest that the Waldensians are treasonous and should be dealt with as such."

"I do not doubt that many of these aspersions come from the Truchiettis', and their friends, who want to destroy us from the earth."

"Perhaps, but I would advise you to prepare a petition confessing your ancient faith, which you claim is the Word of God as written in the Bible and taught by the apostles, refuting the charges that you have adopted strange doctrines."

"Yes, that is what we have planned."

"I think you must make it plain that you remain loyal to the Duke of Savoy, you would defend his sovereignty, and that you have always been true and good Christian subjects, living in harmony with your neighbors."

"You are right; we must remind him of our many years of loyalty," replied Tachard.

"Once you prepare this petition, deliver it to the Duke, his wife, Duchess Marguerite, and the Duke's council. Then I will see it delivered to the court in Nice if you would like to entrust that to me." Tachard quickly agreed and was hopeful they might divert more hostile actions by following his advice. He was actually surprised that Ranconis was so helpful, and thanked him on behalf of the community.

***

Tachard met with the valley ministers, who agreed to draft their petition within the week and deliver it to Lord Ranconis. Most of the petition or "confession of faith," had been written earlier for use by the Reformed churches in France.

The petition began:

"A supplication of the poor Waldenses, to the most serene and most high prince, Philibert-Emanuel, Duke of Savoy, prince of Piedmont, our most gracious Lord...We do most willingly yield obedience to our

superiors; we ever endeavor to live peaceably with our neighbors; we have wronged no man though provoked; nor do we fear that any can, with reason, complain against us.

Finally, we never were obstinate in our opinions; but rather tractable, and always ready to receive all holy and pious admonitions, as appears by our confessions of faith.

And we are so far from refusing a discussion, or rather a free council wherein all things may be established by the word of God, that we desire the same with all our hearts.

We likewise beseech your highness to consider that this religion we profess is not ours only, nor hath it been invented by man of late years, as it is falsely reported; but it is the religion of our fathers, grandfathers, and great grandfathers, and other yet more ancient predecessors of ours, and of the blessed martyrs, confessors, prophets, and apostles; and if any can prove the contrary, we are ready to subscribe and yield thereunto. The word of God shall not perish but remain forever; therefore, if our religion be the true word of God, as we are persuaded, and not the invention of men, no human force shall be able to extinguish the same."

Tachard's accompanying letter to Duchess Marguerite expressed their confidence in her as a protector and friend. She was from France, and it was known she had joined the Reformed Faith before her marriage. Detailing the suffering others had already endured for the word of the Lord. He also reminded the duchess of Esther and other women who had previously saved the persecuted children of God.

MARIANNE
Valley of St. Martin, Piedmont, Italy, May 1560

Marianne was relieved to be back in her own home with her family. The past few weeks had all been like a bad dream. Now with her father reading to them in front of the flickering firelight, it almost seemed like she could pretend it had never happened. But looking toward her right and seeing her Grandmother Peyronel's face, she knew there was no way that Grandma would ever forget.

As her father finished reading the chapter in Matthew 6:34, "*Take therefore no thought for the morrow: for the morrow shall take thought for the things of itself. Sufficient unto the day is the evil thereof,*" he closed the book. Looking thoughtfully into the fire, her grandmother began to speak to the family.

"This feels very much like the violence of 1488," she said.

"I know many people from the villages are talking about it," said her mother, but do you really think it will come to battle?"

"We did not believe it either. Everyone thought our petitions would persuade the Duke and our history as good subjects," Grandma sighed at this, "But they were not persuaded."

Marianne knew the story of her Grandma, how she had been kidnapped as a small child and given to the Catholics to raise properly. She also knew the miracle of her Grandma's life was being reunited with her father, Paul Bertoch, during the siege of Pra Del Tor in 1488.

"If it comes down to it, we must fight," said Marianne's father. "I know many want to turn the other cheek, but after what has happened here, I don't know if we will have a choice?"

Her mother left to put the two younger children to bed, and her father went below to check on the livestock. As Marianne sat by the fire with her grandmother, she said softly, "Grandma, I want to fight too! I know back then, the soldiers did something awful to you. When I get the chance, I want to use my bow to strike back." Her Grandma tried to speak, but Marianne quickly went on. "You know I am better than anyone my age with the bow. Shouldn't I be able to help my people in their battle against the oppressors?" Her Grandma looked at her for a long moment. Marianne knew it was not tradition for women to be at the battle lines, only in rare instances during a sudden attack.

"You remind me of myself, my dear, but even more I think you have your great grandfather's sense of justice."

"When the time comes," Marianne paused, "if the time comes, would you help me do this?" she asked, this time reaching out and clasping her grandmother's well-worn hand.

"I think your mind is such that you will do this with no help, but yes, I will support you. I think your heart is in the right place. If I was younger, I might join you."

JOHN

Ciabas Temple, Angrogna Valley,
Piedmont, June 1560

John Reynaud and his family made their way to the temple. The place where they worshipped on Sunday was being transformed into some sort of court, which John found unsettling. After receiving their petition, the Duke of Savoy declared a public debate at the Vaudois' Ciabas temple. The debate would pit the Catholic authorities against Pastor Tachard. John could feel excitement and tension in the air. He wondered why they couldn't have held the discourse on neutral ground. He noticed the local Catholic clerics there to support the Jesuits led by Antonio Possevino. Lord Ranconis was the moderator for the debate.

John was quite aware that the Catholics found the Ciabas temple a bit of a joke. A plain rectangular building whitewashed in limestone from the local quarries. It had a straw roof with no bell tower or fancy pulpit and did not compare with the beautifully appointed Catholic churches. John liked the visual alternative to the Roman church. His family sat with other members of their faith who had arrived early.

Pastor Tachard looked younger than James had imagined. He guessed he was in his early thirties. He had deep-set eyes that seemed to take in everything around him. His face was clean-shaven except for a neatly trimmed mustache that ended at the corners of his mouth. John expected him to look angry, but he seemed peaceful and confident. John stood as the noble lords entered in company with Possevino.

"We welcome all who have come to find the true word of God on this day," Possevino began. "We do not doubt that your minds have been confused over new doctrine that has been preached, some within these walls. I am sure that after today, many will feel sorrow for their errors."

Tachard then took the podium, "The Roman Catholic church is guilty of many errors in their practice of the doctrine contained in the Bible. But we believe that each person is free to study the scriptures for themselves, and no intermediary is necessary to explain their meaning." At that moment, he turned and looked directly at Possevino, "The mass as a practice is a blasphemous fable!" he exclaimed. The room erupted at his words, with some on their feet protesting, fists raised, while others talked loudly amongst themselves. John, shocked that Tachard would speak out in such a bold manner, could hardly believe this was the same peaceful man he had observed earlier.

"Order, order!" called Lord Ranconis. After a few minutes, the noise died down. "Each side shall have the opportunity to state their case and evidence to support their claims," he continued.

Tachard resumed his speech reaffirming their belief that no one had the power to turn the bread and wine of communion into the literal body and blood of Christ. Jesus Christ made the only sacrifice for our sins, and the bread and wine are just symbols of that sacrifice.

When Tachard had finished his statements, Lord Ranconis stood and addressed Possevino, "Do you have a rebuttal to the questions proposed on the practice of the mass?"

"Certainly, I do," he spat the words out as he rose from his seat, slowly drawing the eyes of the crowd. He waved a sheaf of papers in his hand.

"Here," said he, "is the statement of the doctrines which you profess, which you yourselves have delivered to his highness. Do you abide by it?" he asked Tachard.

"We see no reason to depart from it."

"You will renounce your errors when shown to you?"

"Yes."

"Well then, I will demonstrate that the mass is found in Scripture. The word 'Massah' signifies sent, does it not? The primitive expression, *'Ite, missa, est,'* was employed to dismiss the auditory, was it not?"

"That is true," responded Tachard.

"Well then, you see that the mass is found in the Holy Scripture!" he looked as though he was correcting a small wayward child as he smiled at the Vaudois representatives to his right. "From the primitive expression, we are told 'to go,' to send us toward Christ. So we remember Jesus' life, the Last Supper, and his sacrifice at Calvary at mass."

To this Tachard responded, "Even if the term 'massah' had the meaning in Scripture which you suppose, which it does not. It would in no degree prove the divine institution of the mass, and most definitely not private masses, and other points of contention that are not justified by your proposition."

"Is that so!" said Possevino petulantly, his face red as he tried to recover his composure. "I do not have to listen to this nonsense. You are heretics, atheists, and reprobates! And I will dispute with you no more but shall drive you from this country as you deserve." With those words he gathered his papers, swirled his robe around him, and hurried down the aisle, his assistants rushing to keep up and many of the local clergy behind him.

John had expected the debate to last a little longer. He felt Tachard had pushed the priest a bit too far and knew that sometimes a softer approach was necessary. But he was annoyed that Possevino would walk out of the debate and once again refer to them as 'heretics.' It was obvious that neither side gained additional followers, and most importantly, the Waldensians were not willing to recant. Although Lord Ranconis was in charge, John could not tell from his face what the verdict might be.

TRUCHIETTI
Piedmont Valleys, September 1560

The stubbornness of the Vaudois was notorious. Truchietti and his family had done everything possible to get their Waldensian tenants to recant and return to mass. The debate had been a farce. How could anyone take the Waldensians seriously? Finally, Duke Emmanuel Philibert had come to the same conclusion, and Charles Truchietti and his brother were one of the first to offer their assistance in the inevitable armed conflict. It was September when word came that they were assembling an army to be led by one of the notable Piedmontese nobles Giorgio Costa.

"I am happy to go to battle against these heretics," said Truchietti as he met with Count Costa, who had been a friend of his father's. "I know several hundred of my fellow noblemen are coming to join us, all with fine horses."

"I appreciate all you and the loyal nobles have done," he replied. "We have assembled about 4,000-foot soldiers, including some convicts who have been offered a pardon for their assistance."

"Sir, if I may introduce Monsieur Gastaut, one of the honored veterans who fought in the war with France," said Truchietti as he stepped back so Gastaut could greet the Captain.

"Ah yes, glad to have the help of you and your men," replied Costa. As the army gathered just outside the Pellice valley, they observed the Waldensians retreating up their paths into the mountains, probably to hide in their caves. They could hear the sounds of their singing ringing down the canyon. Singing as they faced certain destruction, thought Truchietti, as he shook his head in disbelief.

At the end of October, they posted a proclamation declaring the people would be destroyed by fire or sword unless they returned to the Church of Rome.

The army began their advance into the Valle Pellice, camping at San Giovanni. The next day Truchietti led twelve hundred men into the Valle Angrogna, which was adjacent to the camp. The soldiers were chanting, "To the Fire, send them to the fire!"

A few small groups of Waldensians armed with slings and crossbows picked off some advancing soldiers and then retreated farther into the hills. Truchietti and his men continued into the valley before camping for the night. Being surrounded by mountains was always a bit unnerving to Truchietti. Then, at about 2:00 a.m., they were suddenly awakened by the sound of a drum booming through the canyon.

"This is not good; they must have sent for reinforcements to surround us during the night!" yelled Truchietti. The Piedmont soldiers rose from their beds and grabbed their weapons. Then they saw the Waldensians coming down the mountain with torches.

Truchietti lost his way in the confusion and became separated from his steward. He ran towards his horse amid a hail of gunfire. As he started to mount, an arrow whizzed past his head.

Caught in the melee, many of the soldiers threw down their weapons and fled down the valley, the shadows of their own bonfires chasing them. Truchietti hid behind some brush as the Waldensians came whooping into the camp.

"Who was playing the drum?" he heard one of the men ask.

"I heard it was just a young boy playing with his toy," was the reply. Truchietti watched as the Waldensians happily gathered the discarded weapons before heading off.

In anger and disgust, Truchieti ordered his troops to burn homes as they retreated down the Angrogna valley.

"They surprised us in the night," was his only report. But he would find a way to get even. His father had taught him to find his opponent's weakness. And he intended to do just that. They re-grouped with Costa at the entrance to the Valle Pellice. Costa then decided on a new tactic. He would extend several proposals to the Waldensians, luring them with offers of peace.

John

Tagliaretto, Valley of Pellice, Piedmont, November 1560

John had spent the last three days gathering the cattle together in the upper pasture, hoping to transport as many as possible to the Pra del Tor. His family planned to join their fellow Vaudois in their mountain sanctuary. But he had arrived home only to find that the fight had come to the hills of his own town, Tagliaretto.

Just yesterday, they received word from General Costa that if the Vaudois lay down their arms, he would take a group of his soldiers to celebrate mass at Angrogna and then appeal on their behalf to the Duke. A meeting was held at the Reynaud home to discuss the matter. John was allowed to stay for the meeting.

"I think we must do all in our power to prove that we have no wish to fight," exclaimed his father.

"But you cannot trust these people," said Pastor Tachard, who had arrived just twenty minutes earlier when he heard of the proposal.

"Perhaps not, but our willingness to live in harmony with others has served us well in the past."

"These are different times," argued Tachard. "We have seen what they are capable of, and who knows why he is making this offer?"

"Perhaps they don't want to lose any more men. Maybe they just want to cut their losses," said their neighbor Monsieur Bergius.

"I do not believe he is ready to march his men meekly out of our valley," said Tachard, "there is more going on here than we know."

"I prefer to live my life taking men at their word," said Monsieur Bergius.

"Then your life may be drastically shortened," replied Tachard. John listened to all the leaders and was inclined to believe Tachard, but he knew nothing of war and was not anxious to leave his herds to find out more. The decision was made to consent to the appeal of General Costa, much to the dismay of Pastor Tachard. Most men had left or taken their discussions outside when John found himself alone with Tachard.

"You, young man, what do you think about all of this?" Since no one usually asked his opinion, John felt unprepared to answer.

"Well, I guess I hope for peace like my father," he managed.

"Of course, we must always hope for peace, but we should also be ready to defend ourselves."

"You do not believe what they say?" asked John.

"I think they will say whatever is necessary to get what they want," he said. "My advice is that you should take this time to prepare yourself so you will be ready to do whatsoever God may ask you to do!"

***

John and the villagers at Tagliaretto brought their weapons to the chapel and laid them down as a sign of good faith. The general for his part celebrated mass at Angrogna, without any of the Waldensians in attendance. Then he approached the village pastors expressing a sincere desire to see the Pra del Tor, about which he had heard so much. John's father was one of the men selected to accompany General Costa on his tour.

"Perhaps this will be the beginning of a new understanding between us," said his father. "But I still feel I must protect the family, and I would like you to be in charge here, John, while I am gone."

"Of course, I will do all I can. But father, can we trust General Costa? Remember what Pastor Tachard said."

"If there is any trouble, go to the hills. The caves will protect you."

That was two days ago. John felt restless; it was too quiet in the village. He yearned to be up in the high pasture where the breezes would blow away all concern. Where he felt he was master of the mountains and his small flock.

Some men had actually gone to the church and retrieved their weapons. John felt that was not in keeping with his father's wishes, so he did not. But the next day, he wished he had done the same. That morning a large group of soldiers entered the village and began sacking and plundering. As the violence started, John grabbed his mother and sister and headed up the mountain. He was thankful he had left the herd in the high pasture. As they hurried up the steep trail, John looked back and saw smoke coming from somewhere in the village.

They had almost reached the cave when they heard yelling coming from within. John pulled his family off the trail on the right, where they hid among the bushes. Directly to the left of the path was a steep precipice. The rocky terrain ended at the bottom with the icy river. Just as they had hidden themselves, an older man ran from the cave, followed by a Piedmontese soldier with a sword. The man ran to the edge of the gorge. John thought perhaps he might jump, but he turned at the last moment and fell to his knees. By then, the soldier had caught up to him, and John was close enough to hear him.

"Have mercy upon me!" he pleaded. But the soldier lifted his sword. Then just when John was ready to run at the soldier from behind, the old man threw his arms around the soldier's knees. Showing remarkable strength he leaned backward, and the top-heavy soldier toppled over into the abyss along with his victim.

In the silence that followed, John crouched in the brush with his mother and sister. Sweat came down his forehead, but he hardly dared to brush it from his eyes. They were frozen together in horror like some statue seen at a fountain in Turin. But John's thoughts were not frozen. He could no longer pretend everything would be fine. It was time for him to decide what he was going to do.

TRUCHIETTI

La Tour Pellice, Piedmont, November 1560

It had been Truchietti's idea to attack the village of Tagliaretto. He was excited that they had done something instead of sitting around waiting. He had not agreed with Costa's proposal to the Vaudois. Although he, too, was disturbed by the losses they had received so far, he was by no means ready to concede anything to these people.

When General Costa returned, he insisted they return the women and children taken at Tagliaretto but did nothing about the looting that had also occurred.

"Stick with me, and you will see how these things are done," said Costa to Truchietti. "Your father would have taught you, but I am pleased to finish your education," he patted him on the back as he led him to the meeting with the Vaudois, where they listed the atrocities they had supposedly endured.

"You gave us your word, we laid down our arms, and then your troops attacked our village!" they cried. The General assured them that this would not have happened if he had been present.

"If you will take your memorial, which you have written, to Vercelli and present it to the Duke, I will continue to do all I can to find a peaceful solution to this problem."

Costa played it all so well that even Truchietti found himself believing him. He had set out additional conditions for which they might obtain a peaceful solution.

"I promise I will withdraw my army if you pay the sum of 20,000 crowns," he declared.

And then, on cue, Trachietti said, "I am sure that I can get the amount reduced to 16,000 crowns." The Count noted they needed the money to pay the soldiers their wages. The Vaudois agreed with the terms of the negotiation, and after hearing of the proposal, the Duke of Savoy responded that he was willing to reduce the amount to half. The Vaudois representatives left the meeting planning to sell their cattle and anything else of value after again proclaiming their loyalty to the Duke.

That evening wine flowed freely in the commander's tent. Trachietti congratulated Costa, "We shall at long last have victory over these people!"

"They are such children. This is much easier than I thought," boasted Costa. The group of men laughed boisterously.

"It is almost comical how they are willing to do anything we ask," said Truchietti. Costa then turned to the two other dukes in attendance, "I am willing to make a deal with each of you, that you three alone shall have the rights to purchase the Vaudois cattle and also set the price," he smiled and passed his glass to his steward for more wine.

JOHN

Tagliaretto, Valley of Pellice,
Piedmont, November 1560

After his father told him the news, John couldn't believe it. "We must raise 8,000 crowns?"

"Yes."

"But how are we to do that when they have taken almost everything we have," he looked around at their meager possessions. They were still struggling to replenish their food stores before winter set in. And also assist the neighbors who had their homes burned.

"We will have to sell our cattle and most of our sheep," his father replied.

John's heart sank. The cattle were his inheritance, and he had taken care of them for as long as he could remember. Especially Ella; surely he wouldn't be expected to sell her. He had bottle-fed the little calf when her mother died at her birth about seven years ago. She was one of their best milk cows, but more than that, they were friends. Granted, most boys didn't have friends that were cows, but Ella was different. She was always the first to greet him at the pasture. And as the sun went down, she waited at the gate for him, her brown eyes thoughtful as he talked about his day. There was a unique pact between them, and he often had a treat for her to find in his pocket.

"Umm, all of the cattle?" John asked tentatively.

"Well, the ones we can sell the quickest."

"What about Ella?" he blurted out. His father looked at him as John kept clenching his jaw.

"We must do our part, son. Everyone has to make sacrifices if we are to have peace to practice our faith."

"I won't do it," John stated.

"Sometimes we have no choice," said his father. A warm tide of anger swelled up in John's chest. He knew he would shout something at his father if he did not escape. He turned and ran from the house, and then he ran to the end of the street. There was nowhere to go, so he turned and ran part-way up the mountain. Hot tears ran down his cheeks as he stopped under a chestnut tree next to a large grey boulder.

"This was all crazy! He could not believe why his father and the other village elders did not fight. They had all heard Pastor Tachard, and then John witnessed their brutality firsthand. He vowed at that moment to find Tachard immediately and volunteer to fight. He was only a farm boy and knew little about combat, but he would learn and somehow make this right.

TRUCHIETTI
Lucerne, Piedmont, December 1560

It had all gone according to plan, Truchietti had fulfilled General Costa's orders, and all were forbidden to purchase the Waldensian livestock except those approved by Costa. He had also set the price at half the current value, hoping to make it impossible for them to raise the needed money. But here they were a few weeks later, wanting an audience with the general. Costa had turned the matter over to Truchietti. The steward ushered four leaders of the faith into Truchietti's quarters at Lucerne.

"We are pleased to report that we have collected sufficient funds from our brethren to pay the $8,000 crowns," said their spokesman Monsieur Beus.

"I see," said Truchietti, who had not risen when they entered.

Monsieur Beus moved forward with two sacks of coins which he put on the table between them.

"Just as we agreed."

"Well, hold on there," Truchietti opened a leather file and took out a piece of parchment. "This document says that you will pay $16,000 crowns."

"But the Duke reduced that sum to $8,000!" exclaimed Monsieur Beus.

Truchietti waved his hand in dismissal, "That is no affair of mine, your representatives signed the agreement we have here, and that is what I expect in payment."

Monsieur Beus looked toward his fellow brethren in dismay. Truchietti knew it was impossible for them to raise any additional funds.

"However," said Truchietti, wishing to appear conciliatory, "My steward here would be happy to draw up a new document that will allow payments to be made toward the remaining balance." The Vaudois leaders, seeing no other alternative, consented to sign the new document. When Monsieur Beus stepped back from the drying ink, he looked directly at Truchietti.

"Now, you will remove your troops?"

Truchietti motioned for his steward to remove the signed document. He looked at his brother, who stood motionless in the corner.

"What do you say to that?" he asked.

"I see no way that the Duke will accept such an action unless the Vaudois send their foreign pastors away," he replied.

"But this was never part of the agreement!" protested another group member.

"Well, unfortunately, that was the primary reason Costa was sent on this mission, and I am afraid we cannot withdraw unless you dismiss those pastors."

Monsieur Beus looked around at his fellow Vaudois, "we will need to discuss this," he said.

"Of course, of course," Truchietti turned to his steward, "please have some wine brought for our visitors," he directed. And so, the Vaudois drank wine from their own vineyards as they agreed to send their pastors over the mountain to Pragelas in French territory.

As they left his quarters, Truchietti was elated as he saw the look of defeat on their faces. He lifted his glass and toasted Costa.

MARIANNE
Angrogna, Piedmont, January 1561

Marianne and her family had traveled from their home to Angrogna and again stayed with Uncle Ribetto while preparing to join their people at La Pra. General Costa had withdrawn his army, but it was only to the valley near Cavour. He had left garrisons in La Tour and two other villages, where they continued to harass the Vaudois residents at every opportunity. To Marianne, it seemed they were trying to starve them out. The army took any wine, oil, or corn left in the villages and destroyed every gristmill.

Marianne was gathering wood a short distance from the house when a company of soldiers came to the village, pounding on their doors and demanding they provide a meal. Marianne hid behind some brush and watched as they broke into the temple. When they came out to the town square, the village men, including her father and Uncle Ribetto, brought out whatever food they could find. The women stayed in their houses, knowing the danger.

"Is this all you have for us?" bellowed one of the men as they continued to feed their bellies. Her father stood close to the soldiers continuing to fill their mugs with wine as soon as they were empty. Marianne's twelve-year-old brother Jacque assisted his father with the wine. Then, as the men began standing and congratulating themselves on the fine meal they had procured, Marianne noticed her father motion for Jacque to get behind him as he moved away from the men.

"And now, perhaps we need a few more volunteers for our army!" exclaimed the group leader. At that moment, the soldiers turned on those who had just fed them. The man her father had been serving grabbed him roughly and pushed him forward. He tied his hands securely behind him with rope and then tied him to his neighbor Monsieur Pascal.

As the men struggled together, Jacque was able to escape and run to the house for help. Marianne slowly made her way to the barn under the house. She rushed in, grabbed her bow and slingshot off the wall, and then crept forward along the side of the barn. Remaining hidden, she saw that the soldiers had tied the captured men together two by two, they moved them through the square and down the path below the village.

The women and children alerted to the danger, ran to the rocks above the path, which led to La Tour. Uncle Ribetto had managed to free himself from his ropes and was beating their captors with stones. Marianne was doing as much damage as possible. Starting with her slingshot, she knocked several soldiers down, allowing some men to escape back up the narrow path. She drew her bow, and her arrows hit one man in the shoulder and one in the back. The other women and children of the village threw rocks down on the soldiers from the heights above the path.

In the commotion that followed, her father and Monsieur Pascal rolled together one over the other down the mountainside out of danger from the soldiers. Marianne thought the soldiers seemed slow to respond to the prisoners, perhaps because their bellies were full of food and wine. Twelve of the remaining fourteen captives escaped the same way by rolling down the mountain with their hands still tied behind their backs. The soldiers finally continued down the path with their remaining prisoners, and Marianne and the villagers hurried home to tend to their wounded men.

"Of course, the men would rather suffer death on the mountain than be taken to the prison or sent to the galleys!" exclaimed Marianne, who was so frustrated that she couldn't help save all the prisoners.

"I wish this seemed more unbelievable," said her father, but I don't think this is an isolated incident. I have heard other stories of the soldiers taking whatever they want from villagers, beating them, or taking prisoners."

"We must hope our messengers to the Duke will return soon with good news for us," said Grandma Peyronel.

Several weeks later, they learned that the two prisoners taken to the fortress at La Tour were tortured to death. Marianne was inconsolable, blaming herself. If only she had been faster and had more arrows. Her parents came to the barn, where she was busy making arrows.

"Marianne, we need you to stop for a minute and listen to us," said her father.

Begrudgingly she put down her tools and looked up at them from her wooden stool.

"It is not your fault what happened in the village," said her mother.

"I was there, and I could have done more."

"Perhaps many things could have gone differently, but you cannot dwell on the past. It will only stop you from going forward."

"I intend to do better next time," she stated.

"Well, I hope there is no 'next time,' but the prospects of peace are looking grim," agreed her mother.

"Please pray, and let God heal your heart, knowing that you did your best to help everyone," added her father. Marianne heard their words but needed time to forget what she had seen and make peace with it all.

MARIANNE
Piedmont, January 1561

After six long weeks, the Vaudois messengers returned from Vercelli, where they had gone to petition the Duke. Apparently, it had not gone well. Marianne's father stomped the snow from his boots as he entered their cottage.

"I heard they pressed the messengers to return to Mass and said we must beg pardon of General Costa," he told the family. Marianne brought him a hot drink to warm his blood as he sat near the fire. "Also, they have appointed Roman Catholic preachers for each village."

"How can we live with their demands," asked Marianne.

"I don't think that we can," replied her father. "Our banished ministers are returning from Pragelas. The church leaders in Dauphine are afraid that their leaders in France may follow the Duke's actions and issue a decree against them!"

It was a cold winter evening two weeks later. The Vaudois pastors and many of the faithful members of the church, including Marianne's family, assembled on a snowy slope near Bobbio. Marianne's heart was as light as the snow that began to fall on the congregation. Surrounded by the silent witness of the mountains, their meeting opened with a prayer to God, asking for strength and direction to do his will at this hour.

"Oh, Father, you know that none of us will attend Mass or reject the truth that we have. There is nowhere for us to escape at this time. Please help us to defend our homes, wives, and children. Please guide our actions so we may protect our way of life and our right to practice our belief, amen."

Finally, the Vaudois churches of Dauphine and Piedmont would stand together. Their allegiance would be to one another and not to their various sovereigns. The ministers and members pledged to sustain one another through life or death in defense of their religion. Marianne quietly promised her loyalty and verbally promised in words spoken in breaths of frosted air that she would defend her people.

TACHARD
Bobbio, Piedmont, January 1561

Tachard sensed a new feeling in the valley. Their messengers had returned safely, but the people seemed to finally realize there was to be no peaceful resolution. The pastors were now prepared to listen to Tachard, who had disagreed with their past decisions. He addressed the crowd in the town square at Bobbio.

"The Turks, Jews, Saracens, and other nations are allowed to enjoy their own religion and are constrained by no man to change their manner of living and worship. Shall we not be allowed to enjoy the same privileges? We, who serve and worship in faith the true and almighty God, and the one true and only sovereign, the Lord Jesus." The congregation murmured their agreement among themselves.

"They have demanded that tomorrow is the day we come to Mass or be burned or slaughtered, so let us show them tomorrow that we will never abjure our faith!" said Pastor Tachard. A cheer rose from the crowd as they stood together, hands clasped or arms linked in unity.

At daybreak the next morning they rushed to their church, which the Catholics had embellished with images of saints, candles, and rosaries. The people threw them into the street, and

Pastor Artus, who joined them, preached a sermon from Isaiah 45:20:

"Assemble yourselves and come; draw near together, ye that are escaped of the nations: they have no knowledge that set up the wood of their graven image and pray unto a God that cannot save...." He continued, "Now is the time where we stand together, now is when we show the power of our faith." The congregation stood for the final hymn. They sang out in perfect unison:

"A mighty fortress is our God, A tower of strength ne'er failing.
A helper mighty is our God, o'er ills of life prevailing.
He overcometh all, He saveth from the Fall.
His might and power are great. He all things did create.
And he shall reign forever more."

The men and boys then took up their arms and followed Tachard two miles down the mountain toward the village of Villar Pellice to free their family and friends imprisoned by the garrison there.

JOHN
Villar Pellice, Piedmont, January 1561

John Reynaud marched with Pastor Tachard. He still didn't know much about fighting, but he believed they had a right to stand up for themselves and not be squashed like bugs. The angry words between him and his father still echoed in his head. He had never gone against his father before.

"I must go with Pastor Tachard," he had said. "I cannot just kneel at their feet and continue to do their bidding, hoping they will let me live according to my conscience!"

"For centuries, we have found a way forward. We must exhaust all our options before fighting," said his father.

"Can't you see there are no more options! If I back down again, then I have no honor." John paused as he swallowed his emotions. "I do not believe God wants me to live without honor. Please help mother to understand." He had just left then. The door had closed between them, and he didn't know if it would ever open again.

John had his pitchfork and a dagger at his waist. The group had formed into columns as they tramped down the road. Halfway to Pellice, they met the troops coming up the road toward them. Tachard let out a cry, and the men and boys rushed forward. The garrison troops scarcely had time to get off a shot before the Waldensian soldiers overcame them. John found he was able to use his pitchfork to disarm several soldiers by trapping their weapons between the forks and twisting them quickly. He also stabbed forward, feeling contact, he heard a shriek, and the soldier stumbled away. With little resistance, the Vaudois group made their way down the road, the garrison troops running before them to the safety of their fortress.

John looked ahead and saw some monks, lords, and what looked like the Podesta, the chief judge from the city, all waiting on a makeshift platform. Ready to accept the solemn renouncing of their faith by the heretics. From their faces, he saw they were shocked indeed, and they barely had time to scramble down and run toward the fortress gate themselves. The officials and their troops rushed for cover from the uninterrupted arrows and musket shots from Tachard and his men.

John and his kinsmen quickly surrounded the fortress. Tachard stationed sentinels along each wall, with several on horseback.

"Gather any supplies you can find, food or ammunition," directed Tachard. A catapult was commandeered outside the fortress. Its bowl was quickly filled with rocks as several men launched them over the wall. Shrieks from the men inside could be heard as they had not expected the Waldensian attack. A few archers were seen atop the rampart but quickly dispatched by the gifted Waldensian archers from below. One man toppled from his post into the shallow moat below. Several men dragged his lifeless body to the bowl of the catapult and launched him back to where he had come. The fight ended quickly, as the soldier's fears overcame them, and they found themselves surrounded and outnumbered.

Later that night John's captain awakened him in his tent.

"Someone just came into camp to see you; luckily, the night guard recognized him."

John dressed quickly and headed out to the large bonfire they kept burning all night. He couldn't have been more surprised to see his father waiting for him. They greeted each other with a hug and kiss on each cheek.

"Why have you come? I hope you're not trying to talk me into coming home," said John, a little apprehensively.

"No, son, I agree with you now that we must fight to preserve our way of life. Of course, your mother was worried, but she understands." At that moment, John noticed the bow his father had strapped to his backpack.

"You have brought grandfather's bow?" he was sure there would be a silhouette left of the bow over the front door where it had hung as long as he could remember.

"Yes, I will join this fight with you; my father taught me well!" A few tears formed in John's eyes, he knew what a peace-loving man his father was, and he knew it must have been an inward struggle to decide to fight.

The next day Costa's garrison from La Tour came to deliver their besieged men. A wall of Waldensian men with pikes greeted them, along with several cannons they had secured from the fort. The garrison was not expecting this kind of intense fighting. Close enough to see the fiery glow in their opponent's eyes which, along with the cannon, artillery, and uncanny archer's skill, sent them running back to La Tour. After the battle, John helped dig trenches and build short rock walls to offer protection while firing on the castle.

TACHARD

Villar Pellice, Piedmont

On the tenth day of the siege on the fortress, the army raised a white flag. The Podesta came out to speak with them.

"There are not enough provisions, water, or ammunition for us to withstand any longer," he said, "We humbly ask you to spare our lives."

"I am willing to end the conflict with you, as we are just defending ourselves and our right to worship," answered Tachard.

"The garrison commander asked if you would allow two Waldensian pastors to accompany us safely to La Tour?"

"We will guarantee your safety if all your weapons are left inside." Then they tied the soldier's hands behind them. After they left, the fortress was destroyed.

***

The community pastors were in total agreement now. The Waldensians would fight for their freedom. Tachard directed the inhabitants of the valleys to station signal posts at prominent positions on the mountains. They would track the movements of

Costa's army. Instructions were given to each household to make bullets, pikes, and all kinds of weapons.

"If you haven't any lead, then sharpen your fighting sticks, and soak the tips in boiling oil to harden them," counseled Tachard, "we must move quickly." When he returned to his troops, he sought out one hundred of his best marksmen.

"You will be our 'Flying Company,' and we will send you wherever we are in the most danger from Costa and his men," explained Tachard. "Pastor Brucioli and I will join you. We will fight with you for our rights to worship, but we will never let ourselves be overwhelmed with unnecessary bloodshed! Now let us all join together at the Pra del Tor and strengthen the heart of our valleys."

La Tor, the small valley meadow high in the alps. Tachard knew it was surrounded by various mountains, on the North the cliffs of L'Infernet and Soiran. To the west were the snowy peaks of the Rora, and on the south rose the Vandalin. Finally, on the east was a massive rock formation called Rocciailla, which provided a barrier between the Angrogna River and Mount Cervin. This was their place of refuge.

Truchietti

Piedmont, Italy, January 1561

After the siege at Villar Pellice, General Costa gathered his nearly 4,000 troops from their winter quarters. He had decided not to waste any more time on outlying villages and to go straight to the heart of the Vaudois, the Pra del Tor.

The snares devised to capture the Waldensians had thus far failed, but Truchietti had one more idea, and the heretics had led him directly to it. Costa's previous guided tour of the area provided by the ever-trusting Waldensians gave him just the information he needed to end this unfortunate war as quickly as possible. Costa offered his complete support as Truchietti carefully unfolded the crude map they had drawn up after the visit to the sacred meadow.

"We will move ahead with a three-pronged attack, as we discussed earlier," said Truchietti as he gathered the captains around him.

"They will not expect me and my men to come from the cliffs to the north, and we will send our smallest group to attack through the regular entrance," explained Truchietti as he pointed toward the different areas on the map. "At the same time, Lord Bianchi will lead his group from Pramol. All three groups will be synchronized to arrive at the same time."

It was finally happening. Costa believed in his plan, seeing the weakness in the Waldensians, who put all their faith in a mountain valley. As he dismissed the captains, Costa shook his hand.

"Your father would be proud of you, just as I am!"

"This is the perfect method of attack," said Truchetti, "We will surround them, and there will be no way of escape. The Vaudois will never have enough forces to wage battle at three locations," he said confidently. "We will deliver the Angrogne valley to you!"

MARIANNE
Pra del Tor, Piedmont, Italy

Marianne had scarcely noticed the icy footpath or towering cliffs in her eagerness to get to the Pra. Her recent battle with Costa's soldiers had only whetted her appetite. She was more anxious than ever to do her part and help her people.

She couldn't stop thinking about how powerless she felt that night in Riclaretto when the marauders stormed her village. Remembering the shock of the cold and the gunshots, she vowed never to feel that helpless again. She liked how it felt to finally stand up for herself.

They were unpacking the provisions they had brought, and she hung her bow and slingshot on the wall of their tent. Her mother noticed the care she took with her weapons.

"I appreciate how much your skills helped our men escape in Angrogne, but I still cannot support my daughter fighting alongside the men!" exclaimed her mother.

"What about Joan of Arc? She led the men!"

"And was burnt at the stake for her efforts," said her mother as she pursed her lips.

"I don't intend to be burned at the stake," retorted Marianne, besides she was fighting for the other side, she mumbled under her breath. "Mother, I love you, but if I have a chance to help in the battle, I have to take it. I couldn't live with myself if I didn't."

"Well, for me, that's the most important thing," said her mother, "that you live."

Her grandmother had been listening to the conversation. "Maria let us talk together," she said to her mother as she patted the seat next to her by the fire. "Marianne, why don't you go check on the goats." Marianne was more than happy to be excused from the conversation. She had intended to leave, but the temptation was too great. So instead, she crouched near the canvas tent flap where she could hear their conversation, pretending to gather rocks.

"Marianne has grown up hearing the stories of 1487. She has my father's need for justice running through her veins. Can we deny her the right to defend her people?" she heard her grandmother ask.

"I want her to help defend her people too. Just in more traditional ways by feeding the soldiers, mending battle gear, and of course, praying," said her mother.

"Your daughter is so talented; I am afraid if you hold her back, she may never forgive herself," replied Grandma. At that moment, a group of children came running around the side of the tent. Marianne stood quickly and walked away, hoping Grandma would help convince her mother that what she wanted was not so different.

JOHN

Pra del Tor, Piedmont, February 1561

John lifted his eyes from the path just in time to see the valley open up before him; he had made it to the Pra Del Tor, herding the five sheep they had left. As he stepped through the rock and into the open meadow, the sheep sensing their journey was over, jumped and frolicked before him. He veered to the right and made his way to a small cottage at the base of the mountain. He herded the sheep into the small adjacent corral and knocked on the wooden door. As if on cue, the door opened to reveal Grandpa Reynaud.

"My boy, my boy, how good to see you!" exclaimed his Grandpa, as he enfolded him in an embrace. Since Grandma Reynaud's death, Grandpa spent his summers with his daughter in La Pra, so he was very comfortable there.

"Is your father on his way?" he asked.

"Yes, they will be here within the hour."

"Good, and then we will plan our reception for the Duke's men!" He looked intently at his grandson. "There is something I want to give you, something I have kept for a long time." John couldn't figure out why he was being so mysterious. He led him out to the small shed where they kept hay. In the corner, several tools were leaning against the wall. John recognized most of them, but then his grandpa pulled out a long wooden pole with two metal blades curving out on one end.

"This is a rancoon, it was used by those who sought to destroy us in 1488. Now it will be your weapon as we fight again," Grandpa handed it to him. The wooden pole had darkened with age but wasn't much heavier than the shovel. John held it in both hands and jabbed forward with the curving blades.

"Can you show me how to use this?" he asked.

"Yes, I think the muscles you have built up working at the farm should help you wield this weapon in defense of your people."

"I didn't want to fight Grandpa," John admitted. "But I watched the village men be tricked over and over and saw for myself their cruelty to an old man for no reason."

"Sometimes, we are forced to fight. You must remember that we are defending our right to live as we see fit and to serve our God." During the next few hours, people poured into the high mountain valley. By evening people were being assigned camp areas and organizing battle units. The following day Grandpa Daniel Reynaud would begin his weapon instruction for the younger recruits, including John.

JOHN
Pra del Tor, Piedmont, Italy

Grandpa Reynaud had asked to meet Pastor Tachard, whom he had heard so much about. That night John invited the pastor to their cottage in the meadow as it was warmer than the tents.

"At last, I am so glad to finally meet you!" Grandpa greeted Tachard warmly.

"John has spoken very highly of you," said Tachard.

"Well, he is a fine boy and has always made me proud," Grandpa beamed as he ushered them to be seated.

"I understand you fought in the great conflict of 1488," said Tachard.

"Yes, being here in La Pra at such a time has brought back many memories. Some good and some not so good."

"Grandpa was born in France. He initially fought under Commander Hugo Palu against the Waldensians in the villages north of here," began John. "He deserted the troops when he realized they were killing innocent women and children." John noticed Tachard's face in the firelight. He seemed disturbed by the news as John rushed to explain.

"He saw the error of his ways and went on to help the Waldensians in their most important battle," he paused as Tachard remained silent. "I hope you are not judging him for what happened."

"No, no, quite the opposite. I know what it is like to live with unbearable regrets." At that moment, he seemed to make up his mind to speak to them of his troubles.

"My mother's grandfather was Hugo de la Palu, the commander of the French troops you speak of." There was a stunned silence among the group. "My parents embraced the Reformed faith in France, where I was born. My father was a local printer in Lyon. My grandfather never knew of their choice. They knew well the wrath that could come upon them if they openly lived their beliefs."

"I wondered why you have been so zealous in your efforts to protect our valley people," exclaimed Grandpa.

"I truly feel that I will never be able to make reparations for the sins of my great-grandfather and the innocent victims of his actions."

"Perhaps it is time for you to put down your burden?" said Grandpa. "I was there, and I do not hold you accountable." Tachard looked as though he might weep. This was the first time John had noticed anything but confidence in his demeanor.

"I have learned that we have a God of forgiveness," continued Grandpa, "For he has also forgiven me for the part that I played in those horrible events so many years ago."

"You have spent your life giving to our family, and all whose lives you have touched, Grandpa," John said as he reached forward and clasped his Grandpa's wrinkled and blue-veined hand.

"There is nothing stronger than love. my boy, and true respect," he smiled at his grandson. "Your Grandma taught me that."

"I am sorry it has come to this," apologized Tachard.

"I have learned to respect you as our leader and those I am training with," replied John.

"I believe we have a chance here if we use our skills and work together," said Tachard. The softness in his eyes was replaced with resolve.

Grandpa raised his glass, "let us toast to the Waldensians who continue to fight on as a light in the darkness."

MARIANNE

Pra del Tor, Piedmont, February 1561

Marianne watched as thirty boys eagerly gathered around Grandpa Reynaud. He began with those who had bows and arrows, as most owned a bow or could borrow one. They practiced hitting targets at various distances. Soon he noticed Marianne sitting near the practice area, watching everything intently.

"Hello there, aren't you Louis Peyronel's daughter? He asked as he approached.

"Yes, I am."

"Your grandmother and my late wife were cousins," he paused as though sizing her up. "Do you have an interest in the bow?"

"Yes, my father taught me, and I love to shoot," replied Marianne, who stood and dusted off her skirt.

"Why don't you join us then?" invited Grandpa Reynaud.

"Oh, could I!" Marianne could hardly contain herself. Grandpa handed her his own bow. Her hands shook slightly as she stepped up to the shooting line. Then, taking a few deep breaths, she brought the bow up and taking careful aim she let her arrow fly. The arrow hit the center of the target. Some of the boys turned to see who had taken the shot.

"Well done!" exclaimed Grandpa Reynaud, "I think you should join us in our training if your family approves?" Marianne could not believe her ears, "Yes, I will go and ask them." She ran as fast as possible to her parent's tent.

She was expecting this to be a long hard conversation. But miraculously, Grandma Peyronel had apparently convinced her mother that a woman should use whatever skills God had blessed them with to fight tyranny.

The next day Pastor Tachard joined their group during practice, as well as Marianne. Marianne noticed John using the rancoon and jousting with another boy. He was taller than the other boys his age and had broad, muscular shoulders.

Later, when he sat down to rest at the edge of the meadow on a large boulder, Marianne sat down beside him, "You did well with the rancoon today," she said.

"Oh, thanks, I didn't really know what I was doing when I started, but I'm more confident now," he replied.

"I hear your Grandpa was a great bowman, especially during the War in 1488."

"Yes, he doesn't talk about it too much, but I have heard some amazing stories about what it was like then."

"I have, too; I just hope when the battle comes to us, we will make our family proud," Marianne looked down at the bow in her hand.

"I've seen you shoot, and I don't think you have anything to worry about," John exclaimed. He was so sincere that Marianne felt warm and happy about making a difference.

"Grandpa wants us all to learn to use the sling this afternoon, he said it has come in handy many times, and there is always plenty of ammunition around here," he bent down and picked up two palm-sized rocks, and began juggling them in front of her. Marianne laughed, "Well, at least they are good for something besides stopping our plows!" After having a drink at one of the mountain streams, they went back to join the training.

At the end of practice, Grandpa Reynaud reminded everyone that they should target the leaders first in battle, as that would cause confusion among the troops. He also told them to wait until the enemy was close enough so that their weapons could actually do damage.

As all the recruits gathered together at the end of the day, Pastor Tachard stood before them and reminded them of their father's pledge of unity.

"Remember, nothing is stronger than all of us together. God has told us that he will not fail us in our time of need. I confirm to you that this is true." He raised his musket above his head. "We will have victory over Satan and our enemies. So go forward, knowing our cause is just. For God's purposes, we know not, but we trust in the strength of his arm." The entire group cheered, but no one was louder than Marianne and John.

TRUCHIETTI

Pra del Tor, Piedmont, February 1561

Truchietti led his troops over the mountain cliffs North of the Pra. The plan had looked great on paper but faced with the treacherous miles of snow and ice, Truchietti began to wonder if it was possible. However, he would never let his men know of his concerns. He would see they achieved their goal.

"Sir, the men must rest, or they will not make it to the top," reported the chief of his forward company, whose words flew away on the icy wind as soon as they left his mouth.

"We cannot rest now. We will reach the summit in twenty minutes, and then we will rest before the descent," Truchietti spoke confidently as he wrapped the leather strap of his walking stick around his gloved hand. Perhaps the leather would protect against the frost he felt permeating his fingers. The first company had beaten a path through the snow, making it easier for his group to follow. His breath was labored as he climbed; his pack weighed heavily upon his bones. The long line of men was now moving single file up the mountain.

As they reached the top of the pass, he signaled to stop. The men fell exhausted to the sides of the path, grasping their water flasks with frozen fingers. Truchietti's lungs burned as he gulped in the cold air.

He knew the hour was upon them, and although the climb had winded his men, he was confident the plan would ultimately succeed. He wished his father were here to see his success. He stared at the clouds until the memory of his mother swirled around him as she had looked that last day with a blue cape around her thin frame.

"I will find a way to see you again," she promised as she hugged him and kissed his cheek. He was only ten years old and did not understand. Then, later his father explained how she had secretly been meeting with the Waldensian Protestant missionaries. And how she chose to embrace their lies and betray her family. Father would not allow her to stay, bringing such a stain upon their family.

Now that his father was gone, it fell upon him to exact vengeance on these people. He did not blame his mother anymore. He blamed those who had taken her away from him. Now he would re-pay them for what they had done.

Truchietti latched on his greaves and thigh plates, then summoned his squire. He stood silently as the squire buckled his metal breastplate and plackart. Then took his helmet and grabbed his sword.

He knew the Waldenses would never expect the three-prong attack. He sent seven spies down into the valley. And awaited the signal from them, soon it would be time.

JOHN

Pra del Tor, Piedmont, February 1561

John sincerely hoped they were ready. He and Marianne had found a small area to practice with their slings. They gathered firewood and made a cone shape leaning the top edges together, then stacking a few more pieces on top. This was their target. John took the first shot, which missed whizzing to the right.

Marianne held the ends of the two leather straps in her right hand. She cradled a large rock in the oval cloth in her left. Marianne let go and circled the sling faster and faster over her head before stepping forward and letting the stone fly. It made a satisfactory smack as it hit the target and sent the wood tumbling.

"Well, I don't think there's anything else I can teach you," he exclaimed.

"I think I was just lucky," said Marianne.

"I think it's more than luck," said John with admiration. He remembered the young Marianne and the sword fight from their youth. She wouldn't give up then, and he didn't think she would now.

"Do you really think we have a chance?" she asked.

"Of course," he paused. "I never wanted to fight," he admitted.

"You didn't?"

"No, I was hoping things could just go back the way they were," he said.

"Even after they kept attacking our defenseless villages?" Marianne seemed surprised.

"I wanted to believe in peace, like my father."

"I understand. It's hard to go against your parents' wishes. But sometimes you have to do what's right for you."

"I guess you're right."

"Do you think my mother is proud of me?" asked Marianne wistfully.

"By tomorrow, she will be," proclaimed John as he went to reset the target.

TACHARD

Pra del Tor, Piedmont, Italy, February 14, 1561

As dawn crept across the mountains on the morning of February 14, General Costa made his move, and the Waldensians were ready. Their scouts had already seen the flames of the fires set in the closest hamlets. And they spotted the first group on the well-used path to the Pra. Tachard heard the clang of their armor in the canyon as they climbed the narrow path southeast of the valley two by two. The trail was on the right, the mountain river wound its way down to their left, and the icy cliffs enclosed them on both sides. The snow and ice made the path more treacherous than usual.

Tachard sent a small contingent of six men armed with matchlock guns to defend the gate of the Pra. Two knelt in front, two stood behind, and two continued reloading the matchlocks to provide a continual barrage of gunshots. History had shown the Waldensians what to expect, but apparently this same history had not been shared with their enemy.

As General Costa's men rounded the bend close to the entrance, they were gunned down, their bodies falling across the path or into the freezing stream below the cliff. Their bodies slowly filled the chasm, creating a human barricade better than any that could be constructed. As the troops began to turn and flee at the barrier, Tachard spotted another group to the northeast of the valley at La Vachere coming from Pramol. He led the Flying Company across the cold ground to challenge the group from the northeast. As the battle continued, the crowd gathered in the center of the valley cried out. That's when Tachard saw another group of soldiers in the high mountain peaks to the north. How was it possible? He thought. Those mountains were considered insurmountable in February.

JOHN
Pra del Tor, February 14, 1561

As the cry went up from the people, John and Marianne saw at least seven soldiers had made it to the bottom of the mountain to the north and were hiding in the rocks near the houses. They started running in that direction, calling for support from those they had recently trained with. John looked at Marianne, and she met his gaze.

"It's up to us now," she said. They knew their best fighters were busy to the east.

"Yes, we can do this!" he yelled.

The ministers and the congregation began praying vocally to their God. Hearing Grandpa Reynaud's voice, John was propelled forward.

As they approached the rocks, John heard some soldiers calling to their comrades on the mountain, "Come down, come down! This day Angrogne shall be taken!" Five older peasant fighters reached the soldiers before John and Marianne, and two of the spies were silenced quickly. John and Marianne came close behind with at least twenty others as the hill began crawling with soldiers making their way down into the valley to fight.

John wielded his rancoon to the right and then to the left. He flipped one soldier up and over the rocks. He stabbed another with the end of his rod, and still, they kept coming. He could not see Marianne; he hoped she was safe. He tried to focus as he circled his next opponent, and they traded blows. He felt the wood crack as he held his rancoon up to fend off a strike from his opponent's sword. An amused smile began on his opponent's face, but it was fleeting and replaced with a look of surprise as John grabbed the center of the rancoon and drove the pike end straight into his stomach.

It was then that John heard the drum. It was coming from behind him in the valley. He turned briefly in time to see the Flying Company rushing towards them with their matchlock guns at the ready. John and those with him began pursuing Truchiettis' detachment up the mountain and through the rocks. As he rounded an outcropping of rock, he saw a fully armored man running across a small meadow ahead of him. The snow was still deep, and as the man tried to escape, he became trapped in the snow to his thighs. As a last resort, he pulled his large sword, shoved it into the snowdrift and tried to pull himself out.

Suddenly to John's right, he felt something whiz by his ear; turning his head, he saw Marianne. She looked triumphant as she lowered her sling. A loud crack brought him back to the scene before him. The stone hit its mark and toppled the soldier over into the snow. John ran forward, not impeded by heavy armor. As he reached the prostrate man, he pulled the sword from the snow. Now, grasping the blade's hilt with both hands, he propelled it downward with every ounce of strength he possessed and lopped off the head covered in the metal helmet.

The helmet clanked, and the faceplate broke open, it seemed only a moment before John was surrounded by members of the Flying Company, including Pastor Tachard, and Marianne. They all stared at the face, stunned. It was Lord Charles Truchietti, the man who had helped lead the persecution of the Waldenses.

***

That evening, singing and exclamations of "Praise be to God" punctuated the valley on every hand. The Flying Company, John, Marianne, and all those that had fought bravely were hailed as heroes. Tachard related that Costa's soldiers had twice turned to fight as they were retreating up the tortuous mountain passes. Finally, exhausted from their climb up, down, and back up the mountain, the soldiers scattered across the hills fleeing before the courageous Waldenses.

As the Flying Company chased the stragglers, Pastor Tachard called for them to return. They could have no doubt caused greater harm, but the Vaudois ministers prevented them from pursuing the defeated army across rivers and through canyon gorges, reminding them of their creed to fight only to protect their homes and families.

***

John wanted to get away from all the attention for a moment. So, while the community shared their story at the campfires, he grabbed Marianne's hand and led her behind some trees. He dropped it when they were alone, afraid she might think he was too bold.

"Are you okay? Marianne asked, her eyes searching his face.

"I was going to ask you the same question," replied John.

"Were you scared?"

"I didn't have time to be," he stated.

"I never expected there would be so many of them."

"I know," he paused. "You're getting pretty good with that sling."

"I guess I am," she paused, looking down, "does it bother you that I'm a girl, I mean?"

"And that you can fight?" Surprised, he looked down at her.

"Well, yes." Then she lifted her head, and met his eyes with her steady gaze.

"Marianne, you're the only one I would ever want to have my back," he grabbed her hand again to prove it. She smiled up at him, so he guessed it was alright.

TACHARD
La Pra, Piedmont, April 1561

It was dark and quiet, and Tachard might have fallen asleep if it weren't for the fact his breath was forming a smoky haze before him. He sat propped against a rock on a cliff overlooking Rocciaglia. He had headed to his sentry position right after evening prayers, his hand resting on his musket, as his eyes scanned below and south for any movement.

The silence pressed upon his eardrums in an almost hypnotic way. Then he heard something skitter across a nearby rock. Looking upward he saw the silhouette of an owl gliding before a background of glittering stars.

At another time this might have lulled him into security. Although peace talks were going on with the Duke of Savoy, Tachard knew better than to let his guard down. The scouts reported a new regiment joined what was left of Costa's soldiers. He knew General Costa or men like him, they didn't like being beaten, and he was pretty sure that Costa would not soon forget the death of Truchietti.

So, he waited silently upon the rock, just one of twenty men stationed at points around their valley stronghold. Costa would not get his revenge on Tachard's watch if he had anything to do with it.

Suddenly an errant sound interrupted his thoughts. It came from far beneath him in the canyon, a clink like metal upon rock. He was instantly alert. Then he heard the hooting of an owl, two short and one long; it signaled enemy movement. He cupped his hands, and turning to the north, he repeated the hooting sounds he had just heard. Below, in the chasm, the sentries had been alerted. Twelve members of the Flying Company were taking their positions at the gate of La Pra.

Tachard knew that John and Marianne would soon be ready with their group along the edge of the canyon, armed with crossbows and slingshots.

At that moment, the light of sunrise began to etch its way across the sky, slowly illuminating the scene below. The Flying Company waited in the still dark shadows of the canyon, and then the leaders of Costa's troop rounded the bend and were met with an explosion of musket fire. Most fell where they stood, while a few managed to stagger a few more steps before succumbing to their wounds. Still, the column continued to move forward, and still, the musket fire echoed on the rocks. Soon, a pile of men blocked any further progress up the defile.

Then Tachard began to shoot into the chasm below, and John and Marianne's group launched their barrage of rocks and arrows. Yelling and swearing could be heard below. From his view, Tachard saw troops trying to move back down the narrow path crash into those still trying to move forward. Other men fell or leaped to their deaths into the cold and rocky water almost 300 feet below them.

In a few hours, the worst was over, the narrow passage was full of hundreds of dead and dying men, and the Angrogna River once again ran red with the blood of the Waldensian enemies. It was a complete rout, and when they were sure of a retreat, Tachard gave the order for a cease-fire.

Tachard met John and Marianne as they returned to their valley fortress.

"I can't believe they attacked us in the middle of negotiations!" exclaimed John, a little out of breath from the climb.

"I'm sure they thought we would never expect it," replied Tachard. "And I don't think this will reflect well on the Duke," he added.

JOHN
Piedmont, Italy, June1561

On June 5, 1561, the Waldensians signed a peace document at Cavour with the Duke of Savoy. This was the first document that allowed subjects the right to practice a different religion than that embraced by the ruling powers. As part of the agreement, Martin Tachard was required to leave the Savoy lands, the goods that belonged to the Waldensians were to be returned to them, and their cattle allowed to be purchased back from their neighbors. It wasn't long before Ella returned home to her pasture, which was a huge relief and blessing for John.

John, Marianne, and their families gathered with their community at the temple at Ciabas to bid farewell to Pastor Tachard.

"You have made your ancestors proud you have met the moment you have been given with courage, and you have secured the right to exist together with your neighbors. Let us all strive to meet the future with the same determination we have shown now, to live as God would have us live." James and Marianne stepped forward as Tachard finished his sermon and walked through the crowd of people,

"Thank you for helping us stand tall even through fear," said John, shaking his hand.

"Yes," agreed Marianne, "thank you for believing in us and never letting us give up."

"You are the future of these valleys," said Tachard, "I know that they are in good hands."

PART THREE

"Unless the same Providence which first planted this vine, and made room for it, shall turn again, and look down from heaven and visit it, it must, it is feared, perish. For nothing short of the divine succors can enable men to bear up against the poverty, humiliation, and deprivations, to which most of the Vaudois clergy are exposed to this hour."
– William S. Gilly, 1827

JAMES

La Tour, Piedmont, Italy,1844

James Reynaud tried to be patient. He was waiting for his supper and couldn't understand why it was so late. His sister was setting the table, while he was glaring into the fireplace.

"Come now, it's time for dinner," said his mother.

"I thought we were waiting for papa. I thought that was why it's late?" he asked and complained at the same time.

"Your father was called out early this morning to join the Piedmont army for military maneuvers on behalf of Charles Albert. He said they would be about nine miles from the village."

Well, that was different, James felt a great loyalty to Charles Albert, King of Piedmont, and wished he, himself, was asked to go with them.

He quietly ate dinner, imagining himself bravely fighting the French or Austrians.

A few days later, his mother called them hurriedly to the house.

"Pastor Brianza has been sent a message that a rowdy Catholic militia group from Lucerne is heading towards us."

"What should we do," asked his sister.

"I can fight them," insisted James.

"Maybe if you weren't just eight years old," retorted his sister.

"Now stop quarreling; we need to go to the square and see what the pastor has decided.

With that, they grabbed their cloaks and hurried to the center of the village. James was happy to see his friend Henri.

"I told them we could fight!" he whispered in Henri's ear. Henri nodded in agreement.

"How did we find out about this plan?" asked his mother.

"Monsieur Odetti, a Catholic captain in the militia, was asked to join the marauders, and he was the one who alerted Pastor Brianza.

"We must send word to our men!" exclaimed their neighbor.

"Word has been sent," replied the pastor.

Two long days passed before the messenger returned. James and his family gathered with the rest of the villagers to hear the news.

"Their commander will not let them leave their posts," said the messenger.

"Then we must send a more urgent message, we must make them understand what is at stake here!" exclaimed Pastor Brianza. And so, they sent another messenger.

The next day Captain Odetti suddenly showed up in La Tour, having traveled across the Pellice River to warn them himself of the conspirators' plan to attack while they were vulnerable. The villagers gathered to meet with him.

"As a member of the Roman Catholic church," he said, "If I cannot save you, I will perish with you. The honor of my religion is at stake." James heard his words but never knew whether he could trust his Catholic neighbors. Then Odetti came to their house and helped James and his family barricade the door and windows. He had brought some wood and precious nails, and while James and his sister held the wood in place, Odetti nailed it across the door frame. Then he went on to the closest village to warn them of the peril.

Jame's family huddled together, praying for the safe return of their father and all the men of the village. Suddenly a great storm descended upon them. The winds howled down the chimney, the rain slashed their slate roof, and cracks of thunder seemed to surround the house. Now the only light came through the cracks in the wooden shutters each time the lightning flashed.

James wanted to escape; he felt trapped. It was dark, a clamoring darkness that jeered at him. The shadows danced in his mind, then someone banged on the door.

"Let me in! It's Joseph; you are safe," he called out. James helped his mother pull the cross boards off the door. His father practically fell upon them.

"Are you all okay?" they hugged one another.

"Yes, we are fine, thanks to Monsieur Odetti," said his mother. They stirred the embers of the fire and added a few logs. Then, as the fire began to warm them, their father explained what had happened.

"Our commander finally agreed to release us. As we hurried home, a great storm descended on the mountains, with much rain. The paths became muddy and slippery, forcing us to slow our frantic pace. But apparently, the great storm and the swollen rivers stopped the murderers from fulfilling their evil plan." All in the family were quiet and thoughtful. James had been terrified, closed off in the dark house, waiting for whatever might happen. He wanted to be brave, but now he became angry, he was ready for revenge.

"Next time, we should get them first," he said.

"Son," said his father quietly putting a hand on his shoulder, "we must be patient, things are changing for our people."

JAMES

Piedmont, April 1845

James was in the high pasture with the family's sheep. His job today was keeping track of the sheep and then bringing them safely home. His family was struggling to survive. They had moved to a small rock house built under a cleft in the rock in the narrow valley of Angrogna. His father had gone over the mountains to Lyon that winter to work in a textile mill and had only recently returned.

James laid back in the grass and just let his mind drift. From that moment, he was never sure if what he remembered really happened. The spring sunshine had lulled him to sleep, and the next thing he knew, he was squinting up into the face of a stranger. A smiling stranger, but a stranger, nonetheless. The fact that he was derelict in his duty made him leap to his feet.

"Hello there, hello," said the stranger. "I'm sorry if I frightened you." The man spoke perfect French as he doffed his cap, revealing a mass of unruly dark curls. "I was hiking about and seemed to have lost my bearings."

"It happens," James said, looking around quickly to make sure his sheep were nearby.

"I am visiting with Pastor Rostaing at Bobbio."

"Oh, yes, well, if you take that path there toward the right of that little bluff," he pointed nearby.

"Right, *merci*. Would you mind if I sat with you and ate my lunch?" the man asked.

"I guess that would be alright."

The man set his pack near a boulder and unpacked a lunch pail and canteen. James had his own fresh water, but his portion of bread was long gone. The man pulled out a flat chestnut cake and, splitting it in half, offered it to James.

"My name is Thomas, Thomas Kane."

"I am happy to meet you!" James mumbled as he stuffed the bread into his mouth, "I am James Reynaud."

James figured the man to be in his early twenties, and he seemed to know a great deal.

As for himself, James didn't feel his grammar school education would be good enough to respond correctly to his questions.

"I have recently become interested in the Waldensians," explained Thomas. "I have been studying in Paris with Auguste Comte. He believes the needs of the working people have to be addressed."

"We want to work," said James, "but we are kept in our place because of our religion. I can't wait until I am old enough to fight. I will do whatever it takes to finally be free." At that, he jumped up, lunging at an imaginary assailant with a sword.

"That is a lot to take on at your age, which I am guessing is about eight years?"

"I am nine, sir."

"I stand corrected," said Thomas, who sat comfortably leaning back on a rock. "And what will you fight for?" he asked.

"The chance to live my religion and not be punished for it, the chance to leave our valleys and go out into the world." James liked how Thomas talked to him like an adult; more than that, it seemed like he actually cared what he thought.

"Those seem like worthwhile goals. However, I have learned that our actions should always reflect what is best in humanity, love, order, and progress."

"We have a lot of love but not much progress!" blurted James. They both laughed.

"I have observed that, but I have also learned that you live your lives serving others, which is very noble indeed."

"I never really thought about that," James admitted.

"Well, I hope when I am gone, you will remember that I admire your people and their lives of goodness, morality and yes love."

LOUISA

Piedmont, Italy, April 1845

All was quiet on the mountain as the stars etched their intricate designs above, framed by points of rock around the valley. Louisa Peyronel had finished her evening chores and stood for a moment admiring the view. She was hoping for a good crop of corn this year. She entered the lower part of her rock home, where the family's cow, calf, goat, and four sheep were keeping each other warm in the straw. She climbed the wooden stairs to the next level, where her father, Bartholomew Peyronel, greeted her. Soon her mother and younger sisters joined them as they gathered around the fire for their family scripture study.

They spoke together in French, although they could also understand Italian. Her sister Maria read from Jeremiah chapter 16:14-16, *"Therefore, behold the days come, saith the Lord, that it shall no more be said, The Lord liveth, that brought up the children of Israel out of the land of Egypt; But, The Lord liveth, that brought up the children of Israel from the land of the north, and from all the lands, whither he had driven them: and I will bring them again into their land that I gave unto their fathers. Behold, I will send for many fishers, saith the Lord, and they shall fish them; and after will I send*

*for many hunters, and they shall hunt them from every mountain
and from every hill, and out of the holes of the rocks."*

"We do indeed know that the Lord does live and continues to
bless his children," commented her mother.

"Is he speaking of the missionaries?" asked Louisa, she leaned
forward to look at the text, and her long dark braids glinted in the
light of the fire. She was a good student at the local school.

"Yes, I believe that he will eventually let everyone know the good
word of the gospel," answered her father. "Although we have been
kept virtual prisoners in these valleys for decades. I'm sure someday
we will have missionaries again."

There was contentment in that thought as Louisa watched the
embers of the fire. There were periods of peace for her people,
most recently under Napoleon Bonaparte, when they had rights
like any other citizen. But the nobility wasn't anxious to give up
their power to the people, especially the Protestant people.

"We should always remember that Christian kindness towards
all our brothers and sisters will often be rewarded in some day or
hour that we know not," said her mother. Louisa sincerely hoped
that were true. She hoped that someday her Waldensian people
would be treated the same as other Christians in the valleys.

TORONTO

Boston, America, June 1845

As Joseph Toronto guided his boat through Boston harbor, he noticed a much larger vessel headed right towards him. He used every maneuver he knew to get out of her way, but the ship continued to bear down upon him. He waved both arms, trying to get the attention of someone on board. He desperately did not want to desert his ship. At the last moment, as he prayed fervently, the larger vessel turned, thus avoiding a direct hit.

But the boats collided. Joseph and his full cargo of fruits and vegetables were thrown into the water. He caught his breath as he plunged sideways into the cold water. He was pushed down by the weight of his cargo until he managed to break free of the debris. Then, when he couldn't hold his breath for another moment, he surfaced, gasping. But he was confused. It had been daylight when he went into the water, and now it was pitch dark. It took a moment before he realized he was underneath his capsized boat.

He was getting tired and knew he must dive down again and swim outward if he stood a chance of getting rescued. With a gulp of air, he dove, kicking with as much strength as he could. He hit his leg on the edge of the boat before bobbing up six feet away.

With a few strokes, he managed to reach the side of the boat, where he grabbed onto a rope that hung down into the water.

As he caught his breath, he heard someone yelling from the other side of the boat.

"Joseph, Giuseppe, where are you?" It was the voice of another merchant sailor, Tommaso, whom Joseph knew. The words in broken English were some of the happiest Joseph had heard.

"I'm here, over here, on the other side!" he called out. Tommaso had his two brothers working with him, and they soon hauled him aboard another small boat like his. They tied a rope to Joseph's vessel and managed to get it to shore along with their own.

"You are very lucky," said Tommaso, "I am glad we came along when we did."

"Yes, grazie, thank you," Joseph said when he could finally breathe. Toronto sat quietly on the bank with a blanket around his shoulders. His mind traveled back to another time when he sat on a riverbank in Boston, completely wet, with a blanket on his shoulders. At that time, he had just been baptized a member of the Church of Jesus Christ of Latter-Day Saints.

"You need to join your fellow brethren in Illinois," encouraged the missionaries. "That is where you belong." But the ocean was his life. Even as a young boy, he had been drawn to the sea, beginning as a ship's boy and then as a sailor in the Italian Merchant Service. He had worked on the ocean since he was ten, saving all his money to take home to his family. Now at seventeen, he did not want to give that up. He sold fruits and vegetables to the large ships in the harbor and was saving to buy his own boat. Well, until today. Maybe this was a sign that it was time to take that leap of faith.

TORONTO

Nauvoo, Illinois, July 1845

The following month Joseph Toronto arrived by steamboat in the bustling city of over 20,000 in Nauvoo, Illinois. He walked from the ferry landing through the town's main streets with a mixture of log, frame, and brick homes. The tall white temple stood on a small bluff above him. He continued up until he faced the temple. He was surprised to see no one working around the temple site, although there was scaffolding in place. He was amazed at the beautiful building 65 feet tall in front of him. It looked just like the sparkling temple of his dreams. When he had first come to America, he had been worried about thieves stealing the money he had saved from eight years of hard toil. One night he had dreamed of a "Mormon Brigham," a man standing in front of a tall white building. He was told to give his money to this man in the dream, which would bless his family.

Pulled back to the present by the sound of a wagon coming toward him, Toronto called out to the driver, who brought his team to a stop next to him.

"Where is everyone?" asked Toronto, "Why are there no workers?"

"There have been no workers for a few weeks now," said the man, "there is no money left to finish the temple, and everyone is busy preparing to leave the city."

"Let me introduce myself. I am Joseph Toronto, just arrived from Boston," he tipped his hat to the man and his wife in the wagon. "Pleased to meet you, folks."

Toronto knew his clothes were worn, but they were clean. He also knew his English wasn't perfect. His dark hair, eyes, and dark complexion made him stand out from most of the American settlers here.

"I am Parshall Terry, and this is my wife, Hannah. We are just on our way to the bowery to hear President Young speak. Would you like to come with us?"

"Yes, very much!" Toronto exclaimed. President Brigham Young was just the man he was looking for. Upon entering the bowery grounds, they found places near the front and to the side of the podium. Brother Terry pointed out President Young and some other apostles.

Toronto could hardly believe he would hear the president's address in person. But after about twenty minutes, the tone of his sermon changed.

"I am sorry to report that work on the temple will have to cease, for the tithing funds have been depleted, and donations from the Saints in Europe have not been enough," he stated. "But somehow we must continue to build this house, and get an endowment, preach the gospel, gather the Saints, build up Zion, and be prepared for the coming of Christ."

After hearing the words of President Young, the congregation began to disperse, and Toronto went up to introduce himself. Young was the president of the Quorum of the Twelve Apostles and the current leader of the Church of Jesus Christ of Latter-Day Saints.

"I was told to come here in a dream," he said. "May I meet with you tomorrow and tell you my story?"

"By all means, come to my office at one o'clock tomorrow, and I will be glad to receive you," said Young.

The next day could not arrive soon enough for Toronto. He felt he was finally doing what he had been told to do. Parshall Terry and his family offered him a place to stay for the night. They had a small home several blocks from the temple and a farm on the outskirts of Nauvoo.

"Everyone is preparing to leave next spring," Terry told him before they went to sleep. "We are being driven from this place. Mobs continue to attack outlying farms. As you know, our prophet and his brother were murdered in cold blood at Carthage jail. We have recently made a truce with the authorities and those who have attacked us. Our leaders will leave first, and the rest of us will be left in peace to sell our property and follow them as soon as a new place for settlement is chosen beyond the Rocky Mountains."

The next morning Toronto climbed the stairs to President Young's office, carrying his carpet bag with him. He knocked on the door, and Young's assistant welcomed him.

"Would you like to leave your bag out here?" he asked.

"No, thank you. This bag is why I have come to speak with President Young today." As he stepped into the office, President

Young came to greet him. Young was taller than him, clean-shaven, with a piercing gaze.

"Welcome, welcome; I believe you are the first of your Italian countrymen I have met, who have joined the Saints." He seemed genuinely glad to meet him, and although Toronto was sure he was extremely busy, he felt he was given his full attention.

"Yes. I traveled alone from my home in Sardinia, Italy. I have worked as a sailor and fisherman and recently delivered goods along the coast. I hoped eventually to buy my own boat."

"It sounds as though you have been very resourceful."

"I have done my best, President," responded Toronto. "I'm so glad I arrived in time to hear you speak yesterday. I knew then what I must do." At that moment, he opened his bag and took out three smaller drawstring bags. He placed these on the desk between the two men.

"I would like to give myself, and all that I have, fifteen hundred dollars to the building of the Kingdom of God and the construction of the temple."

President Young opened one of the bags and found it was indeed full of gold coins. He was so surprised he could hardly speak.

"I never expected such a gift," he said at last.

"I am used to doing the unexpected," said Brother Toronto.

"You will have blessings upon you and your family for doing this thing," Young declared.

"I only wish I had come sooner, as instructed," Toronto lamented.

"It is just in time," said Young. "We will not have to halt construction. We can finish the carpentry work and painting inside and erect the steeple. Many people will receive the blessings of the temple before we must leave this place for the west."

"Now I shall look to you for counsel and protection," said Toronto, who felt he was putting his future into the Lord's hands now.

"Thank you, Brother Toronto. May you find your home in peace among us," he said as he rose and shook his new friend's hand.

KANE

Philadelphia, Pennsylvania, May 13, 1846

The hall was filled with men and women of different ages. As Thomas Kane made his way to a vacant seat at the end of a wooden bench, he noticed all manner of people present, merchants, tradesmen, and farmers. He listened as Elder Little introduced himself. He was a missionary for the Church of Jesus Christ of Latter-day Saints. Elder Little told of the trials that had befallen his people since they had been driven out of their beautiful city of Nauvoo. Although now spread across vast distances of prairie, they still firmly believed that God had not forsaken them and that the people would somehow receive the desperately needed assistance.

Kane was confounded by religious people who looked for salvation from a distant God. He thought that deliverance would only come through one's own efforts. Although short of stature at 5'6", Kane had never let his size determine what he could do in the world. His father, currently serving as Attorney General of Pennsylvania, and his mother, had both allowed him to believe that he could accomplish anything he set his mind to. He had studied abroad and then got his law degree in Pennsylvania. Kane had a deep concern for those less fortunate, the "downtrodden of society," as some liked to call them. As he listened closely to Elder Little and the other gentleman who spoke that evening, he felt a keen interest in this group that he had only heard rumors about. He hurried to the front of the hall to introduce himself to Elder Little.

"I have been impressed by the story of your people that you shared tonight," he said as he hastily introduced himself. "I am the district court clerk here and believe I could help you." Elder Little seemed pleased to meet him.

"Would you be willing to accompany me to my home, where we could have a more extended conversation about these matters?" Kane asked.

"By all means!" exclaimed Little, "I feel very fortunate to have met you."

***

Kane was bold. He wrote letters of introduction to his political friends in Washington. Then, two weeks later, he joined Little and, based on his father's reputation, arranged a meeting with the United States President, James Polk.

The Latter-Day Saints, or Mormons, as people commonly called them, were anxious to prove their loyalty to the government of the United States. Although, as Kane could see, they had been treated most egregiously and had every right to call out their injustices. At this point, the survival of their people was their highest priority.

Brigham Young had asked Elder Little to get whatever aid possible from the government. With Kane's encouragement, Little agreed to supply the government with 500 men to form a battalion and march from Iowa to California to assist in the Mexican War. Kane felt this would not only show loyalty but help the people and their families with money the government would pay the army.

KANE

Council Bluff, Iowa, 1846

Kane had a personal interest in the success of the Battalion. So, he traveled to "Winter Quarters," a little northwest of Council Bluffs, Iowa, on the west side of the Missouri River. The Saints had established a winter encampment there. As he rode his horse into camp, he was amazed at the cleanliness and organization he saw. The hills were all crowned with white canvas tents, and smoke from 1,000 cooking fires filled the air. Cattle, sheep, horses, and oxen were all grazing together, and he observed large groups of women gathering at the river, washing muslin and calico clothing.

"How can I help you?" The voice came from a young lad who had broken away from his playmates to address him.

"I am looking for the leader of this camp," replied Kane. The young man gave him precise directions, and as Kane dis-mounted, he insisted on leading his horse across the bridge, which he said was a bit tricky and unstable.

Kane found his way through the camp and met President Brigham Young at his tent.

"Well, your people are lucky to be camped among Indians who understand your plight so well," commented Kane. "I know the

Federal government has moved them from the Mississippi to the Missouri and now the Kansas Rivers."

"Yes, the Pottawatomi and Omaha have been kind enough to let us camp on their lands on either side of the Missouri," explained Young.

"I think it would be wise if we make a treaty allowing this to continue," Kane advised. "Many of the Pottawatomi speak French, having learned it from the fur traders. Since I also speak French, I would be happy to negotiate the terms of the treaty on behalf of your people and the United States."

"That would be very much appreciated," replied Young, he added. "The Indians seem to admire our sacrifice of worldly wealth in pursuit of a greater vision." The truth was that Kane also found himself admiring the Mormon people. He continually witnessed remarkable faith and sacrifice in these people that had so little, including their willingness to send off 500 of their most able-bodied men to serve in the army.

Soon a solemn peace council was held with an officer of the United States, the Mormon leaders, Kane, and the chiefs of the Potawatomi. During the conference, Chief Pied Riche Le Clerc, spoke to the group in French:

"My Mormon Brethren, the Potawatomi came sad and tired into this unhealthy Missouri Bottom not many years back. When he was taken from his beautiful country beyond the Mississippi, which had abundant game and timber and clear water everywhere. Now you are driven away the same, from your lodges and lands there, and the graves of your people. So, we have both suffered," he continued. "We must help one another, and the Great Spirit will help us both. You are free to cut and use all the wood you may wish. You can make all your improvements and live on any part of our actual land not occupied by us. Because one suffers and does not deserve it, is no reason he shall suffer always. I say we may live to see all right yet. However, if we do not, our children will. Bon Jour."

***

That evening under the bowery of branches, Kane danced with the camp's men, women, and children. The earth was packed tightly under their feet as they stepped, hopped, and sashayed to the merry tunes of the fiddle, horns, and sleigh bells. The night's celebration was a send-off to the Battalion, which left with their commander early the following day.

"Thank you for your help, Mr. Kane," said Army Captain James Allen, the Battalion's leader.

"Yes, this will greatly benefit our people," agreed President Young. Unfortunately, the Battalion was barely out of sight when Kane was struck down with congestive fever. As he languished in his tent with fever and chills, he heard fellow sufferers moaning in nearby tents. Through his delirium, he instructed Young to send for the doctor at Fort Leavenworth. He wanted no aspersions made toward the Mormons if he should die. The doctor was duly summoned and gave him a powder they administered each day. Kane was vaguely aware of a kind woman who brought him soup and medicine. Perhaps this is the end? He thought, after weeks of suffering. But finally, after a month, he was ready to return home.

"Thank you for all you did to preserve my life, such as it is," said Kane.

"It was my pleasure. You seem like a man worth saving!" exclaimed Sister Browning, who he now recognized as his angel of mercy.

"Indeed!" added President Young, who had come to bid him goodbye. "Your efforts with the Battalion and negotiations with the Indians have been invaluable. You have proven to be a true friend to our people."

"I wish I could do more for you. But you can be assured that I will continue to speak out against your wrongful persecutions and any injustices that come to my attention." The two men clasped hands, then Kane mounted his horse to begin his journey home to Pennsylvania.

TORONTO

Nauvoo, Illinois, September 1846

Joseph Toronto and Parshall Terry stood shoulder to shoulder as they loaded the last cannon onto their wagon.

"We won't be able to defend ourselves much longer. Can everyone get across the river in time?" asked Toronto.

"They will be right behind us!" said Parshall, speaking of the mob. The anti-Mormons of Hancock county planned to drive the remaining Mormons out of the city.

"There is no peace for Hancock while a Mormon remains in it!" proclaimed the local newspaper. The last stragglers from the city camped across the river. They were those who had waited until the last minute to leave. Toronto was part of a small group asked to stay behind to defend the Nauvoo temple so that the people would not see it destroyed as they looked back on their beloved city.

Parshall's daughter helped her aging parents tie the last of their belongings to the wagon.

"Will we ever find a place of safety?" she asked her father.

"I believe if we have faith and keep moving forward, nothing will stop us now." The family climbed aboard the wagon as Toronto urged the two horses onward as fast as possible with their load. The wind whipped the scarf around his face. Finally, they reached the broad bank of the Mississippi River.

Toronto guided the horses out onto the ferry. He looked back one last time at the city they had worked so hard to build. He thought of the well-kept farms, green gardens, and fine homes their persecutors would now enjoy. He saw the temple spire peeking up through the trees, and then it was gone. Sounds of yelling and some cannon fire seemed to signal that all indeed was finished here, and they must move forward, as Brother Terry said. The wagon creaked, and the horses stood silently. The yells of the mob drifted away until he could hear the sounds of the town no more.

The ferry headed toward some light on the opposite bank. Soon, Toronto found himself among several hundred people, the young, old, and sick, huddled together on the ground. These were those who had nowhere else to turn. The next day they would gather what strength they had left and follow their brethren to the western desert.

He had just knelt to help a feeble woman with her meal when the sounds of renewed revelry rose and carried across the river, a bit of vulgar song or a loud oath. Then the drunken men began to whoop and shriek, beating a drum and ringing some sort of bell from the top of their sacred temple. His heart broke as he thought of the years of toil it had taken to drain the marsh and build a city, not to mention his personal sacrifice. But he was not sorry. He would do it all again, knowing he had helped build up God's kingdom on earth.

His fellow sailors had always thought he was strange, not spending his money on women or wine. Toronto always felt he was working for some higher purpose. His resolve grew even more as he helped the feeble souls on the bank of the river eat their soup and make a rough shelter. He would be true to his God and go wherever he asked him to go.

JAMES

Piedmont, Italy, March 1848

James Reynaud marched as he had never marched before. He felt proud parading in formation with his youth militia before the Duke of Savoy and thousands of cheering civilians. He thought this day of freedom would never come to his people, the Vaudois, those of the Piedmont valleys. But, under the Albertine Statute implemented by King Charles Albert, all had been granted civil rights! They would, at last, be able to own property in other areas besides their prescribed land. They could now hold public offices and vote as they saw fit. Most importantly, although Roman Catholicism was confirmed as the state religion, freedom of religion was granted to all other existing forms of worship.

James and a large number of Vaudois, along with many Protestant residents of Turin, gathered around a large banner. It was embroidered in silver with the words, *"To King Charles-Albert, THE GRATEFUL Waldensians."* Then, the group of more than six hundred moved to join a larger procession of at least 50,000 people, to parade throughout the city. Soon they were approached by a delegation sent from the central committee, and a gentleman called out to the assembled Vaudois.

"Vaudois!" he said, "Until now, you have been the last. Today let justice be done, and march you at our head!"

James could not believe his ears. His group moved swiftly to the head of the parade, followed by hundreds of the residents of the valleys. Their banner was waving before them as a dozen children dressed in costumes of the 16th century followed along.

James marched in the procession along the streets of Turin. He was aware of handkerchiefs being waved all along the route. He glanced at the crowd, where he observed a priest throwing his hat in the air. Would wonders never cease? he thought.

"Evviva ai Valdesi, evviva l'emancipazione! Cheers, the Waldensian, long live the emancipation!" The shouting was thunderous. Forgiveness was somehow found for centuries of oppression. Suddenly, through the crowd, he spotted his father, who broke in on the procession, clasping his son in a bear hug. As he marched along with his father, he pointed ahead to where his mother and sister waved a flag and cheered.

It was some time before the procession ceased, and the family was reunited. As they returned to their valleys that evening, all was ablaze with light. In celebration, bonfires burned upon every mountain and valley of Piedmont.

***

The next day, all gathered at the small church at Ciabas, situated half a mile from La Tour, one of the speakers was their beloved benefactor, General John Beckwith.

"Finally, our dream of so many years is being realized," he said. "You must maintain the reputation of your ancestors who shed their blood for liberty. Now our friends swarm on all sides, and our enemies retire into the shade. It is striking. But I hope you are equal to the task of the times," Beckwith paused for a moment. "If you have courage, you will succeed; if not, you will remain concealed among the crowd, and we will hear nothing more of you. Your first duty is to assert your civil rights, for it is on this your future depends."

James completely trusted Beckwith. He knew how he had served in the British army until the battle of Waterloo when he lost his leg. In 1827, he discovered Dr. Gilly's book outlining the history and deprivations of the Waldenses. Although he was a member of the Church of England, he chose to live among them and use his fortune and contacts to help the Waldensians.

James pondered on his words. Was he, in fact, equal to the task before him? Able to find his place in society? James was struggling. He felt he should be happy but sensed something was missing in his life, and he wasn't sure what? After the meeting ended, James told his family he would meet them at home. He sought out Beckwith to speak with him. He had to wait for many enthusiastic villagers to leave the church as Beckwith ushered him into his office.

"I know I should be happy. But I can't help it; I'm still angry," James blurted out. "This change has taken so long!" he exclaimed.

"I understand your frustration. But I believe real change is possible."

"I have heard that for so long, I'm not sure I believe it," said James. "I have watched as the authorities gave our neighbors opportunities for better farmland and jobs. I have felt held hostage by my faith. And that I will never be accepted just for who I am."

"Have courage, my boy. Your answers will come. I lived half my life before God called me to his great purposes. Your ancestors have given you a good foundation. What you do with that will be up to you!"

James thanked General Beckwith. He walked slowly home up the path that zig-zagged across the mountain.

KANE

Pennsylvania, 1850

The door to the jail clanged shut. Thomas Kane sat down on a metal bed with a meager excuse for a mattress. So, this was it. How many months was he in for? He thought his father was jesting when he had threatened to send him to jail. Apparently not.

Kane tried to explain his feelings to his father, who was also his boss, the attorney of the District Court of Philadelphia.

"I cannot live by this Fugitive Slave Act. I won't assist in returning these people to a life that is repulsive to me!" He didn't believe owners of enslaved people and their agents had the right to search his free state for escapees. Pennsylvania shouldn't be an open ground for bounty hunters or kidnappers. And now, they would deny enslaved people the right to a jury trial. As the court clerk, he refused to comply with the new federal mandate for the state, and so he had new living quarters. But Kane was proud to go to jail, if only on principle.

His soul was still on fire since meeting with the Free Democrats in Washington in January. Their fearlessness and honesty impressed him. He believed in their motto; "Free Soil, Free Speech, Free Labor, and Free Men." He resolved to be brave in standing up to what he believed was a crime against men, even if it meant standing up to his father.

A week later, his sister visited him at the jail. She shared a recent newspaper story about him in the local paper.

"Well, what do you think? Am I a "renegade to my parents' faith?" he asked.

"I'm not sure if they mean our Presbyterian faith or their faith in you personally," she said, always objective. Perhaps he was a renegade, he thought. He had always questioned the status quo, and the answers he came up with often put him at odds with his family and others. Since he left the Utah territory, he had written articles and organized committees in Philadephia and Boston to solicit contributions for the "suffering Mormons," as the newspapers called them. Kane would continue using all his resources to help those without power, including slaves or Mormons.

TORONTO

Italy, July 1850

Joseph Toronto had been called as a missionary to his brethren in Italy. He was thankful God had seen fit to send him back to his native country. He had helped drive Brigham Young's cattle across the plains and had been excited when Young announced his plans to open missionary work in non-English speaking countries.

He peered out the square window of the diligence hired to carry his party to their final destination, Genoa. The waters of the Mediterranean winked at him around each curve of the road. Welcome back! They seemed to say. His heart was fairly bursting. He had finally come home. It had been nearly nine months since he left the Salt Lake valley. As the coach entered the city, Toronto had an excellent view of the harbor. Ships from every nation passed one another as they traveled in and out of the harbor. Sailboats, steamers, and war frigates together. He inhaled the sharp salt air like a man denied oxygen. Whatever may come, he thought, it would be worth it.

Soon, Toronto and his companions, Elder Snow and Elder Bingham, were able to teach a few people. He spoke the language fluently but could not write it. Initially, Mr. and Mrs. Romano had agreed to a visit.

"So sorry, we cannot meet with you again," said Mrs. Romano.

"What has happened to change your mind?" asked Toronto.

"We felt compelled to talk with our priest at confession this week," explained Mr. Romano. "And he forbade us to continue listening to your message."

"We cannot go against the priest," added Mrs. Romano as they said goodbye.

Their prospects seemed bleak. They were prohibited even from giving a Bible to a Catholic. But, as the missionaries pondered this problem, they received inspiration concerning the people of the Piedmont valleys to the northwest. The Waldensians who had maintained their homes and stood for freedom of religion for many long centuries.

"Reading about these people, it is amazing they have survived all these centuries," said Elder Snow.

"Yes," agreed Toronto. "I feel it's important that we go there and share our message."

"It does seem the Lord has hidden a special people in those Alpine mountains," agreed Snow.

The three Elders made plans to travel to La Tour as soon as possible. They found rooms at the local Inn, and sought out General Beckwith, who had become the civil leader of the Waldensians. Under his direction, 120 elementary schools were built or restored. In addition, he constructed a college for secondary education at La Tour and a school for young women.

Beckwith agreed to meet with the missionaries. They felt if they were received favorably by him, they would gain the citizens' trust. A personal assistant greeted them at Beckwith's door and ushered them into a large drawing room at the girl's school where he was currently living. They exchanged greetings and enjoyed an English tea before Elder Snow broached the subject of their visit.

"We thought there was an opening for our missionary efforts here in Piedmont since the new statute is in place, and the people are free to proselyte and have public meetings," said Elder Snow.

"In reality, it is a little more difficult than it sounds. I know you have been in England, where they embrace free speech, but this place is quite different. So many of the people are superstitious and set in their ways," said Beckwith. "There are about 21,000 Waldensians here and only 500 Catholics. Based on their seclusion, I worry about their abilities to take their place on a world stage."

"The people we have met seem honest, virtuous, and most kind to strangers," said Elder Toronto. "Although, many seem to suffer from numerous mental and physical maladies."

"Yes, these people have known much suffering. They are indeed honest and virtuous, almost to a fault, but are not prepared for the wiles of men." Beckwith continued, "Their families continue to increase, and lands are divided and re-divided amongst them with more mouths to feed. Each year it becomes a greater necessity either to emigrate or to resort to commerce and the occupations of large towns."

"It seems economic circumstances will force them to spread out into Italy or even emigrate to other lands," said Elder Snow.

"We are here to help these people rise above their current circumstances," said Elder Bingham.

"I have been ordained as an apostle of the Lord, for the Church of Jesus Christ of Latter-Day Saints," said Elder Snow. "We believe that the Lord's church is organized with apostles, prophets, evangelists, pastors, and teachers to move forward the work of the ministry and to build up and unify the church. These callings are still necessary today."

"I, too, believe that the Lord's church cannot go forward without proper organization and emphasis on missionary labors," remarked Beckwith.

"It seems that especially here in this country, whenever a man has dared to think for himself and search for truth amid the labyrinth of opinion, he has quickly been removed to a dungeon!" exclaimed Elder Snow.

Beckwith laughed at that, "I know it is sad but true. First, the Catholics persecuted the Waldensians, and then the Protestants oppressed those who disagreed with their creed. That is why I am so excited about expanding the Waldensian church out into all of Italy, where we can at last study the Bible together." As they gathered around a large table, Beckwith showed them his plans for building a large church in the capital of Turin.

"We can see that you are grounded in love, as the Apostle Paul has asked us to be," said Toronto, "You have sought to do great good for these people, and I am sure you will be blessed."

At the end of their meeting, Beckwith said, "If indeed you follow the Apostle Paul and have eyes to see the goodness of the people, you shall not receive any opposition from me. If you preach the gospel as faithfully to these valleys as to me, you need not fear reproach at the Holy Altar of God."

After the meeting, Toronto felt a new sense of purpose. He spent his time getting to know the people of the valleys, observing their lives of toil in the alps to provide a meager living for their families. He walked up and down the mountains to visit the Waldensians in their rock homes that climbed the edges of the steep canyons. Everyone in the families worked hard to glean whatever could be grown on their small patches of land. Most discussions occurred while the families were weeding their gardens or tending their sheep or goats. The people had very little knowledge of anything outside their own valleys, and many were intensely loyal to the religion of their ancestors.

Toronto was starting to feel discouraged again the same week their innkeeper's young son became ill. Despite the efforts of his parents and the doctor, the boy's condition grew worse, and they had no hope of his recovery.

The missionaries found a secluded spot on the mountain where they prayed fervently for the boy's recovery. That afternoon they anointed the child's head with oil and offered up a blessing that he might be healed upon the will of the Lord. The next morning when they visited, his father met them at the door with a smile.

"*Mieux beaucoup*, better, much better," he said. The boy's mother then expressed her joy to them. As word of this miraculous healing made its way among the valleys, the Elders dedicated the land to preach the gospel, organized the church, and began to actively minister among the Vaudois.

LOUISA

La Tour, Piedmont, July 1850

Louisa heard that the foreign visitors from America were coming to meet with General Beckwith at the girls' school she attended. She was fourteen now and always curious about anything new, quick to volunteer to help serve the refreshments to the guests. She knew Beckwith liked a proper English tea in the afternoon, a tradition he had kept most of his life.

As Louisa brought the trays of food into the drawing room, Beckwith motioned the girls to come forward and introduced them to the guests touting their astounding progress at the school. She understood that they were missionaries from America. One spoke fluent Italian, and the other two were learning the language. One man with kind eyes said that he was ordained as an apostle of Jesus Christ.

When Louisa took the used plates from the room, she looked back at the men huddled together around Beckwith's plan for a new church in Turin. A beam of light came through one of the drawing room's long windows, illuminating the figure of the man with kind eyes. She felt a great desire to talk to him. As school was out for the day, she waited outside, hoping that she might have an opportunity as the guests left. Trying to be patient, she noticed several women walking down the street carrying heavy loads in their gerla or large shoulder baskets. She was glad her days of bearing loads up and down the mountain trails were over.

Luckily, she didn't have to wait too long. When the men came out to the street, she approached them.

"Signore, I was inside serving your tea when I heard what you were talking about. I would like to know more," she said to the nearest gentleman.

"We would be happy to talk with you," said the man, who introduced himself as Brother Toronto and spoke perfect Italian. "Can we give you a pamphlet that explains more about our message and our church?"

"Yes, please," said Louisa, as she took the parchment, "I am anxious to read this."

"We are staying at the Inn, and would be happy to come visit your family," he continued.

"Our farm is out on the plain east of La Tour. After they enacted the new constitution two years ago, we moved there."

"That is not far. You share the pamphlet with your family, and we will visit you. What is your name?"

"Louisa, Louisa Peyronel."

JAMES

Angrogna, Piedmont, July 1850

Twilight was James' favorite time on the mountain. Soft beams of light stretched behind the tall rock peaks and lit his path. He led the sheep down the grassy knoll toward the safety of the barn. He heard the bells' various musical tones echoing across the hillside as the villagers herded their cows down from pastures for the night. The sheep followed him contentedly, knowing he led them to water and sleep. He secured the sheep in their pen, and then took one last look at the magnificent sky where pinks and purples mixed with the wisps of darkening clouds.

"Is all well with the sheep tonight?" asked his sister Anne as he stepped into his family home. "Yes, they are almost as content as me," he said as he saw she was serving one of his favorites, chestnut hand pie. He couldn't resist pulling a small taste from the edge as his sister tried to swat him with her dishcloth. Then the door opened, and his father came in.

"Are you behaving yourself?" he asked, not expecting a reply. "I hope so because I have some interesting news!" His father's tone made them both stop and listen. "I have just heard of a miraculous healing of a young boy in the Grey family. The family that owns the Inn at La Tour." His father opened their Bible and read from James 5:14:

"Is any sick among you? Let him call for the elders of the church; and let them pray over him, anointing him with oil in the name of the Lord: And the prayer of faith shall save the sick."

"These three missionaries that have come to La Tour, say the gospel has been restored to the earth. That many things were lost by error and sin; finally, the church as constituted by Jesus Christ has returned."

"My goodness, that is quite a claim," said James.

"Yes, they are teaching at Monsieur Malan's in La Tour tonight. Why don't we go and listen to what they have to say?"

"I can have dinner ready in just a few minutes," offered Anne. His mother returned from helping a neighbor and after dinner, they took the trail from Angrogna to the village of La Tour. Monsieur Malan welcomed them along with about twenty-five other villagers. The strangers from America introduced themselves:

"I am Joseph Toronto. I emigrated to America from the island of Sardinia. After finally arriving in the valley of the Great Salt Lake, I was called by Brigham Young, a prophet of God, to serve as a missionary in my native country," he paused, visibly emotional, "I am so happy to be here among you. Please call me Brother Toronto."

He then turned to the other men, who introduced themselves, Brother Jacob Bingham and Brother Lorenzo Snow. The latter stood and addressed them,

"My dear friends, I am here as an apostle of the Lord Jesus Christ. I have seen your people as a light in the darkness, the darkness of many centuries. I have read your history and have been sent here with more light for your people."

James was astonished. Now, fourteen years old, he knew the history of his people all too well. The stories were told around family hearths and at church meetings, permeating every aspect of their lives. They were the Vaudois or Waldenses. They had stood against corruption and had fought for their freedom to worship God how they wished. They had been tortured and burned for not renouncing their faith in the face of many persecutions. They had been driven from their mountain homeland, only to return triumphantly to reclaim it. And through it all, the miracles of the Lord had preserved them. Preserved them through to this very day, and to this very hour.

Brother Snow continued, now speaking about Moses, "The Lord appeared to him in the burning bush and commanded him to go forth and accomplish a certain work, which concerned the peace, happiness, and salvation of a great people. His success and prosperity were made perfectly sure by the fact that the work he was assigned was not a thing of his own invention but emanated from Jehovah. I testify that our work here is also from God."

"Through the centuries, many of the doctrines and ordinances of the gospel have been changed or lost," said Elder Bingham, standing up. "This made it necessary for God to restore those things to the people. He called the Prophet Joseph Smith to restore his church and the priesthood authority that had been taken from the earth."

Brother Toronto brought the meeting to a close with his words, "I testify that this is God's work, and he has restored his church through the prophet Joseph Smith. He has also provided another testament of Jesus Christ, a companion to the Holy Bible, the Book of Mormon. I pray we may listen and follow our Lord and Savior, Jesus Christ."

There was much discussion on the way home. When the family reached their own fireside, James spoke of his grandfather, "I know he was dissatisfied with the church because he saw the differences between what was being taught and the teachings of the Savior and apostles. He once said to me, 'The young will see the day when the gospel shall again be preached in its purity.' His words kept coming back to me as I listened to the missionaries tonight!"

"I was impressed with their sincerity," said his father.

"I also felt a great joy in hearing their words," said Anne. "How will we know if what they are saying is true?"

LOUISA

Piedmont , July 1850

Louisa wasted no time. Sometimes her impetuous nature got her into trouble, but tonight she was too excited to care. When she got home, she helped prepare dinner, and that night as her family gathered around the fire for their regular Bible study, she quickly pulled out the pamphlet entitled "The Voice of Joseph." She explained the unusual meeting at the school.

"I felt like I needed to learn more," she said. Her father then reached into his coat pocket and pulled out the same pamphlet.

"I have been reading this since last week," he said. "There is a lot of information about the history of the Mormon people in America. Apparently, they have been persecuted and driven from their homes several times. Every time they build up a fine community, they are attacked by mobs who are intent on driving them away."

He continued, "For example, it says here they were attacked in Missouri: '*In November 1833, a ruthless and murderous mob, composed of many hundreds, armed with weapons of destruction, came suddenly upon the Saints, who were unprepared for defense. They drove men, women, and children from their lovely habitations. Their deep distress, the severity of their sufferings, it is no pleasing duty to relate. Women were shamefully abused in the presence of their husbands, daughters in the presence of their parents: defenseless men were shot down like wild beasts: some while fleeing for their lives. So suddenly were they compelled to flee that they could not take sufficient apparel to preserve them from the cold wintry blasts. The reader may easily imagine the extreme suffering of women and children. In consequence of these severities, many perished by the way before any kind hand of hospitality offered its relief.'"*

"This history sounds like the many persecutions that our people have endured," Louisa said as she put her arm around her younger sister.

"It also says that although they appealed to the state governor for aid and justice, none was given. Instead, he issued a proclamation for their Extermination and Banishment. Several thousand troops marched into their settlements in Caldwell County where they burned fields and homes, shot their livestock, and butchered some eighteen or twenty defenseless citizens."

"I must say I am somewhat astounded, as sometimes I have believed we were the only people on earth who have suffered such horrible things," her mother agreed.

The following week the Peyronel family invited the missionaries to visit their home. Elders Joseph Toronto and Jacob Bingham came for a fine dinner that Louisa and her mother had spent all afternoon preparing. Her little brother Pierre was too young to understand, but he was well-behaved and played with his wooden blocks after dinner while the others talked.

"Please tell us some of your experiences during these trials of your church?" asked her father.

"My friend Parshall Terry said the local ministers riled up the people to put down the 'evils' of the Mormons," explained Elder Toronto.

"What were some of their concerns?" asked Louisa.

"Some of the issues were the declaration that miracles had been performed, cures achieved among the sick, our belief in angels, and the gift of tongues," added Elder Bingham. Basically, they were different, thought Louisa, just as the Waldensians had always been different from those around them.

"However, being led to the western desert, we have founded a new city," continued Brother Toronto. "It is there that the new Zion will be built, and flourish, as spoken of in Isaiah chapter two. Could you read that for us, Louisa?"

"And it shall come to pass in the last days, that the mountain of the Lord's house shall be established in the top of the mountains and shall be exalted above the hills; and all nations shall flow unto it."

At that moment, Louisa felt a connection with these people that she could not describe. Perhaps she thought, her faith was like a mountain stream going on its course for centuries until it joined with a larger river and became something more remarkable. The fullness of the gospel was thunderous to her like a great river. All that was missing before was filled, including her heart.

Her father closed their family meeting by praying to God that they could know his will concerning them. He prayed that the light of truth would dwell with them and show them their path.

JAMES

Angrogna, Piedmont,1852

James knew his ancestors believed in miracles, and so did he. One day he walked up into the mountains, high into the pasture where he used to take his flocks when he was young. The chestnut tree was just as he remembered at the edge of the forest. James had always loved this tree. It stood almost 90 feet tall on the mountain. Its limbs angled out in an expansive canopy overhead interspersed with patches of blue sky. He knelt near the trunk, reaching out and letting his palm rest on the deeply lined aging bark. There he prayed. He prayed to know if what he was learning was true. He prayed to know what God wanted him to do. And then he just sat by the tree and listened. A quiet feeling of peace settled over him, and then he knew. His heart and mind together said it's true! Tears pricked his eyes.

James had always felt he had a greater purpose. After hearing the missionaries, some of his questions had been answered. He knew that God had a plan for him and hoped he had enough faith to see it through, wherever it might lead. When the sun hid behind the tree line he started back down the trail.

One cold night six weeks later, the Reynaud family huddled together, waiting to be baptized. Elder Toronto baptized them one at a time, immersing them in the frigid water of the mountain stream. No matter how cold the air was, the family felt warmed by the feelings in their hearts. James wrapped a blanket around himself and his sister, and the small group made their way up the narrow path and back to their home.

His mother, Henriette Reynaud, had fallen ill a month earlier. Despite all they could do for her, she died just a week ago. The sorrow was still profound. However, the hope the family held in the resurrection gave them strength. And the teachings of their new faith gave them a reason to rejoice. One day their family would be sealed together in a temple of the Lord, never to be parted again.

James knew he was taking a big risk. At first, it was okay to attend the meetings. None of his friends knew anything about it and didn't care. But then the ministers began to ban together in a "holy alliance." Neighbors were pitted against each other. Because the people of the valleys had lived and died together for centuries, many people were related. Sometimes it was nice to have everyone know all about you and help in times of need. But this time it was not very nice.

The ministers began to use their sermons to speak against the missionaries and the new religion. They reminded their congregations in no uncertain terms, "Your forefathers have sworn to die before they change their religion or quit their country!"

James knew some people who had lost their jobs upon joining the new religion. As the rhetoric became more intense at the Waldensian temple, and as the ministers told the people falsehoods or half-truths about his new faith, things just got worse. Now, as their crops suffered from grape rot disease, some blamed the arrival of the American missionaries for the blight. James was defending himself with his neighbors and even in the marketplace.

"Brigham Young hired those missionaries to convert you and make you his slaves in the desert," taunted one of his old schoolmates.

"I'll never be anyone's slave!" he retorted.

"You're dirty enough to be one!" James lunged toward the boy, and they rolled around in the street, with James getting in a few good punches here and there. Then, suddenly, he was pulled to his feet by Brother Toronto. His friend Henri Chastain had grabbed the other boy and held his arms.

"Now, what is going on here?" asked Toronto.

"Oh, he's just a hothead," said the boy.

"I'll show you a hothead," muttered James, as the presence of Toronto had extinguished this particular flame. As they went their separate ways, Toronto walked next to James.

"Do you want to talk about it?" he asked.

"I don't understand this. Don't we all love Jesus Christ and try to follow his teachings?" he said in frustration.

"Sometimes people are more concerned with being right than showing love to their neighbor."

"Or than listening to the facts!" he exclaimed. "They believe everything bad the pastors say but hear none of the good."

"Satan is the father of dissension," said Elder Toronto. As James walked by the schoolhouse, he thought of General Beckwith, who had left the valleys in 1851 to oversee the building of the great

Waldensian church in Turin. James wondered what he would think of the current persecutions.

One night, Elder Toronto came to visit a neighboring house in Angrogna. The converts in the area prepared to gather at the planned time--others who felt differently piled big logs and stones to block the narrow path up the mountain. Finally, after trying an alternate route, some decided it wasn't worth the extra climb to attend the meeting.

James felt his persistence rewarded by the message from Brother Toronto. He spoke of forgiveness, the need to forgive people of their backbiting and slander against them. He said this would free them to be genuinely committed to one another. He also expounded on Hebrews 10:32:

"'But call to remembrance the former days, in which, after ye were illuminated, ye endured a great fight of afflictions.' As in the days of Paul, after we have received the light of the true gospel, we will most likely have to endure afflictions. And I ask you to continue to remember how you felt when you received the spirit of the Holy Ghost testifying of the truthfulness of what you now embrace. Hold on, little flock, hold on!" He continued, "Do not retreat down that mountain that you have already climbed."

The meeting ended, but as they opened the front door for the missionary to leave, the lamplight that reached into the night showed some dark figures waiting, and a barrage of rocks began pelting down. It looked like Toronto avoided injury as he ran away from the nameless people who felt empowered by the cloak of darkness to throw stones.

Later that night, James lay in the manger of the stable. During the colder months, his family often slept among their animals to stay warm. James wasn't sure he wanted to endure any more afflictions. He had always been shorter than the other boys, and after his family's fortunes had turned, he felt more inferior than ever. It felt like the rock walls were closing in on him. He tried to remember what his mother had taught him, "Breathe, James, breathe and be thankful."

LOUISA

Near La Tour, Piedmont, 1853

It had been three years since the missionaries had first come to their valleys. Regardless of the rumors of mob violence, the little band of Latter-Day Saints was intent on having their Sunday meeting. Louisa and her sisters had been baking bread in their outdoor oven for two days. No one who attended would go hungry, in body or spirit, thought Louisa. The people gathered from the nearby mountains and valleys. Louisa knew some had started walking before daybreak.

"Welcome, welcome," said Louise's father as he greeted everyone, "we are so pleased to once again hear from the brethren who have traveled such a great distance to bring us the good news of the restoration of the gospel of Jesus Christ."

Elder Toronto rose from a chair and began to speak. At precisely the same moment, the people heard yelling coming from outside.

"Bring out the wolves in sheep's clothing!" they shouted. "Bring out the wolves!"

Toronto kept speaking about Joseph Smith and how he had read in the Bible, the scripture in James 1:5:

"*If any of you lack wisdom, let him ask of God, that giveth to all men liberally, and upbraideth not; and it shall be given him.*'Joseph had felt if any needed wisdom to understand which of the many different religions was right, it was him. And so, he decided to take his private prayer to the Lord in a grove of trees on his family farm," he continued, "and that is where he received his answer. The Lord made known his plans to restore the gospel in all of its fullness, restoring all that had been lost over time, including the authority of the Holy Priesthood of God."

The yelling became louder, and they could hear it on three sides of the house.

"Who is helping the wolves? Let them come out!"

"You better bring out the wolves in sheep's clothing, or we will come and get them ourselves!" shouted another voice.

At that moment, Louisa, armed only with her Bible, stepped out of the house and descended the stairs to face the mob. Those in attendance, including the missionaries, looked at one another and followed her. She walked up to one of the Vaudois ministers who was part of the mob. This man she had known since childhood.

"It is a fake Bible!" the men yelled.

"You have been disloyal to your church," the minister accused her.

"I have been loyal to truth and righteousness," said Louisa. "I believe our duty as children of God is to seek knowledge. I have a better understanding of the Bible now." Louisa's hand that held the Bible did not shake. She felt perfectly calm as she stood amidst the ministers and men who continued to yell.

"You have all been deceived!" they yelled, taking in the crowd behind her. Just as it seemed they would move forward as one body to attack any who should oppose them.

Louisa lifted the Bible in her right hand and declared, "I demand that you depart immediately! The elders are protected, and you cannot harm them!" Louisa knew God was with her, just as with her great-great-grandmother Marianne, who had stood and fought Trachetti's troops at The Pra. She could feel their blood coursing through her veins, and she would not back down. In that one moment, the fierce group of men was dispersed, their heads bowed in shame, they mumbled among themselves as the ministers among them told them to return to their houses.

All returned to calm. Louisa, her family, and all who had gathered there marveled at the protection of God.

"Weren't you afraid?" asked James Reynaud, who was at the meeting with his father.

"For some reason, I wasn't," mused Louisa. "I have a habit of doing things before I think them through, but I guess in this case, it worked out alright."

"You were fearless," said James. It seemed that James admired her, but she wasn't sure. Most boys thought she wasn't very ladylike when she spoke her mind. Louisa had noticed him earlier at the meeting; he had a long face with high cheekbones and deep-set eyes. He seemed kind of the quiet sort to her.

The following Sunday, Elder Snow secretly returned to the valley. After hearing of the week's events, and the other persecutions that had gone on, he encouraged all who could to emigrate to Zion. As they met together, he said the Perpetual Emigration Fund would provide some monetary help, but they should try their best to sell what property they could.

"Church members in the Great Salt Lake Valley, having come through great tribulation, have not forgotten their brethren who are still in adversity, scattered among the nations. Therefore, they established the Perpetual Fund to help poor immigrants so they too can gather to Zion. Brother Toronto will lead you there."

Elder Snow also related a fantastic dream that he had, where he found himself in the company of some friends on a fishing excursion:

"We were delighted with seeing large and beautiful fish on the surface of the water, all around, and to a great distance. We saw many people spreading their nets and line. I discovered that a fish had got upon my hook–I drew in my line and was not a little surprised and mortified at the smallness of my prize. I thought it very strange that among such a multitude of noble, superior-looking fish, I should have made so small a haul. But all my disappointment vanished when I discovered that its qualities were of a very extraordinary character."

"I see the fine character of those before me," he continued. "I do not doubt that you will continue to progress and grow in the gospel and be an example to your friends and family in faith and commitment to Jesus Christ."

Louisa was excited at the thought of gathering with those across the great ocean. The idea of building something of worth, something greater than each individual. She thought it must be wonderful to live in America, where they could finally meet together without fear.

Kane

Philadelphia, America, July 1855

July 1855

Brigham Young, My Friend,

I was pleased to receive your letter in the last mail. I am glad to hear that your community is thriving in your mountain home. I appreciate your salutation, "that I may long live upon the earth to enjoy the sweet society of wife, children, and friends." And I am happy to see that come to pass as I am now the proud father of a new baby daughter.

You know I shall never forget those who helped and nursed me on the prairie. It was the observance of your noble self-denial and suffering for the sake of your conscience that first made a truly serious and abiding impression upon me. If God spares me, I shall always labor for your justice.

It is gratifying to hear of your efforts to pacify the Native tribes in your region without resorting to arms. You have undoubtedly prevented the shedding of blood, including your own people. Helping feed and clothe them seems to me a wise course of action. As well as operating strictly on the defensive. Please let me know if I can offer you or yours any service.

I remain your friend,

Thomas Kane

JAMES

La Tour Pellice, Piedmont, Italy,
November 1855

James' father, Joseph Reynaud, had served in the fourth company of rifle soldiers for ten years. But now, he was getting James, who had turned eighteen, released from his garrison conscription so that he would be free to immigrate to the new land. James would be traveling with the Chastain family, as his father did not have the means for them to go together, and he would have more time to try and sell his farm.

James walked to the cave above his home slowly. He wanted to savor every moment he had left on the mountain. How many times had he run and played on this trail? His footsteps made no sound as he entered the cave. A sliver of light came down into the darkness from a crevice high above. He had brought his lantern to see the names scratched into the wall. *Daniel Reynaud*, and *Madeline Jaquet, 1488*, there were his ancestors' names left long ago. Somehow touching those names made them feel closer. What would they say to James, knowing he was leaving the valleys they had fought so hard to defend?

He returned home. His sister had gone to bed as James sat with his father one last time, looking at the dying embers of the hearth.

"I have always been so proud of you, father, the way you served your country and worked for our family."

"And I have always been proud of you, my son. Whenever I was gone from home, I knew you would watch over the family and the farm." He continued, "You have a great legacy left by your ancestors. Although you are leaving the mountains, you will carry their blood with you. Their courage, resilience, and belief in the freedom to serve their God will always be with you," he paused a moment. "I understand it is a hard thing to leave all that you have known and venture so far out into the world."

"I couldn't do it if I didn't have the conviction I have felt since first hearing the missionaries," James said quietly.

"And I couldn't let you go if I did not know of myself that this work is from God. And after all my years on the mountain, I know that when God calls us, we must answer the call or suffer the consequences."

"Father, you know well of my fear of closed places," he paused, "do you think I can do it? Travel in a ship?"

"Yes, son, I think you can do it and will. Pray for help and it will be given to you to overcome all obstacles."

"I will do my best to make you proud, father, until you and Anne join me in the Great Salt Lake Valley."

"I will look forward to that day, but if we do not meet again on earth, we will embrace each other in the resurrection." Tears filled both their eyes as they stood and hugged one another.

***

It was dark, and the morning air was cool as they loaded the carriages at La Tour. About one hundred people had come with lanterns to say goodbye. James felt thankful that a few twinkling friendly lights marked his last moments in the valley. He was traveling with his best friend, Henri Chastain, and his family, which included Monsieur and Madame Chastain, along with his siblings, Catherine, fourteen years old, Frederic, eleven, and Mary, who was five. Louisa Peyronel, a girl he had long admired, also traveled with them. Along with her parents, two sisters, Maria, twelve, Suzanne, nine, and her brother Pierre, who was six. They were the second group to emigrate from their Italian valleys; the first had left with Brother Toronto in March 1854.

James knew he was lucky to have Henri. But the two friends couldn't have been more different. Henri had light brown curly hair contrasting with James' straight and dark. Henri was also taller by several inches.

But the real differences were in how they looked at the world. Henri had always been satisfied with his lot in life. He didn't struggle against anything. He seemed just as content toiling on the farm for years or now, leaving the valleys forever. Whatever life he was currently living was fine with him. This was always a little frustrating to James, who sometimes felt Henri didn't care about the future or didn't plan to shape it in any way. But, on the other hand, maybe this difference helped their friendship. Henri was the steady one. James knew he would always have his back.

From La Tour, the group traveled twenty-two miles to Pinerole and then on to the Piedmont capital of Turin. James had been to Turin only twice previously. At this time, as before, priests and soldiers filled the streets. Priests in their flowing robes and large flapping hats, moving about amongst the people, and of course, the soldiers keeping the peace.

The travelers then caught the newly completed railroad north to Suza. There they hired coaches that were put on sled runners to take them over the mountains. It was November, and the mountains could be treacherous. Sixteen mules pulled their large coach filled with twenty people. James couldn't help but notice that the sled conductors seemed to delight in guiding the coaches as close as possible to every precipice.

Mary hid her face in her mother's cloak, but James and Henri pressed their faces to the windows, not wanting to miss a moment of this great adventure. The roadway cut into the rock, in places supported by bridges, wound its way up Mount Cenis. Gusts of wind from Piedmont rattled the coach from time to time. The sled conductors got out of the carriage several times to drag it over a rough patch.

After about two hours, they reached the highest point of the road and proceeded across the plain of Mount Cenis. They passed the hospice founded originally by Charlemagne and about twenty-five houses of refuge built to house weary travelers. The coach stopped there, and the occupants found lodging for the night.

They slept together in a large room with cots. When Brother Chastain awoke early, he discovered that his small money bag had been stolen. Luckily, Sister Chastain had sewn the bulk of their money into the hem of her garment. They knew that none of their Waldensian friends would have done such a thing, but other unknown travelers were at the lodge.

They did not wish to cause a disturbance, so they ate their breakfast of bread, cheese, and milk in silence, then loaded the carriages. They then proceeded down the mountain toward France. The road made a gradual descent, with switchbacks coming down. When they reached Loundsburg in Savoy, they took the coaches off the sleds and proceeded on to Lyons, France.

LOUISA

Liverpool, England, December 1855

The group from Piedmont waited three weeks at Liverpool before word came the ship was ready! This would be the inaugural voyage. The William Tyson was the biggest ship Louisa had seen, but she would have to find out if it was large enough for all the passengers. She heard there were over 500 Mormon immigrants on board, with over 400 Scandinavians, forty British citizens, and her group of thirty-one from Piedmont. Finally, the cargo was loaded, and they were allowed to board. James and Louisa helped stow their luggage below deck. They discovered that wooden bunk beds lined the sides of the steerage hull. There were no mattresses except for the blankets they had brought with them. The passengers stacked their boxes in a long row between the bunks. Canute Peterson from Denmark was elected President of the entire company.

The ship finally left the harbor on December twelfth. However, waves of sea sickness soon tempered the excitement of being on the ocean. Louisa's mother and sisters were down for at least a week. James, Henri, and Louisa felt better after a few days. They enjoyed walking the deck as the ocean sprayed out before them. Although the sky was grey and the weather dreary. The first storm at sea had all the passengers running for cover in steerage.

"Here, take Pierre!" Louisa's mother called out as she thrust the boy into her arms. Boxes were sliding across the floor while pans, utensils, and anything not tied down flew through the cabin.

"Watch out, Mother!" she cried as a copper pot fell from a bunk and started rolling toward her. Louisa scrambled up onto the top bunk with Pierre in tow. They watched the chaos below as the Elders did their best to lash the boxes together. Her mother and some women more adept at keeping their footing were running from side to side of the heaving ship, trying to collect flying household goods.

Pierre started to chuckle as the ship continued to roll from side to side. He was actually enjoying himself! Then, when the ship paused and began moving up and down, he started bouncing.

Louisa felt a bit unsteady when she finally emerged from the hull at the end of the week of storms. The passengers found the foremast had split and was held together with heavy chains.

Louisa and the rest of the saints were so happy to have some fresh air that they met in their ward groups praising the Lord for his deliverance and singing hymns. A few days later, the captain of the ship, Captain Austin, bellowed:

"There will be no more singing on this vessel. It has done nothing but bring us bad luck!" But President Petersen told everyone privately that they should continue singing silently and also continue with their prayers.

Louisa was a fine seamstress, having been taught by some of the nuns in La Tour. She was quite proud of the dresses she had sewn for her mother and sisters. On the first day of sunshine, Louisa and others were busy sewing tents and handcart covers from the strong muslin they brought on board. Louisa noticed James watching her sew, but he didn't say anything.

"Hi there, do you want to join me? It would be nice to have some conversation while I work," said Louisa.

"Why yes, I wouldn't mind," he managed as his face turned crimson. He pulled up a wooden crate. "You seem like you know what you're doing."

"The nuns were good teachers, and I've been able to practice sewing lots of dresses. I guess that comes from having sisters."

"Your stitches look almost perfect," he commented. Now it was Louisa's face that turned pink.

"Well, thanks; I'm glad I can help with the things we will need crossing the plains."

"Can you believe we'll soon be crossing the American plains?" he asked.

"No, not really, I'm not sure what I expected, but it has already been a bigger adventure than I imagined."

"I think if I could have stayed in the valley and still served the saints, I would have. But my family was dwindling. The mountain had given all she had to give to us."

"That is a wonderful thought!" said Louisa. "The mountain had given us a home, a sanctuary from evil. It had fed and clothed us throughout all the centuries of our ancestors." As she pondered this, she also pondered James, there was much more to him than she expected.

JAMES
Atlantic Ocean, January 1856

James tried to spend as much time as possible on deck, with the big open sky above him. And that was where he was one week after the big storm when an argument broke out with the captain and one of the crew.

"If you weren't such a lubber, maybe you could have reefed the sails in time! How do you like being a swabbie?" he taunted. "That's all you're good for! A good flogging will teach you!" The crewman kept his head down as he continued to swab the deck. Finally, the captain stormed off and returned with his first mate and his black whip, the handle of which held nine ropes. He continued to verbally abuse the man while whipping him mercilessly, soon, his shirt and back were shredded and bloody. Captain Austin looked down in disgust when the man collapsed while the first mate dragged him away.

James did his best to melt into the barrel where he was standing, but just then the captain noticed him.

"You there, grab that mop and get busy!" He gestured for him to take the mop and clean the deck. He thought it best to do what the Captain said after what he had just witnessed. James knew what it felt like to be angry and want revenge, but the Captain seemed to relish hurting other people like some kind of sport.

During the next week, the Captain asked three other young men of the company to take over some of the crew's duties, which were worn out from fighting the storms or injured by the captain and his continual beatings.

***

James planned to make himself indispensable to the crew, so he could spend most of his time on deck, even if it meant more work. At the beginning of January, they endured another horrible windstorm. After mending the ship's sails, they continued their journey and shortly came upon another vessel. Initially, people were excited, but then it became apparent that the boat was in great trouble. It was a clipper ship whose mast and spars were missing, and her bulwark smashed. Everyone onboard voiced concern about the crew of the sinking ship.

"Captain, I request permission to send a relief boat to save the crew," said the first mate.

"Denied!" said the captain. "As if we don't have enough mouths to feed as it is. The way we're going we'll run out of food before we reach New Orleans."

"But sir, the men don't have a chance without our help!" he continued.

"Well, I say they should look to their Captain, who got them in such a fix in the first place. Maybe they should serve him to the sharks." He laughed at that remark, dismissing the first mate.

Francis, the first mate, sent the word among the rest of the crew about his conversation with Captain Austin.

"We can't leave 'em!" said one. "It could just as easy been us in that last storm!"

"I won't have this on my conscience tonight!" said another crewmember. Frances was the one who came up with the plan. James was considered trustworthy and became a party to their proceedings. Within the hour, Frances and two of the stronger crewmembers had locked the captain in his quarters. The rest of the crew were anxious to help the ailing ship. They dropped anchor and lowered a rescue boat. Because of his size, Frances asked James to carry a lantern and sit at the boat's prow. They quickly rowed to the struggling craft.

"Ahoy there," shouted the men from the clipper.

"Ahoy!" shouted Frances, "How many of you are there?"

"Twenty-six, with several wounded."

"It will take us three trips then. Why don't you send eight at a time, with your wounded first?" said Frances. One man seemed to have a broken leg, and two others had broken arms. The rest were loaded in, and they commenced rowing back to the ship. Crewmembers on the William Tyson had made a sling from canvas and some rope. They lowered it to the rescue boat and hauled the wounded men up. The others were able to climb a rope ladder. When all were safely aboard, they repeated the trip.

"Where are you from?" asked James in his broken English as he helped the last man aboard.

"We were traveling from New York to Liverpool with a cargo of flour," he replied. "The storms have been terrible this season."

"They certainly have," agreed James.

"Thank you for coming back for us," added the man. It made James feel good to help rescue the sailors. The crew accepted him, and several even tried to convince him he would make a good sailor and should sign on for the next voyage. They released the captain the next day, but because they had put a gunnysack over his head, he didn't know who had forced him into his cabin. This fact made him angry at everybody, and since the captain of the clipper had been washed overboard in the storm, he was the captain of the new crew as well.

LOUISA
Atlantic Ocean, January 1856

The next morning, Louisa and her family were below deck getting dressed when smoke began filling the steerage area. Louisa picked up her little brother, yelling for her mother and sisters, who had been dressing. They grabbed their shoes and scrambled barefoot up the stairs, away from the smoke. Some passengers looked ready to jump off the ship, but the voice of their leader, President Peterson, pierced through the commotion.

"Stay on the ship, stay on the ship! We will get the fire out and make it safely to America," he shouted. Finally, the crew got the fire under control, but not before it burned through the floor, ruining some of the baggage.

The crew discovered that Captain Austin was drinking the night before. Staggering around his cabin in the early hours, he knocked over his coal stove and started the fire. Louisa and her family were afraid to return below for several hours.

The saints continued to hold their Sunday services in Danish, English, and Italian. They divided the company into wards of about 30 people, and the Sacrament was blessed and passed among the members. President Peterson occasionally talked to all the immigrants and chose to address them the following Sunday.

"I have noticed a bit of rivalry between some saints concerning whose country should be ranked above another." At that, there was a bit of whispered comments among the congregation. "We should do all in our power to resist nationalism and instead see ourselves as brothers and sisters in the gospel of Jesus Christ. Be proud that you each dared to overcome your individual obstacles, leave your native countries, and come together for the cause of building Zion. I encourage you to love and work together to achieve our noble goals." Louisa agreed. She had made some Danish friends while sewing the tents and learning English together.

Besides meetings, the saints held a few dances on deck. That was new to the Waldensian converts, as dancing wasn't allowed in their former religion. James, Henri, and Louisa learned the double cotillion, Virginia Reel, and several folk dances from other emigrants. Louisa's favorite was the Virginia Reel. Six couples faced each other with a large space down the middle. The couples would travel forward and back and swing their partners with a right and left elbow. At one point, the boys and girls peeled off following the head couple to the foot of the formation where the first couple made an arch with their arms, and the boys and girls meeting under the arch would join hands and slide across the floor together back to their original spots.

"I can hardly get my breath!" Louisa exclaimed to James after one vivacious series.

"Well, I think that's part of the fun of it," he said. "We can't let the rest of these dancers get the best of us! Come on, let's go back for the next round," he insisted, so together, they learned to dance with the best of the group. Louisa liked dancing with James, who was quite good but didn't think he was. She noticed that he was rarely below deck but never got a chance to ask him about it. During their Sunday service, she made a point to sit next to him.

"Thanks for dancing with me. I know I'm not nearly good enough," he said.

"You do a great job," she whispered as the meeting began.

"He doesn't think he's good enough to dance with you because your family comes from the valley, and he's just a mountain boy," Henri explained to her after the meeting.

"Well, that's crazy, we're Italian Waldensians, and I think we better stick together," she replied.

Unfortunately, the dancing ceased when measles broke out onboard the ship, and many children died among the Danish converts. Finally, they thought the worst had passed, but one night Louisa was awakened by her mother.

"Come help me with Pierre. I'm afraid he has the measles!" she exclaimed. The small boy was resting fitfully on his parents' lower bunk. A flat red rash covered his face and stomach.

"He feels so hot," said Louisa as she put her hand on his forehead.

"Please stay with him while I get some more cold water." Her father had brought some sugar tea with a dose of cod liver oil. He was able to rouse the boy enough to have him drink the mixture. Her mother returned and continued to apply cold compresses to the back of his neck and forehead. Finally, they called for the elders, who gave him a blessing. Louisa and her parents continued caring for Pierre for a week until he succumbed to the disease.

It was a horrible day for Louisa and her family losing their six-year-old son and brother. The mourners gathered on deck as President Peterson spoke comforting words to them.

"You have taught your family to love the gospel as contained in the holy scriptures. Those blessings will sustain you, as will your new faith that your family will be together again in heaven," he said.

Louisa would never forget witnessing her brother's burial at sea. She had sewn the little body into a muslin bag with a lump of coal at its foot. Her father laid him upon a long wooden plank that extended over the ship's side. A prayer was offered, and they sang a hymn as the plank tipped forward and the body slid down and out into the endless waves of the sea.

What more could she have done? Louisa thought. Wasn't it her job to protect her siblings?

"How are you doing?" said a voice that pulled her back. It was James who had come up beside her.

"Not too good," she admitted. "It's just so hard; I keep thinking I could have done more."

"I think that's normal," said James. "We all felt that way when my mother died."

"How do you get through it?" she asked, tears hanging on her lashes.

"Mostly faith. Faith that God has a plan for us. Even though Pierre's mortal journey is over, I know you will see him again one day."

"Yes, I believe that too," Louisa said softly through her tears.

LOUISA

Outside St. Louis, Missouri,
February 1856

They had made it to America. The steamship "Benjamin Webster" ferried the Waldensians and the other emigrants from New Orleans up the Mississippi River. Louisa observed neat farms and plantations with cotton and tobacco fields from the boat. Unfortunately, the ship was quarantined two miles from St. Louis after cholera broke out among the passengers. The captain dropped the immigrants at a small island where a broken-down ferryboat served as their habitation.

Louisa now scarcely noticed her dreary surroundings. For three days and nights, she was busy nursing many people. They found that hot baths, and vigorously massaging the people seemed to save some. But not all; at three a.m. one morning, Louisa and James attended the funeral of Sister Christiansen, one of the Danish sisters they had helped care for. The only light they received for the burial was from the moon and a few lanterns.

One of the elders said a few consoling words over the body, which was laid with nine more in a common grave quickly prepared on the island. Louisa hurried back to help her mother and father. She found her father gripped with the illness, and for an hour, they administered the remedies of a hot bath, massage, and a ginger drink. When he finally spoke, he whispered to Louisa between the severe cramping that was racking his body, "Get me away from here, or I will die!"

Who could help her? She quickly found James and Henri also assisting the sick.

"I have to get my father off the boat," she said quietly in French, knowing most could not understand her.

"But how will you get past the quarantine officers?" asked James.

"I don't know, but I have to try and save Papa. Will you help me?" Louisa did not know what the punishment was for leaving quarantine. She only knew she must do all in her power to save her father, and the boys were willing to help. So, it was agreed they would take her father off the ferry just after five o'clock in the morning. James had noticed a small fishing boat anchored at the far end of the island during the burial last night. Hopefully, it will still be there, thought Louisa.

Her father walked gingerly between the two boys as they quietly made their way across the island, staying close to the shadows cast by the trees. Henri was the first to spot the boatman. His clothes were shabby, but he had a kind smile. They had brought money, and the man agreed to transport them to the other side of the river. James had volunteered to go with him, but the boatman said it would be better if Louisa went, as she understood the language better. He also said a woman would not be suspected.

Louisa and her father lay in the bottom of the boat with a blanket for cover. James whispered goodbye and good luck to them both, and the boatman struck off for the far bank. Luckily, the moon, which had been so bright the night before, was covered in clouds. Louisa listened for any sound of shouting, but all she heard was the oars turning on the sides of the boat. After a short time, the boatman removed the blanket. He insisted on helping her father onto the shore. After securing his boat on the bank, he accompanied them along a path that led toward the city. After about ten minutes, her father, gripped by an intense attack, could not walk any further. With the boatman's help, Louisa dragged him under a tree off the path.

"He needs some whiskey!" the Boatman declared.

"But he has never drunk it in his life," Louisa explained. "We have always had wine made from our own grapes." Her English was improving a great deal.

"Well then, you go and get a bottle of Port Wine," he responded. "I will stay here with him." Louisa could not believe the kindness of this stranger. He told her where to purchase the wine on the city's outskirts. Louisa set off as dawn was approaching. Traveling alone, she moved quickly. She secured the wine and hurried back to where she had left them on the trail.

On returning, she could see that her father was failing. They had to pry open his mouth to get a bit of the wine down his throat. They continued to massage him and administer the wine. His body slowly relaxed, and his breath came easier. Eventually, he finished the bottle of wine and could speak again.

"God bless you both; you have saved my life!" he exclaimed. He insisted on paying the man extra for his efforts.

"See now, that is just what he needed," said the boatman. It was noon when they reached the city. It was crowded. The boatman helped Louisa find them a place for the night. All that was available was a bed on the hotel's second floor. There were three other beds in the room already occupied by men. After they washed and helped her father into clean clothes, he fell asleep.

Now Louisa's father was doing better; the boatman remembered he had left his boat unattended too long. He needed to return as quickly as possible, fearing what might happen if the quarantine officers found out what he had done.

"I'm so sorry if we have brought trouble upon you," said Louisa.

"I was the one who insisted on coming with you," said the boatman. "No matter what happens to me, I saved a man's life today, so I am happy." Louisa shook his extended hand, thanking him once again for his charity toward her father.

LOUISA

St. Louis, Missouri, February 1856

Louisa was now alone, alone in a room with strange men, alone in a strange city, and alone in a strange country. She had never felt this way in her life. All she had ever known, the strength of the mountains, the certainty of her religion, and the presence of her family, was now gone. She sat on her father's bed for a moment and was comforted by the easy sound of his breathing. Her stomach grumbled. She had eaten nothing all day since four o'clock that morning.

She decided to hurry down to the hotel's dining area and eat quickly so she could return and care for her father. But as she sat alone at the end of a long wooden table, she found her appetite was gone. She was so exhausted she could barely stay awake, and on top of that she worried about spending the night in a room full of strange men. She began silently praying that somehow, she would find help.

"Well, bonjour there!" a familiar voice spoke to her, making her look up from the table. "I am surprised to see you here! I thought your ship was in quarantine?"

Brother Jacob Bingham, one of the first missionaries to teach her family in Italy, stood before her. She was as shocked to see him in this place as he was to see her. He had left Piedmont about a year before. She started explaining her predicament in English but quickly changed to French when she noticed the crowded dining area.

"Father was very ill, he asked me to get him away from the boat, or he knew he would die!" she explained hurriedly, her face pale. "We found a kind boatman who brought us across the river. Through his efforts, my father is finally recovering upstairs."

Her family had fed and sheltered Brother Bingham many times on his mission. He did not hesitate to offer his services and said he would be happy to sit with her father and care for him throughout the night. Louisa was exhausted from the ordeal and didn't have the strength to object when he insisted on taking her to stay with his family a short distance away in the city. His dear wife was very kind, and he assured her he would return and take her to her father in the morning.

Within a few days, her father was up and around. He also came and stayed with the Binghams until they got the news a few days later that their family and fellow passengers were finally out of quarantine and on their way to St. Louis.

Such a joyful reunion had perhaps never taken place before. Louisa had never seen her mother so happy as when her husband and daughter appeared on the dock. James and the Chastains were equally glad to see them and pleased to report that no one else had succumbed to the horrible disease. Now they prepared to get passage on the next ferry up the Missouri River. This would take them to Florence, Nebraska, where the Saints gathered to start the trail west.

As soon as Louisa found a moment to be alone with James and Henri, she quickly explained all that had transpired since she had left them on the island that morning.

"Do you know what happened to the boatman?" she asked. "I was worried about him." James and Henri exchanged glances. She could see that they didn't want to tell her.

"I'm sorry," James began. "We hid in the underbrush at the end of the island after you left. We watched you tie the boat and go. After several hours, we noticed three quarantine officers by the river. They seemed to be looking over the boat, and then one gave some orders that we could not hear, but they all hid in the area.

"We were terrified," said Henri. "We didn't know what to do. We were afraid that you would come back and be arrested. But we had no way to warn you."

"I thought of swimming across to try and find you, but we know the dangers of the current, so we just prayed for your safe return," explained James.

"It was dark when we saw the boatman return, and the quarantine officers sprung upon him. One was holding him, and the others were beating him. He cried out, and we heard his pleadings. It was so dark by then that we couldn't see what had happened. We just had to return to the ferry and pray that he would be alright."

"I never knew his name," said Louisa quietly, "I never knew his name."

JAMES

St. Louis, Missouri, March 1856

Out of necessity, the traveling party waited one week before securing passage on the next ferry to Florence, Nebraska. Brother Bingham asked James for all the news from Piedmont. The community of saints in St. Louis had grown to four hundred, with many immigrants choosing to work there before continuing across the plains. One evening Brother Bingham invited them to attend a lecture given at the St. Louis Historical Society. Most of the family just wanted to rest from their ordeal, but James thought it was a great idea since he hadn't left the house since arriving. Louisa and Henri agreed to come along, and Brother Bingham arranged for a carriage to take them. As they rode together through the lamplit streets, James thought how strange it felt to be back in a town after months of traveling.

"Tell us more about the speaker, Thomas Kane?" said Louisa.

"Thomas Kane?" asked James.

"Yes, that's right, he is a true friend to the Mormons," said Bingham. "This man used his connections to help us secure the commission for the Mormon Battalion."

"I met a Thomas Kane once, back in the valleys," mused James, "It must be someone else."

They entered the large hall. James noticed a line of gas lamps and several oil paintings on the walls. They found seats near the front on a wooden bench, whispering together until a large man came to the podium.

"Welcome, welcome! as president of the Historical Society, I am happy to see you this evening. It is my pleasure to introduce our speaker, Thomas L. Kane, who has served in the courts of Pennsylvania for many years and regularly speaks on topics of general interest to our society. Tonight he will talk about his travels among the Mormon people as he found them in 1846."

As soon as Mr. Kane stepped forward and addressed the crowd, James knew it was the same traveler he had met years ago when he was on the mountain. The man had a pleasant face, a little older perhaps, and curly dark hair slicked back. He figured they were pretty close in height now. The story of his travels among the Indians and the Mormons was fascinating. He gave many personal observations, including the deaths he witnessed during the difficult times on the prairie.

"Those bereaved along the trail were forced to makeshift burials, grieved to leave loved ones in one of the undistinguishable waves of the plain. To be forgotten, with no tombstone or rock to pile a monumental cairn. After prayers and psalms were said they would seek out landmarks or the surveyor to help determine their position so that it could one day be recognized. Such graves mark the path of the first years of Mormon travel."

James was carried along until the very end of his remarks. When he made his closing statement, James felt the same intensity and admiration he had felt when Kane spoke about the Waldensian people.

"I said I would give you my opinion of the Mormons: you may deduce it from my presentation. But I will add that I have not yet heard a single charge against them as a community, against their habitual purity of life, their integrity of dealing, their toleration of religious differences in opinion, their regard for the laws, or their devotion to the constitutional government under which we live, that I know from my own observation to be unfounded."

The speech ended with an intense round of applause. As people gathered their cloaks and scarves to exit the building, James asked Bingham if they could go speak to Kane. They waited for him to finish a conversation, then he turned to face them.

"Sir, I am James Reynaud. We met once many years ago when you traveled through my valley home in Piedmont, Italy." Kane looked at him intently.

"Why, so it is you! Grown up a bit now, almost as tall as me. And what kind of a story you must have to be here." He clasped his hand in a warm grip of friendship. "Your English is really improving," he commented. "I want to hear all about your adventures.'"

"First, let me introduce you to my friends, Louisa Peyronel, Henri Chastain, and Brother Bingham, one of the missionaries who originally came to our valleys." Kane shook each hand in turn.

"Very pleased to meet you all," he said as he turned back to James.

"So, you joined the Mormons and left Piedmont behind? That must have been a hard decision." Said Kane.

"As you saw, there was a lot of poverty among my people. But poverty we were used to. My grandfather always felt there was more truth to be discovered. So, when the missionaries came, God inspired my family to join them."

"And how were you accepted among your neighbors?"

"Not well, as you can imagine after seeing how important our traditions are to us. People could not understand, and not understanding made them angry." Relating the story now, James realized he was sad about what happened.

"My dear boy and all you young people," he said, including Louisa and Henri, "you have learned something of great value. An unfortunate reality of mankind is that people begin to hate those things which they don't understand."

"It didn't make sense to me," said Louisa. "I kept thinking, 'aren't we all Christian brothers?'"

"One would think that is enough. But there is no shame in being different," Kane paused as the light of the lanterns lit all of their faces. "I have always believed that defending those who are despised or seen as outcasts from the majority is important. Perhaps others will respect you less, but what matters most is if you can respect yourself."

It was getting late as they said their goodbyes. Kane hugged James and wished them all a safe journey.

"Please, if you ever need my assistance, contact me in Philadelphia at the district attorney's office," said Kane. "May our paths meet again, and may you have safety and guidance as you cross that desolate prairie."

JAMES

Florence, Nebraska, July 1856

James, the Chastains, and Peyronel families were part of the 30 Italians who joined the handcart company in July at Florence, Nebraska. A month before, their company had left Iowa City with 273 souls, three wagons, and fifty-four handcarts. Already, many delays had beset the journey, including oxen wandering off in the night and families abandoning the company.

Clearly, the handcarts needed strengthening, so James and the men of the two families worked along with others to replace axles and add a piece of iron to each cart preventing the wheels from wearing away the wood. Each handcart weighed 60 pounds and was loaded with from 250 to 500 pounds of goods.

They held a camp meeting that Sunday. A motion to sustain Brother Alfred Eckersley as president, with Brother William Walters and Brother John Morley as his assistants, carried unanimously. As Brother Eckersley rose to address the congregation, James noticed his piercing blue eyes as he surveyed the group. He removed his hat and held it during his address.

"This emigration has already cost more than expected, and we cannot expect plentiful amounts of meat and sugar," stated Eckersley. "Much is expected of this company. If we fail, we will discourage others who are gathering to Israel. It will be our own fault if we fail, for the Prophet Brigham Young has said it can be done. So far, the carelessness of some has caused axles to be broken and cattle to be lost. I do not want to hear any more grumbling, or the judgments of the almighty will be upon us."

Nothing could dim James' excitement for this last leg of the journey. The group set out early the next morning. Brother Chastain and Henri pulled their handcart for the first few days, but Brother Chastain had not been feeling well for a week. James soon took his place alongside his friend. It was up to each of them to do their part, and he was happy to pull the handcart if it would get them to the valley faster. The large canvas tents that Louisa had sewn on the ship were packed with their poles in the wagons. Each tent sheltered twenty immigrants.

As he and Henri pulled the handcart, the rest of the family walked, sometimes forward and sometimes behind. James became personally acquainted with the tall grass and sagebrush of the trail.

"What are you looking forward to when we get to the valley?" asked Henri.

"I guess I'll need to find a job so I can send money back to Papa."

"Yes, I think it would be great to have a large piece of land to farm with no rocks!" exclaimed Henri.

"That does sound like a dream come true," agreed James.

The two boys were not able to do much talking by the afternoon. The harsh sun, the dust, and the heavy load demanded most of their energy. The trumpet sounded early each day. They had a quick breakfast of fried dough cakes and helped put the tents in the wagons.

LOUISA

American Prairie, July 1856

Louisa was doing her best to be useful. Useful meant keeping the younger children away from the oxen and handcart wheels. It also meant singing songs, finding new flowers, or doing anything to distract the children from the constant walking. She also spent as much time as possible practicing her English. It was clear to her that language was either going to bring them together or divide them on this journey.

The initial shock of the prairie landscape had worn off, and now she was kind of used to the tall prairie grass going on forever before her and the expanse of blue sky stretching like a bright canopy over them all.

Captain Eckersley made it clear that the wagons were to be used to transport food and tents, not for weary travelers. They circled the handcarts and finished dinner when Eckersley again weighed some of the emigrant's belongings. Each person was only allowed seventeen pounds of baggage, which included clothes, bedding, and cooking utensils.

He specifically called the new Italian emigrants and a few others to bring their handcarts to his tent so he could weigh their baggage. Louisa and her family brought their luggage forward.

"Brother Green, could you please hand your baggage to Brother Butler to be weighed," requested Eckersley.

"Unfortunately, you are overweight," said Brother Butler. A box of books was confiscated, and the process continued. Louisa and her family were next.

"Sister Peyronel, I'm sorry but you must discard some of your clothing to meet the weight requirement," said Brother Butler. Louisa sadly left several of her beloved dresses at the side of the trail.

Later that evening, after prayers, Louisa and James observed several young English women who occupied Eckersley's tent looking through the clothing that had been discarded and taking several items for themselves. As they moved closer, they heard one girl laughing as she leaned closer to her friends.

"Brother Eckersley is surely correct that the Italians are ignorant and lazy, but there are some who are good seamstresses!" If James wasn't there to stop her, Louisa might have lost control. Possibly not just using her well-worded English reply, she might have actually punctuated it with a slap to the girl's pinched white face.

JAMES

American Prairie, July 1856

On the morning of July 26, they came to the Wood River. It was too deep to cross on foot, so James spent several hours helping to ferry the handcarts and wagons across. They finally resumed their journey on the other side, where they encountered sandy soil, which caused two of the handcarts to break down. A few men stopped to fix these including one of Eckersley's counselors Brother Walters, while the rest of the company continued forward.

A dark cloud was quickly making its way toward the group, and it wasn't long before thunder and lightning began accompanied by torrents of rain. Suddenly, they heard a thundercrack overhead and saw a lightning bolt strike the ground. Ten of their party fell to the earth.

James and Henri quickly pulled their handcart to the side of the trail and rushed forward to help.

"What happened, what happened?" one woman kept repeating as she sat stunned. It looked like the side of her face was burned, and her husband lay motionless a few feet away. James ran to the man but felt no pulse. Several men tried to revive him but to no avail. A young boy of about eleven seemed unable to move. Two men came forward and carried him to a covered handcart. All the carts stopped now. Everyone tried to stay dry by huddling together, with the younger children under the handcarts.

As the storm finally passed, they received the order to proceed. James and his companions traveled about two more miles before they camped for the night. Some went to dig a shallow grave for the fallen man. Fortunately, the young boy caught in the lightning strike could move and began to talk. James, Henri, and Louisa huddled together at the campfire that night, hoping to dry off.

"I'm glad you're well," said James. Just the sight of Louisa was somehow comforting.

"I'm glad you two are uninjured! I can't believe how close you were to the lightning."

"After all the storms we've lived through in the Alps, it would have been pretty sad to die in a storm on the prairie," said James. He sounded like it didn't matter, but he knew it did. It was hard to witness such a horrible thing. And the thought that it could have been him or Henri was not comforting. They had come so far, and he desperately wanted to make it to Zion.

JAMES
American Prairie, July 1856

A few nights later, James substituted for Brother Chastain on camp guard duty. He was near a wagon when he noticed Brother Eckersley and Brother Walters moving away from the campfire and coming toward him. They stopped short of his position, and he assumed the shadow of the wagon cover concealed him. Brother Walters quickly began talking.

"Brother Eckersley, I think you should know there has been some talk among the brethren about the speed that we are takin' the journey. Many cannot keep up at four miles an hour, and Sister Newey and her daughter were vomiting before they made it into camp yesterday."

"I walk ahead with people from my tent, including several women. They have had no complaints of our pace."

"Unfortunately, not all are as young as your companions, and though committed to making the journey, many suffer from exhaustion. Also, there has been some dissatisfaction that those in your tent are receiving special treatment," continued Walters.

"This is all nonsense. We are hastening to Zion, and if we did not have to wait for the oxen and the wagons, I think we would move even faster," Eckersley seemed to be greatly bothered by the conversation.

"I know that you want to make a statement of what the Saints can achieve, but maybe we should consider slowin' our pace to allow all of us to complete the journey together."

"I will never do that! If we cater to the least and weakest of our group, it will make us all weaker. Weakness is unacceptable! Only through strength will we achieve our goal."

"I'm sorry this has upset you, but...," Eckersley cut him off.

"The thing that upsets me is that these people are so easily influenced by evil. It is the evil one who tries to slow our pace, and preys upon our weakness. He will never win as long as I lead this company." The conversation was apparently finished as Eckersley stomped off towards his tent, and Walters stood looking after him. James had heard some talk about Eckersley's tent receiving better rations, but he was surprised that there was disagreement among the company's leaders.

LOUISA

Plains of Nebraska, August 1856

They met a group of California pioneers who were returning to the states, apparently disillusioned, having not found the gold they sought.

"We passed a couple of supply wagons a ways back," said the group leader. "They are headed your way with flour, salt, pork, and other provisions." Louisa and her family were so happy to hear the news but didn't have much money left to buy the items.

They mainly burnt buffalo chips for their fires now, and part of Louisa's job with her sisters was collecting the chips each day. At this point, Louisa was happy with small things. Her shoes had worn through many miles back, and she was now barefoot. The heat during the day was not too bad until they got to a sandy area, where the heat from the sand burned her feet.

James and Henri joined Louisa and her sisters as they searched for prickly pears. This red fruit grew on the cactus just off the cart trail, but it took the boy's knives to make it edible by cutting off the ridges of spines along its sides. They split up the fruit among the two families. They knew the only food back at camp that night was a broth made from boiled ox hide. As they walked back to camp, the girls held the fruit in their aprons

"So, Louisa, what is the first thing you will do when you get to the valley?" Her sister asked. This was the start of a game they had played for many miles now.

"I will soak my feet in warm lavender water," she replied. "And you?"

"I will fall down and kiss the ground," said her sister.

"And you, James?" They had not included Henri and James in the game before, but they caught on quickly.

"I shall build a big bonfire and use the handcart for the wood!" he exclaimed.

"And you, Henri?" he continued.

"I will make a feather bed from all the chickens I shall own," he said. And to Susanne, the smallest, he said, "And you?"

"I will drink all of the grape juice I can find!" she exclaimed. Their dreams seemed small, but they were enough to get them up the next morning in hopes of what the future might bring. They were all happy to have a bit of fried bread for breakfast, and Louisa pretended to wash her feet in lavender water, even if it was only sand.

They pulled the carts through some tall grass that morning, before camping earlier than usual to repair the handcarts and do some laundry and cooking.

Louisa was glad the company was stopping, even if it meant she had to do the laundry. She took her basket down to the stream and began rubbing the clothes with soap on a rock. She was intent on her work until she heard the sound of horses on the path. She looked up in time to see a beautiful, shiny buggy pull up about four yards away. A tall man in a somewhat shabby suit jumped out and came toward her. She stood up and dried her hands on her apron.

"How about going for a ride with us?" asked the man.

"No, thank you," replied Louisa.

"Do you have any parents?" he asked.

"Yes, I do," she said as she looked behind the man to the carriage to see if there was any way around them back to camp.

"Have you ever seen one of these before?" asked the man in the buggy.

"One of what?" Louisa asked. Were they trying to sell her something, she wondered.

"Well, come on over her, and I'll show you," the man in the buggy replied.

"She don't seem to be interested in seeing something new," the taller man said with a laugh.

"Just take this handkerchief and tie it over her mouth, then you can bring her along," said the man in the buggy, pulling something out of his pocket.

At that moment, Louisa's father and sister appeared over the bluff at the buggy's side.

"What's going on here?" Brother Peyronel called out. Instead of grabbing the handkerchief, the tall man jumped into the buggy, whipping the horses; they drove off, leaving dust behind them.

Louisa seemed rooted to the riverbank. Her father and sister hurried to her side.

"Are you okay?" asked her father. "I had a feeling I should come and check on you."

"Well, I am thankful," said Louisa. "A bit shaky, I guess," she paused, "they wanted to take me for a ride."

"Well, that's a ride you definitely don't need!" he exclaimed. "I guess they were part of the California group we met yesterday, and they must have circled back. It's good to keep your guard up. I didn't expect to have a problem doing the washing."

Louisa hugged her mother and sisters more tightly when they gathered around the campfire that night.

JAMES

American Prairie, August 17, 1856

It was six o'clock, and the morning light was slowly creeping over the sand and sagebrush that lay between the Italian emigrants and Zion. James and Sister Chastain helped the weakened Brother Chastain into the back of the freight wagon. He leaned forward and spoke softly. His voice was hoarse,

"I will not make it to the valley, but you will all live to see Zion and always have enough bread to eat."

"My dear Pierre, if you rest a little, I am sure you can recover," Sister Chastain said the words, but even James didn't know if she believed them.

They quickly left the wagon so as not to attract unwanted attention. It was well known that the captain disapproved of emigrants who rode in the wagons. Today was just a continuation of the last week. They traveled about four hours, half of that pulling or pushing the carts through heavy sand that came almost to the wheel tops. Frederic and Mary began complaining that they were hungry, and James was unsure how much flour they had left. He, Henri, and Sister Chastain were doing all they could to make it through the sand. When they, at last, stopped to eat what they had, Henri stayed with the children as James escorted Sister Chastain back to the wagons. Later, he told Henri what had happened. Sister Chastain stepped up onto the tongue of the wagon and peered inside. She called out her husband's name, "Pierre, Pierre!" He had feebly gestured toward her, touching his fingers to his mouth and sending her a kiss. Suddenly, there was a harsh voice behind them, and they turned just as James saw a black whip flick Sister Chastain's back.

Who was this? What had she done? The whip again struck her shoulder as she scrambled quickly off the wagon.

"Stay out of the wagon!" it was Captain Eckersley, and he was shouting at her. She did not understand his English words.

"You are lazy and need to commit yourself to the Lord. Where is your faith, woman? Where is your faith?"

As she backed away, tears started down her face as she said, "Mon mari est en train de mourir!" *My husband is dying. My husband is dying!* Her French words fell on ears that could not or would not understand her.

All at once, James stepped forward.

"What are you doing?" he said in almost perfect English. "She has done nothing wrong, and you have no right to treat her like this!" Righteous indignation made him strong and unafraid. He reached out and grabbed the end of the whip. "This is not God's will."

"How dare you!" yelled Eckersley.

"If you're so anxious to whip someone, then go ahead and whip me," stated James. And so they stood facing one another. The man with the power– and the boy with the truth.

Eckersley looked down. He yanked the whip away from James and stalked off away from the wagon.

***

Traveling that afternoon, they left the sand behind and pulled the cart across several small creeks before camping at about four o'clock beside the Platte River. They had traveled twelve miles that day. It was several hours before the wagons caught up to the handcarts. As James Reynaud and the Chastains went quickly to wagon number two, Henri climbed up asking for his father; an older women gestured to his father's body, which lay slumped against the side of the wagon cover.

"He passed away an hour ago," she said simply. James understood her words and noticed her eyes were sad. He climbed in next to Henri, and with the teamster's help, they lowered his body from the wagon and carried it to their tent. Sister Chastain bowed in grief, took some cool water from the stream, bathed his face, and cleaned his hands. Someone had a clean sheet, which they wrapped him in. Other men in the tent found shovels to dig a proper grave.

JAMES

American Prairie, August 20, 1856

In the three days since Brother Chastain's death, they had traveled between eighteen and twenty miles per day. Captain Eckersley had given each man on the carts a much-appreciated extra can of flour. The sweat soaked through James' shirt, and he had permanent grooves in his back from the handcart harness. They finally pulled into camp for the night, but Brother Walters had several handcarts to repair. James didn't know how he would have accomplished the task without his help. When they officially met, Walters had been working on their cart a few weeks earlier. James had carefully observed him. He made himself helpful by handing him tools and was interested in the work he was doing to help so many continue their journey. James found out that he was from Yorkshire, England, and enjoyed listening to his stories about his homeland. James was also useful in interpreting English words as needed for the adults.

At seven o'clock at night, the camp assembled to receive the sacrament, and several elders spoke, including Brother Eckersley.

"I am cheered by the improvement made in the last week. There has been much less quarreling and complaining. But I call to repentance all those who have robbed the handcarts or wagons and taken any food," Eckersley continued. "Your flesh will rot from your bones, and you will go straight to hell! Those I speak of know who they are!" James noted Eckersley's face was flushed, and there were beads of sweat on his brow. "The destroyer will not conquer us. He may use sickness, fatigue, and the breaking of our carts, but he will not break us. I regret that we have wagons in our company. They have served only to destroy your faith. If there were no wagons, there would be none sick or weak, but their faith would have made them strong."

James felt that the people were so exhausted that they listened mostly with glazed eyes. He felt sorry for those whose hunger had compelled them to steal. But there was something else. His anger had made him stand up for Sister Chastain. Now he was just frustrated that this man seemed so detached from what was actually going on in the camp. And that, once again, his people were being mistreated.

"There is honor attached to pulling handcarts into the valley, more than having to be carried in a wagon. Let it be said that you were faithful before God and did what was required of you," Eckersley finished with a flourish.

At that moment, the clouds gathering overhead decided to divulge themselves upon the travelers, and all ran for cover.

JAMES

Echo Canyon, Utah Territory,
September 22, 1856

James had come to check on Brother Walters, who was so weak that he had been unable to drive the company stock ahead of the handcarts that morning.

"Now don't you worry about me," said Walters, "I'm sure I'll start feeling better right soon."

"I'm staying with you," said James, and he wasn't leaving it open for discussion.

The pair did their best to keep up with the group, but a huge thunderstorm overtook their party and soon soaked them to the skin. Evening approached, and the darkness swallowed up everything around them. Up and down, up and down they went, over a rocky divide, with the Captain insisting they continue. Walters fell to the ground.

"What is it?" asked James, who knelt beside his prostrate friend.

"My stomach," he gasped, "I can't go on." James knew that he would be left behind to live or die. James was feeling pretty weak himself. He could sense the company moving farther away with every minute.

"Why is this happening?" he yelled to the sky. "We have done all we've been asked to do!" Tears ran down his cheeks along with the pelting rain. Was this how it would end?

A thunderbolt pierced the sky as though his anger had reached the heavens. Suddenly he heard his mother's words in his head, "Breathe, and be grateful." He bowed his head.

"Father in Heaven," he pleaded. "Forgive me, but please strengthen Brother Walters. Help him to finish the journey. Extend us your mercy so we may serve your purposes here on earth and in heaven. Amen." Not long after his prayer, he helped Walters to his feet.

"My pain is gone," he said. The trail was now only visible during the flashes of lightning. Thunder echoed on the rock, and human voices were lost. James tripped over some stones that jutted from the earth and landed sprawling on the wet ground. He crawled a few feet, then stood and continued moving forward.

Suddenly, they saw a handcart up ahead. The occupants had stopped and seemed to be seeking shelter under a blanket next to the wheel. Walters approached the man, one of the Danish brethren, with his daughter.

"Come with me!" Walters exclaimed, "We mustn't be left behind the company in this weather." The man spoke in a foreign language.

He gestured toward his handcart, then to his mouth and stomach, and throwing his hands up toward heaven; he finished speaking.

James was not ready to give up. Motioning to the man to leave the cart behind, he said, "Save yourself and your daughter. Leave the cart!" He had to yell over the howling wind and rain. The small man just shook his head sadly. James knew all the family had left to start their new life was contained in the cart. Their eyes locked together in one moment of desperation, blue eyes and brown. Please, understand me?

"I understand."

LOUISA

Echo Canyon, Utah Territory,
September 22, 1856

Louisa and Henri were also walking that day, only having had a half-cup of flour for their daily ration. They, too, were stumbling along when the thunderstorm began. Shortly after Brother Chastain's death, one of the handcarts had broken beyond repair, and Brother Beus and his group had put some of their belongings on the Chastain cart. The good news was that another man and boy could now take turns with the cart.

The three wagon teamsters had tried their best to make the climb and the descents required over the last six hours, even doubling up the teams. But now they were stopped together at the top of another precipice, unwilling to descend in the dark. It seemed the elements were conspiring against them. The animals lifted their feet in place and twitched a little nervously every time there was a new flash of lightning. Louisa noticed it was all the teamsters could do to keep them calm.

Louisa, Henri, and about sixty immigrants huddled around or under the wagons to avoid being soaked by the oncoming rain.

"Do you think someone will come back and help us?" asked Louisa glumly, shivering under her blanket.

"Eventually, once they realize their tents aren't coming in the wagons," said Henri. Louisa's clothes clung to her shivering limbs. She huddled next to the wagon wheel with her arms around her sister. It was hard to imagine anything good. But she tried for her sister.

"Let's imagine that we have all the nice firewood we want. We are back home, and Papa has just put a new log in the fire. The flames shoot up and embrace it. We stare into the flames seeing fleeting shapes and feeling the warmth on our hands and faces." They gazed into their make-believe fire. In the moment before Louisa dozed off, she wondered briefly if this was the end of the trail for her?

Two hours later, Louisa awoke to the sound of someone hollering for the teamsters. A few men yelled back, and soon Brother Hinckley peered at them through the dark.

"Glad you found us," said one of the teamsters. "Could use some help. We need someone to lead the teams while we drive." Brother Hinckley explained it was about five miles more to the camp. Just then, Brother Eckersley came into the camp in a rage.

"What is the matter here? We have been down there waiting for you for hours!" Brother Hinckley turned to explain the matter, along with the teamster, but Eckersley did not want to hear their explanations. "Wake up, wake up, can you all be so lazy as to sleep when your fellow travelers are in the open waiting for their tents! Will we let a little rain stop us? will we let thunder keep us from Zion?"

"It was too dangerous for us to continue," offered the teamster.

"Too dangerous! If we feared danger, we would be back in our beds in the East. You will never make a success in Zion, with this sort of attitude." He started off and then turned back abruptly, "Maybe you could follow me this time," he said pointedly. Louisa looked into the faces of her fellow immigrants, their hair plastered to their heads, shivering, as they silently turned and followed the captain. Louisa felt she had no choice but to join them.

The rain had let up by midnight when they reached the handcart camp. Everyone did their best to get the tents up and circle the handcarts. Louisa and Henri talked quietly together.

"This man is nothing like the missionaries that came to the valley," said Louisa. "It took every ounce of energy I have left not to say what I thought to his face."

"No, he is full of himself," added Sister Beus, who overheard them talking.

"Sadly, he can't see the people are doing all they can," said Henri.

"He doesn't think the Italians are doing all they can. He thinks we are lazy and looking for a handout," said Louisa.

"Well, I personally will take any handout I can get!" joked Henri. "Especially if it is food." The joking in the tent ended suddenly when Sister Madsen came by looking for her husband and daughter, who had never caught up with the main camp.

JAMES

Echo Canyon, Utah Territory,
September 22, 1856

As James and Walters continued to make their way toward the camp, James saw something small moving on the path up ahead. Was it a deer caught out in the storm? As he got closer, he saw that it was a young girl, maybe five or six years of age. She was sitting on a rock, sobbing, and taking large gasps of air every now and then. He approached slowly, not wishing to scare her, and from about eight feet, he spoke to her. The girl raised her head, obviously startled by the sound of a human voice after hours of hearing nothing but howling wind and thunder.

"Is it you, Papa, come to fetch me?" she cried out.

"No, I am not your Papa, but I have come to fetch you," he replied.

"I don't know where to go," she said as she continued sobbing. "I'm tired; I just sat down," she paused, "then it was dark... and I couldn't see anyone."

"Are you ready to go on now with me," he asked softly.

"Can you take me to my family?" she asked.

"I will try my best," said James, "What is your name?"

"Hannah, Hannah Clarke."

It was about one o'clock in the morning when Walters, James, and Hannah made it to the camp. They asked the guards for directions to the Clarke family. Lamplight illuminated a group of people around the tent. They must be searching for the girl, James thought.

"Brother Clarke, Brother Clarke?" he called out as he approached. A man turned to him and hobbled forward on legs bent with years of toil. Walters was carrying Hannah on his back. He lowered her to the ground, where she stood dazed from her experience.

"Hannah, oh, it is you! The Angels be praised!" he shouted as he lifted the girl in his arms. His wife and two older children joined the group celebrating the safe return of their wandering lamb. As his wife hurried off to get the child something to eat, Brother Clarke turned back to Walters and James, "I can never thank you enough for restoring to us one of our only treasures on earth! We have already buried three of our children in England. You have restored our faith!"

"Seeing your joy is more than enough thanks," replied James. "I am glad that God has allowed us to do this." Exhausted, they left quietly, returning to their own tents.

In the morning, a search party found the Danish man, Brother Madsen, dead beneath his cart. His daughter survived the ordeal and reunited with her mother. They did not travel that day, as they built fires and allowed their tents and clothing to dry.

***

Three days later, the company came to the mouth of Emigration Canyon. Emerging from the mountain gorge, they began their descent into the Salt Lake Valley. It wasn't what James had expected. He could see no trees, just some rolling hills about thirty miles distant that created a valley of what looked like sand in between. But his spirits rose as they finally saw the city laid out before them in squares of ten acres, with fields of green and neat houses of log and stucco.

"I can't believe it's been ten months since we left Piedmont!" James exclaimed. Louisa stood quietly beside him looking down on the strange land before them.

"How do you feel?" he asked.

"I feel like we traveled not only 1,300 miles across a prairie but also across time and space. The distance seems even farther when I look at this desert valley. But I am so grateful we made it all together."

"So am I," agreed James. They allowed themselves a few moments to take in the view together.

"This is the beginning of a new life for us," he said softly.

"Yes, a new beginning," agreed Louisa. Louisa suddenly moved forward and hugged him. After the shock, he hugged her back. She also hugged Henri, but he felt his hug was special. James then went to help Walters with the company stock and say goodbye.

"Thanks for not mentioning my accent," said James.

"That's not a problem," replied Walters, "You haven't mentioned my limp! It's what's inside here that counts, my boy," at that, he pointed to his heart. "Remember, the voice that tells you

you're not good enough is not from God. Your Heavenly Father loves you, and he knows your name," the two hugged one another.

"Will you be all right?" asked James.

"I'm sure I will. When I was hurt in the mining accident, I thought it was the end. So, every day since has been a bonus."

TORONTO

Salt Lake City, Utah Territory,
September 1856

Toronto could hardly speak when he beheld the handcart company pull the last of the thirteen hundred miles and set down their carts for the last time at Pioneer Park. A brass band met the group, and many dignitaries congratulated them on their extraordinary achievement. However, their sunburned faces and parched lips told only part of the story. The Waldensian families seemed happy to see his friendly face among the crowd. Some also had friends and relations to welcome them.

"Why have we received no letters or information during your journey?" asked Toronto.

"We went faster than anyone else on the trail," explained James. "An ox train started ten days before us, and they planned to make the passage as quickly as any company could, but we passed it, and they are still behind us!" He reached into the pocket of his worn and dirty trousers and pulled out a folded letter to his family in Italy.

Toronto took most of their group to his house on First Avenue near the center of the City of Salt Lake. It was a fine two-story house, the first story built of cobblestone and the second of adobe. There were also several small cabins along the north wall of his property, where he offered sanctuary to various emigrant families. He knew how difficult it was to start over in a new country and vowed to do all he could to help his Waldensian friends.

They all gathered for a meal of potatoes, corn, and stewed plums.

"I am in charge of the church herd of cattle and horses out on Antelope Island," he said. "I can offer James and Henri a job there where they can work off your passage money owed to the Perpetual Emigration Company." James quickly agreed, and Henri, after securing his mother's approval. The Chastains and Peyronels had been invited north to Fort Bingham by one of their neighbors from the Piedmont valley.

"We have made a lot of progress since we got to the valley," noted Toronto. "If you are resourceful and willing to work, you can prosper here." He knew the language could be a barrier, but he was pleased to hear the English conversations among the young people at the table. "I hope to one day return to Sardinia and bring my family members to the valley," he declared. For now, he considered these Italian brethren as family. A few days later, they made preparations to leave.

"I guess this is goodbye," said James.

"No, I'm sure we will see each other again soon," stated Louisa.

"I hope you're right," said James. Toronto observed them quietly. He knew how it felt to have no prospects and yearn for something more.

"It's a fine day to go to the island," said Toronto. "We have frequent storms on the lake, so you must always be on the lookout." James and Henri traveled with Brother Toronto to the

Jordan River, where they were surprised to see a small paddleboat. It was about forty-six feet long, and as they boarded the boat, James noticed that two oxen were positioned on a treadmill to power the craft. They waited as they loaded twenty sheep onto the deck.

"We mostly use the Timely Gull for transporting livestock," explained Brother Toronto. The Timely Gull glided out onto the Great Salt Lake.

The island was about fifteen miles long and five miles wide. The group headed to Black Rock on the eastern shore. When the boat reached the shore, Toronto jumped off and secured it to the pier. He herded the sheep off, and they scurried up the bank.

"We have sheep, horses, and cattle that graze here," he explained as the boys walked down the ramp and onto the shore. "Most livestock is received as payment for church tithing or to pay back debts to the Perpetual Emigration Fund, but some are privately owned. We have almost 600 horses here this year."

"Where will we stay?" asked Henri as they approached an adobe house toward the island's south end.

"Well, our foreman, Mr. Stringham, stays there. So, I'm planning to enforce the lean-to out here by the stable for you two." The lean-to had a fireplace and a bunk bed built into the wall.

"Your job consists of checking on the cattle and doing farm chores as needed," explained Toronto. "There are enough supplies for two weeks, and I will return twice a month to replenish them and check on you." Toronto waved to them as the Timely Gull moved out onto the lake and toward the city.

LOUISA

Bingham's Fort, Ogden, October 1856

After bidding goodbye to James and Henri, Louisa traveled north with her family and the Chastains. They headed to Bingham's Fort, built by settlers just a few years before. Some of their neighbors from Piedmont had encouraged them to come to Ogden, where they had settled after emigrating the previous year. The Ogden valley was a crescent shape nestled against the Wasatch Mountains, whose rocky towers served as a boundary on the east and north.

Louisa was surprised to see the size of the fort. The walls were twelve feet high, with a gate on the west and east ends and a road going through. Inside, log cabins butted up against the walls, with a separate schoolhouse, a molasses mill, and several stores. Her father said the fort encompassed forty-five acres. Her family moved into one of the cabins, planning to build in the city boundaries in the spring. Louisa noticed Indian families spread out among the residents of Ogden, with many spending the winter camping in the fort.

They had only been there a few weeks when one day Brother Brown, the leader of the fort, galloped through the east gate shouting.

"To arms, to arms, turn out and help disarm the Indians!"

Women and children ran for cover, and the men grabbed their rifles. Louisa peeked out from the edge of the cabin. Just then, a young Indian came galloping through the gates of the fort toward the Indian camp in the center. Brother Brown pulled his horse in front of him at the west gate. He reached forward, grabbing the Indian's gun. They wrestled over the weapon while their horses whinnied and pawed the ground. Finally, with one last tug, Brother Brown took the gun from the Indian. The Indian dropped his head.

"Give me my gun and let me go free. You can have my wife, my children, all that I own. We are only women now."

Louisa watched as Brother Brown disarmed all the Indians in the camp and placed their weapons under guard. Later that night, her family gathered around the fireplace in their small cabin.

"The Shoshone Indians have been entreated to live among the people during the winter," said her father. "The settlers feel that feeding the Indians through the long winter will serve them better than having them kill their cattle or steal food and burn fences as has happened before." He continued, "Luckily, Chief Little Soldier received a letter from Brigham Young this afternoon outlining the plan to help us all survive the winter. The chief has approved, and the braves now go along with the decision." After winter set in, Louisa could see the wisdom in working to survive together.

Snow fell early, and although the fort was quite far from the mountains, it was almost two feet deep. The snow was too deep for their cattle to find grass, so many starved. They had a limited amount of hay, which was soon exhausted. With no animals to haul wood, the residents gathered willow branches from along the creek to build their fires. Due to crickets infesting their crops the past summer, all were suffering. Louisa dug sego lily bulbs and pigweed, which her mother boiled with water and flour. They made molasses by simmering the juice of squash, beets, or cornstalks. It was a poor imitation of molasses or honey, but it was all they had. They also built some fish traps out of the willows.

The Indians had a store of pine nuts, which supplemented their diet. One day Louisa noticed a young woman about her age mashing the pine nuts into flour. This reminded her of grinding the chestnuts back home in Piedmont. As she stopped and watched, she spoke to the girl in French, hoping she would catch a few words, as the Indians knew some of the language from meetings with French trappers.

"I also grind nuts to make flour," Louisa said while her hands explained what her words couldn't. The girl nodded and offered Louisa the pestle so she could try it herself. Louisa eagerly helped, and soon the two girls had a pan of flatbread cooking. Their friendship continued as their people learned to get along to survive.

Louisa's new friend's name was A'niki, which meant "mountain chickadee" in Shoshone. She explained that it was because she liked to hum or sing as she worked. They started working together every day, dying wool, which would be spun and woven into cloth to help clothe their families.

Brother Brown taught a class to learn the Shoshone language, and Louisa begged her father to let her attend with him. When

Brother Brown found out what a good student she was, he allowed her to stay. One day Chief Little Soldier visited their classroom.

As Louisa unbraided her hair that night, she remembered the unique way the chief had braided his long black hair, crossing the braids in the back and then over his shoulder. A'niki had told her that only his sons were allowed to wear their hair the same way. Shoshone traditions were very different, but Louisa planned to learn everything she could about them during the next few months.

JAMES

Antelope Island, October 1856

The first day after Toronto left, James had a chance to really look around. This was an island with a mountain that ran down the middle from north to south. To James, it seemed like a barren wasteland after coming from their lush tree-covered mountain valleys. What struck James the most was how quiet it was, a quiet that seemed to press in upon his ears. In Piedmont, there was always the sound of water, streams, and rivers, gurgling and sometimes crashing full of ice in the winter.

He was amazed at the great distance that he could see. From the lake shore, he could see east clear to the Rocky Mountains and then north and south with no mountains in between. The lake lay silvery blue between James and the City of Salt Lake. The boys hiked to the west side, where the same expanse of water stretched away to the west.

During that long winter, they had about two feet of snow. It was bitterly cold, and James was forced to tie his shoes on with string as they were falling apart. His diet was meager, consisting of some squash, cornmeal, and harvesting roots and weeds to survive. They chopped their wood from the small canyon nearby. Toronto had brought some grain and hay for the horses, but even that was getting low. One time, Toronto came and killed an old ox, divided it up, and cooked it. The meat was so tough James decided they could have eaten the hide and known no difference. The best thing about his visit was that he brought a letter from Louisa:

Dear James,

I hope this letter finds you well and you have more to eat than we do. My family has a small wooden cabin that protects us from the storms. I am learning to speak the Shoshone language! I guess that will make me more foreign than I already am. We are planning to send for some silkworms from Piedmont. My mother thinks we could do well with that again. I do miss our talks. Say hello to Henri, and remind him that spring always comes.

Your friend,

Louisa

James had to admit the letter couldn't have arrived at a better time. He was feeling pretty sorry for himself. His conditions seemed no better than what he had left in Piedmont, and in some ways, they were worse. But Louisa had written that was enough for now.

That night he opened his worn copy of the Book of Mormon and read Helaman 5:12:

"And now, my sons, remember, remember that it is upon the rock of our Redeemer, who is Christ, the Son of God, that ye must build your foundation; that when the devil shall send forth his mighty winds, yea, his shafts in the whirlwind, yea, when all his hail and his mighty storm shall beat upon you, it shall have no power over you to drag you down to the gulf of misery and endless wo, because

of the rock upon which ye are built, which is a sure foundation, a foundation whereon if men build they cannot fall."

James thought about the sure foundation that his parents and ancestors had provided. Their faith and trust in God had been enough to survive all the "mighty winds" that were sent to bring them down. He now realized that his own faith was strong. As hard as things had been on his journey, he was beginning to feel a peace that God did indeed know him. And somehow, he was not alone.

***

On the rare days of clear weather, James and Henri would track the horse herd. They were somewhat elusive but occasionally let themselves be found. James loved the dark chestnut with the white markings on its brow. She was beautiful when she tossed her head and looked at him with her big dark eyes. They had their own communication, which was saying something since he felt pretty much cut off from all humanity on the island.

The foreman, Mr. Stringham, tried to communicate with the boys, whose English was improving. On Sundays, they met with Brother and Sister Stringham and their four children. Brother Stringham blessed and passed the sacrament of bread and water. Then, they sang a hymn, and Brother Stringham or one of the boys gave a talk based on the scriptures. Finally, they also read speeches by the twelve apostles from the church's general conference.

Brother Stringham let the boys ride two of his horses around the island. He taught them how to saddle and groom the animals and even told them they were "natural horsemen." James felt very comfortable on the horse as they moved together across the ground. He got the animal to respond with only a little prodding and some coaxing in French.

The wild horses loved to hang out at the very top of the island. It was toward the north end with low hills and hollows, and some cedar trees mixed in. There was a freshwater pool fed by an underground spring, and James had to agree it was an enjoyable place to stay. The horses pawed the snow away until they could nibble the grass underneath, much like James and Henri cleared the snow to find edible bulbs and weeds.

"Yes, we are in this winter survival together," he thought.

"Look at the way they travel across the rocks," said James one day, admiring their delicate footwork. Being raised on the island, the horses had no problem going up and over boulders or navigating the craggy, uneven ground. They moved so quickly that James was hardly aware of the obstacles they had overcome.

"I guess you become good at what you know well," said Henri. "Remember, we come from the steep valleys of the Piedmont, where we learned to climb up and down and around rocks our whole lives."

"That's true," replied James. "They know this island as well as we know our valleys." That day he had tucked a bit of hay in his jacket. He held it out to the mare, "Bright Dancer," he called to her in English. She lifted her head and looked him over, apparently judging favorably; she came over and took the offered hay.

JAMES

Antelope Island, Spring 1857

T hings began to thaw the second week in March. By April, it was spring, and the boys' spirits warmed up with the weather. James could finally grab Dancer's mane and climb on her back. She seemed okay with him riding her around the island if she mostly decided where they went. One day they were coming down the hill near the middle of the island when Dancer began to whinny and broke into a trot. He almost fell off but managed to hold on as she moved fast along the sandy beach. Where was she going?

He looked out over the lake, and to his astonishment he saw a large reddish-brown stallion swimming out in the middle of the water. As Dancer stopped, the swimming horse got closer until it could stand on the bottom of the lake and walk the rest of the way to shore. By this time, a group of horses had gathered as if to greet the new arrival. James slipped off his horse's back and approached the new horse. She was wearing a bridle, and the long leather straps hung dripping from the sides of her head. He reached forward and grabbed the straps. The horse whinnied and seemed happy to have James lead him as long as it was north to the hill, but whenever he headed toward the coral, the horse stopped dead and refused to move. Not knowing what else to do, James took off the bridle, and the horse galloped off with his friends.

About two days later, the weekly ferry came from Salt Lake. Soon James observed a strange man coming toward him.

"Hi there, so Brother Stringham said you're the boy who saw my horse?" he exclaimed, "I am Lot Smith," he said as they shook hands. The man was taller than James, with red hair, a fuzzy red beard, and a windblown face. James figured that Lot was about five years older than himself.

"Well, yes, I saw him. He was wearing a bridle, and I tried to get him to the barn, but he wasn't having that," said James.

Lot laughed easily, "That darned horse! This is the second time he broke away like that," he continued. "He grew up here on the island, and whenever we're out at my farm in Farmington, his ears perk up, and he starts looking longingly toward the west."

"Well, these horses seem to have something special," agreed James. "I'm pretty sure I can show you where to find him."

The two men headed out toward the top of the island, where James was confident he would find Smith's horse and Dancer. As they got closer, James saw that Dancer was near the pool. He made a low throaty call and reached inside his jacket for a treat. Dancer lifted her head. She eyed the stranger for a moment, then, deciding he wasn't a threat, came over to the two men.

"Say, I'm kind of surprised at that," said Lot. "These horses don't take to too many people," he looked at her flank. "She's one of my herd," he paused, "it looks like you two are pretty good friends?"

"I would say she is the most amazing animal I've known," said James, his eyes lighting up. "She's taught me so much about living on the island and let me have a ride or two."

Lot seemed shocked, "You mean you just rode her bare-back?"

"Yeah, that's what I did," he looked down for a moment. "I hope that's okay, Sir."

"My gosh, of course, I wasn't thinking that. And please don't call me Sir! That's for my dad, Lot is good enough." It took them about fifteen minutes to find Lot's wandering horse. When he called, it came, although he kind of dropped his head when he got there.

"Knows I'm not too happy with him, I s'pect," said Lot. Dancer had followed them to the spot. "Look, I've got a proposition for you. I could use some help on my ranch this summer, and I think Firebrand would be happier if one of his buddies joined him on the trip back. I don't want him jumping off the ferry," they both laughed at that. "I mean, I can take – what did you call her Dancer – and get her saddle trained with some others I'm working with. And I think maybe as payment for working this summer I could let you have her. What do you think?"

James stood there in his bare feet and a dirty pair of coveralls, which was about all he had to his name. This offer was more than he could imagine.

"That sounds just great!" exclaimed James as he shook Lot's hand. "This winter has about done us in here."

"Been pretty bad everywhere," Lot agreed. Lot had brought an extra bridle, so he put that on Firebrand, and James put a rope around Dancer's neck. They walked the horses back to the stable.

Before Lot left for the ferry, James wanted to talk things over with Henri. He explained everything that had happened, and Henri said he knew how much James loved that horse.

"Besides, Toronto said he's thinking of moving his herds to the south side of the lake where there's better grazing. I'll have a job with him as long as I want it," said Henri. So, James agreed he would come work for Lot in June after he finished up his time on the island.

JAMES

Cottonwood Canyon, Salt Lake
Valley, July 24, 1857

Brother Toronto had invited James and Henri to a celebration at Silver Lake in honor of the tenth anniversary of the first pioneers to enter the valley. James was excited to get a break from work and see some new surroundings. The sounds of a lively band greeted them, and all kinds of games beckoned them. James and Henri chose the food line, which ended at large banquet tables serving hundreds at a time. As he waited his turn, he saw a small dark-haired girl in the crowd. He wasn't sure until the girl pushed her bonnet off her face. Yes, it was Louisa! She looked so happy, and most of the trials from their trip seemed to be gone from her face.

"Louisa, Louisa!" he called. She turned but could not see him until he removed his hat and started waving it over his head. At last, she saw him, and they made their way toward each other through the happy group.

"It's so good to see you again!" Louisa exclaimed. James couldn't help himself, but he reached out and gave her a big hug. Luckily, she didn't seem to mind.

"How are you? And your family?

"We are all well. It was a hard winter. But our crops are doing pretty good, and we have been selling charcoal, which helps feed us all." She looked so grown-up now, her hair was pinned up, and her dress was to her ankles.

"Well, Mademoiselle, could I escort you to the table this afternoon?" James said, with his most formal voice.

"Of course, you can, but we know each other too well for any formality," she replied.

"I just don't want anyone else beating my time with you," James said honestly. This made Louisa blush a little.

"Well, in that case, Monsieur, lead me to the feast!" and with that, she held out her hand very demurely, which he took only too gladly.

The evening picnic and dancing convinced James he didn't want to spend another hour without Louisa. He wasn't entirely sure that she felt the same, but he had great hope.

Brother Toronto gave a closing prayer. "We praise the Giver of all Good," he said, "and the dawning of this new day when the Children of the Kingdom can have peace in their houses, with none to make them afraid."

Four men rode into the camp looking for President Young as the celebration was winding down. There was a great deal of activity and discussion. Finally, they rang a large bell, and President Young addressed the crowd.

"I was just informed that an army sent by the President of the United States is on its way to the valley to remove me from my office as governor, with force if necessary." James, along with the rest of the crowd, audibly gasped. How could this be? More details would come forth. But for the time being, President Young had declared martial law in the territory and called for the Nauvoo Legion to be assembled to protect the Saints and their property from unlawful invasion. He also made an official proclamation.

"All armed forces of every description are forbidden from coming into this Territory, under any pretense. All our forces must be ready to march at a moment's notice to repel any such invasion," he declared. "And no person shall be allowed to pass through this Territory without a permit from the proper officer."

Then President Young compared the Mormon people in the Rocky Mountains to the Waldensians of the Alps.

"Did their enemies ever overcome the small band of Waldenses in the mountains in Piedmont? No. They slaughtered army after army sent against them and maintained their position, notwithstanding to reach them was only like sending an army from here to San Pete. They were within easy reach of their enemies."

Louisa and James looked at each other. James was surprised to hear the history of their people at a time like this and in this setting. He was pretty sure that no one around them knew exactly where the two were from. Young continued,

"This territory and its people are perfectly able to defend themselves with the help of our God. And if the world combines against us, if we are united, all will go on well and work together for our good."

A sad group made their way down the canyon that night. Louisa had promised James that she would write to him at Lot Smith's address in Farmington, and he had promised to visit her as soon as

possible at their settlement in Ogden, about thirty miles north of
Salt Lake.

KANE

Pennsylvania, August 1857

Thomas Kane continued to correspond with Brigham Young after their first meeting on the Utah prairie. He was aware of some action toward the Utah church members but was rather surprised when he received a letter in early August from his young friend James Reynaud:

Dear Mr. Kane,

I hope this letter finds you and your family in favorable conditions of health and prosperity. I am writing to you because of your kind offer to assist us if we need your help. We could definitely use your assistance, including all the Latter-Day Saint people at this unfortunate time. You know well the false accusations and rumors that have driven our people across the desert to the valleys of the Utah Territory.

Now we are again faced with an army of extermination being set against us by our own President! I do not understand all of the reasons behind the action. I know there were some false charges that President Young had destroyed the records of the Supreme Court of Utah. And that judges had pardoned Mormon criminals while innocent Gentiles were imprisoned. According to my friend Brother Toronto, a dishonest and immoral man holding a grudge against the brethren is behind some of the charges. Toronto said there had been no investigation of the allegations. Still, President Buchanan has sent a new governor for the territory, accompanied by the army to suppress rebellion among the Mormon people. They are assembling at Fort Leavenworth to march to Utah. All mail to Utah has stopped, and President Young received no official notice of this action.

You know that I came to America hoping for the religious liberty that the Constitution of this country guarantees. But instead, we continue to suffer persecution. I sincerely hope that you can help us. I will end with what President Young said in a recent meeting.

"If these people must burn their property to save it from the hands of legalized mobs, they will see to it that their enemies shall be without fuel; they will haunt them by day and by night. We have been twice driven by tamely submitting to the authority of corrupt officials, leaving our houses and homes for others to inhabit. But are now determined if we are again robbed of our possessions, our enemies shall also feel how pleasant it is to be homeless for once."

Sincerely Your Friend,
James Reynaud

JAMES
Echo Canyon, October 1857

Companies of militia from several districts throughout the valley were ordered to report to the Echo Canyon base camp and bring thirty days' worth of provisions.

James reported to the camp leaders. Then he joined a group of forty men who climbed to the canyon's edge. Inspired by his Waldensian ancestors, they gathered rocks to be used as missiles, if necessary, to send down upon the oncoming troops. They were also busy making rock breastworks where men could find cover to shoot down into the canyon.

James looked down the sheer rock wall into the gorge, where a group dug large trenches across the canyon floor. Cedars clung perilously where they could get a hold of the rock. On the opposite hillside was a bramble of willows and wild cherry trees. The men were building a four-foot dam across the mountain creek below lined with breastworks leaving a small space for travel. James couldn't help but think about his treacherous trip through that very canyon a year ago. Yet, even from this perspective, things still looked perilous.

James went with Lot Smith to meet with Lieutenant General Daniel H. Wells and other leaders in charge of the defensive operation. James was glad to see Apostle Lorenzo Snow again.

"We must be vigilant and delay any movement by the troops," said Snow. "They are well supplied and eager to show their strength against ours."

"Yes," agreed Wells, "our orders are to annoy them in every possible way, to stampede their animals, and set fire to their trains. Burn the whole country before them and on their flanks. Blockade the road by felling trees or destroying fords."

"Watch for any opportunity," agreed Snow.

"Leave no grass before them that can be burned, and keep your men concealed as much as possible," continued Wells, "do all in your power without shedding a drop of the enemy's blood." At that moment, he looked inquiringly at Lot. At twenty-seven, he was an imposing figure with his long shaggy red beard and piercing grey eyes. James knew he was fearless. He had also shown his prowess by serving in the Mormon Battalion, territorial militia, and other exploring expeditions.

"Do you think you could take a few men and turn back the supply trains or burn them?" asked Wells.

"I can do whatever you tell me to do!" he replied confidently. "How many men will I have?"

"About forty-five, but I believe they will appear as more to our enemies," said Wells. Thus, James found himself once again riding alongside Lot. He trusted him as a leader and personally looked up to him as the brother he never had.

The group left on October third and traveled about thirty miles before they camped by Black Fork. The next day James left camp with Lot and twenty-three men. They started for the Sandy Fork to intercept approaching army supply trains. They observed some dust in the distance and sent out scouts who reported there were twenty-six large freight wagons.

After dinner, the group saddled their horses and rode almost fourteen miles to the train. Staying hidden, they observed that the teamsters were drunk and had no wish to start a fight with the men. They decided to wait until most had gone to bed.

Unfortunately, as they began to approach the camp, Lot realized he had misunderstood the reports from his scouts and that there were actually two lines of twenty-six wagons each.

"Well, that is a little different situation, isn't it?" James said quietly under his breath.

"Yes, indeed!" replied Lot.

"Do you think we should just say 'Hi, we're just passing on through," quipped James.

"No, actually, I think there is no time like the present," Lot said. And he led the men forward in a long line up to the campfire. Then, just as their horse's heads made it into the light of the campfire, the men turned, and one stood up so fast he spilled his coffee.

"Good evening, gentleman. Could you please direct me to the captain of your wagon train?" asked Lot. A short, wiry man stepped forward.

"I'm the captain, Dawsons' the name," he said. "What would you be wanting with me?" At that, James saw that Dawson's eyes were looking at the train of horses. As James looked back, he saw that it was impossible to tell how many men were riding with them or where the line of men and horses ended.

"Well, I need you to get all of your men and their belongings out of the wagons, as we're meaning to put some fire into them," said Lot.

"Oh, for God's sake, don't burn the trains!" Dawson exclaimed.

"It's actually for his sake that I am going to burn them," replied Lot. "Now, if you will please have your men stack their weapons over here, I would be much obliged." James was sure the captain thought he was outnumbered. Dawson told his men to comply with the instructions, and they vacated the wagons. Two of Lot's boys guarded a large pile of weapons, and the men by a few more. At that moment, a messenger from Ham's Fork came riding into camp.

His surprise at the sight before him was equal to the surprise of James and the other men at his presence. James was the closest to him, and he walked his horse until they were nose to nose.

"Do you have a dispatch for us?" James asked.

"Yes, but it is a verbal message," he replied. Just then, Lot rode up beside them.

"Give it to me!" he commanded. "If you lie, your life is not worth one of these wagons." The man tried to speak but was so frightened he could not get a sound out. Obviously, he was doing his best to comply with the order, but it took several seconds before he could utter a word.

"My orders are from Camp Wingfield," he managed to say. "The men must not sleep, as we have spotted Mormons in the area. Keep a guard on the trains. Four companies of cavalry and two pieces of artillery will come in the morning to escort you to camp."

"Thank you for your message," replied Lot. "As you can see, we have a good guard on the train now. Please dismount and join your friends here," he motioned to the group of teamsters gathered nearby under guard. The teamsters and the messenger were all pretty calm when they found that they wouldn't be hurt.

"Glad you're burning the damn wagons!" exclaimed one of them. "Then we won't have to bull whack no more."

"Well, we just aim to help you out," replied Lot. He got a torch ready and asked James to help him as they used some saltpeter to help accelerate the blaze. They lit about ten of the wagons when James returned to Dawson and his group.

"We need a few men to get some provisions out of those front wagons. We could use several of those overcoats in that fifth wagon," James said specifically as three men got up. "We could also use some sugar and coffee, as some of our men camped below are fond of it." Lot and James had already decided to make it sound like they had other men nearby in camp.

As James looked up from the group of wagons, he noticed an Indian coming from the Mountaineer Fork. Now what? he thought. The Indian approached, and as he spoke, James was surprised to hear him speaking French. He had noticed the "big fire," and now he wanted some presents.

"I want two wagon covers for my tent and some flour," he said. James alerted Lot to the new visitor, and he agreed to give him the items.

By three o'clock in the morning, the wagons were blazing and lit up the area for miles around. Lot told the wagon masters his group would move off but warned them they would shoot them if they tried to put the fires out. Then, the boys returned to Big Sandy to camp for the rest of the night.

JAMES
Big Sandy, Utah Territory

The next morning, James' company received news that the Mormon militia had burned Fort Bridger. They also heard that Colonel Sidney Johnston had finally left Fort Leavenworth and was on his way to take command of the troops.

The boys were flush with excitement from their victory the night before. They had collected a bunch of gun caps from the wagon train, and everyone gathered around to get their share.

"Looky here, what I got!" yelled one of the boys, holding up a fine rifle that had been taken from the supply wagons.

"Hey, I'm the one that found that," shouted another.

"I was right there, and you were nowhere around that wagon!" exclaimed another. Then, just as he grabbed the gun, it suddenly went off.

The gunshot went through the group, hitting Orson and wounding him in his thigh. The bullet had also grazed the side of someone's head, but luckily no one was killed.

The boys were suddenly sober. It was like the gunshot had brought them to their senses.

"This is what arguing does for us," said James. "We then hurt one of our own!"

The group parted to let James through. Another man with medical training stepped forward. They set the bone and dressed the wound. Then, James and several men gathered some willows at the river to make a stretcher.

As they returned to camp, the picket guard spotted 200 mounted troops moving in their direction. Fear stood out on the faces of many of the men. Some said they should run or surrender. There was confusion in the camp as the boys gathered their supplies and argued about what they should do. Finally, Lot stood up and faced his company. It was the first time he had addressed them with such passion.

"We are not here for ourselves. We are out here for our people!" his voice echoed around the camp. "We are engaged in the Lord's work and have been called to protect our homes and religion. If God allows those troops to come upon us, we will trust Him, and no matter how many there are, we will beat them." His words settled everyone down. They soon realized there was no cavalry, just the burnt-out teamsters making their way to camp.

At sundown, James and the company set off toward Green River to get some help for their injured companion. The distance was twenty-five miles, and four men had to carry the stretcher on their shoulders. They took turns carrying the stretcher as they tramped through sagebrush and up and down hills. They kept on for hours until they were exhausted, and the captain let them sleep for a few hours. Then, they traveled on until they saw the river. Worried about the possible enemy cavalry, most stayed back while James and a few scouts went to get water from the river. Upon reaching the river, they were thrilled to find out the party they had been evading was actually some of their own militia members who were out searching for them. Lot brought the rest of the group to camp, where they found a wagon to take Orson back to the valley.

"It has been a pleasure to serve with you men," he said, as he was lifted into the wagon.

"Thank you for your service," said Lot, "you have done well."

"Don't you worry," said James. "I'm sure they can patch you up when you get back to the valley." At that point, he pulled out the gun that had caused such a problem. "The boys would like you to have this as a going-away present," he explained.

"Well, I'll surely take good care of it," replied Orson.

LOUISA

Ogden, Utah, October 1857

The fall wheat harvest had gone better than expected. The gristmills worked non-stop, grounding the wheat into flour. All had been encouraged to store what food they could. Louisa was now teaching eight pupils at the small log cabin where they also held meetings. A bit overwhelmed by this assignment. Louisa had welcomed donations of scraps of letters ripped from old books. She had taken these and pasted them onto wooden paddles. Arriving early, she swept the packed dirt floor and put kindling in the stove.

"Miss. Peyronel is this correct?" one of the students asked. Each pupil had a piece of charcoal which they used to write words on the back of their paddles or their hands.

"Yes, that is right," said Louisa, as she walked behind the children who sat on a long log bench together.

"Will you also teach us French?" asked Joel.

"I think your parents would prefer English," she responded. "But perhaps a few French words would round out your education." The children rubbed off the charcoal and prepared to write a new word. She was glad the students were curious to know more. As for herself, she never wanted to stop learning.

"La Foi means faith. Let's open the Book of Mormon and read Nephi 7:12." There was a rustling of pages as the children opened their shared books and followed along.

"Joel, you start us out."

"Yea and how is it that ye have for...got," he paused.

"Yes, that's right," said Louisa, "just keep sounding out each syllable."

"...forgotten that the Lord is able to do all things accord...ing to his will, for the children of men, if it so be that they exercise faith in him."

"La Foi!" the children chanted together.

"Alright, that is enough," said Louisa. "Faith, F-A-I-T-H." The children silently scribbled with their charcoal, as Louisa hoped her faith would be enough.

She had been so busy at school and on the farm that she scarcely had a moment to think of James. Usually, at night, before she went to bed, she prayed for him and for all the men who were with him. Occasionally, she let herself pray for James to come home safely to her. She hoped that he felt the same and it wasn't just her imagination that he cared about her as more than a friend. They had been through so much together, and she hadn't told him how much she missed him when she saw him at the Fourth of July celebration. But, somehow, she hoped he knew it, knew the same way she did, that they would be together someday.

JAMES

Ham's Fork, Utah Territory, October
1857

James and the militia spent most of their time day and night following the United States army's movements as they traveled up Ham's Fork. One night they camped about a mile away from the army. In the morning, they heard some commotion and sounds of braying. Thinking they might surprise the soldiers as they took their mules out to graze, most of the group saddled up, leaving their pack mules with a few guards.

James was riding close to Lot as dawn approached when they realized it was the jackass cavalry of Captain Marcy, that was mounted and looking for them! The American soldiers didn't have enough horses for a proper cavalry, so they were mounted on mules. The boys surprised the men, who immediately whipped their mules into line and, taking their knees, pointed their guns. James was determined to remain calm. He estimated the guns were about sixteen feet away when Lot and Captain Marcy dismounted and approached one another.

"So, what are you boys doing in this part of the country?" asked the captain.

"Well, I was just about to ask you the same thing," replied Lot.

"We're looking for a way down the Bear River to Salt Lake," said the captain.

"Well, I wish you luck in that pursuit," said Lot.

"Why don't you go meet Colonel Alexander, I'm sure he would be happy to meet with you, and you could visit the Hickman brothers as well," added the captain.

The soldiers had taken the Hickman brothers prisoner about a week before, which James knew well. He tightened the saddle on his horse as Lot expressed no desire to meet with the Colonel.

"Well, we need to be on our way," said the captain.

"Yes, so do we," said Lot agreeably. He mounted his horse and turned away, coming toward James. The boys let him pass and then followed at a gallop back to where they had left the pack mules.

However, Captain Marcy and his soldiers had no further interest in looking for the supposed new route to Salt Lake. Instead, they followed the boys by traveling along a high ridge to the right, almost opposite their position. When James reached their pack animals, he could see several companies of infantry coming to meet them. So, the footmen were coming from the left, and the jackass cavalry was on the right.

"Come on, boys, we can do this!" Lot yelled. James jumped on his horse and galloped across Ham's Fork, water splashing up his pant legs. They climbed the steep, rocky bank on the opposite side. It was a hazardous area that was difficult to navigate when not being pursued. James patted Dancer's neck and whispered encouragement. When the foot soldiers saw the boys were out of reach, they turned back toward camp.

After finally gaining the ridge, Lot and the boys stopped for a moment at the top, seeing no sign of Marcy.

"Don't you think that would be a nice place to stop and have breakfast?" Lot asked, pointing to a grassy valley below them.

"No, actually I don't!" said James, surprised that Lot could be joking at a time like this.

"If we had them down there, we would have a clear shot," said one. So, the boys descended into the valley, thinking Marcy and his men had turned back. Unfortunately, when they reached the bottom, James looked up to see the soldiers on the ridge they had just vacated. And sure enough, the soldiers began shooting at them from about 100 to 150 yards away. The bullets came so fast there was no counting them.

They galloped away at full speed as the bullets whizzed passed them. Miraculously, none of the shots killed horses or riders. James' hat came off, and later on closer inspection, he saw a bullet hole had pierced it. They traveled quickly to the other side of the valley and up the hill. They slowed the pace a little but didn't stop to camp until well after nightfall. There was no bread or flour, as the army had taken the men bringing the supplies prisoner.

For James, the initial excitement of battle had worn off. Getting the better of his enemy had always been important, but now he was beginning to feel that other things were more important. Maybe not getting shot just to prove a point.

KANE

Pennsylvania, October 1857

Kane made good on his word to help his Mormon friends. He immediately sent out requests to President Buchanan and a close friend in his circle to set up a meeting to clarify the position of the Mormons. Two weeks later, he was appalled to read a column in the New York Times written by someone unknown to him.

"It is obvious from this article that this man, whoever he is, had privy to my letter dispatched to the President!" he exclaimed, crumpling the offending paper in his hands.

"You can't be sure," replied his wife, Elizabeth.

"I am doubly sure there is a direct correlation to his remarks–and not only that, he has called me out by name, saying Buchanan should not be influenced by anything I have to say, as I am obviously tainted."

"Dear Tom, perhaps it isn't as bad as it sounds," said his wife trying to appease him.

"The fact of the matter is I have received no answer to either of my letters but instead receive a personal rebuff in the New York paper!" The offensive incident struck directly at his character. A blow that he took personally. It seemed that his motives were still suspect even after all he had done to lift the downtrodden of society. He washed his hands of the matter and chose to back away.

Finally, a visit from Captain Van Vliet a month later shed new light on the whole affair.

"I understand you have received no answer from President Buchanan or his staff. I have also read the unfortunate column in the Times," he began. "But I believe I have information that may change your view on the matter and hopefully encourage you to defend the defenseless once again."

"At this point, I'm not sure what that could possibly be," responded Kane, whose despondence over being misjudged had caused physical illness.

"It has come to my knowledge that Judge Drummond wrote the column in the Times under an assumed name. He had received information that you might enter the fray and counter his accusations. So, he resolved to do his best to stop you.

"I don't know what to say," responded Kane, astonished by the news.

"Well, I hope you will request another meeting with the President, and this time not be deterred. I also have it on good authority that Drummond's supreme desire is to be appointed himself as the next governor of the Utah Territory and enter accompanied by an army." However, William Drummond wanted to present himself now; Kane knew that he went to Utah as a dishonest and immoral man. Drummond left his wife and family without means in Illinois and brought his mistress to Utah, whom he represented as his wife. When found out, he left the territory and began his anti-Mormon campaign.

The recent news of the burning of the army supply wagons had caused a fervor of concern among the American citizens. And Congress demanded to see what evidence had caused President Buchanan to intervene with such drastic measures without their approval. Perhaps now the timing was right, thought Kane.

JAMES

Ham's Fork, Utah Territory, Fall 1857

James was on scout duty on October tenth when snow began to fall. All the American troops had gathered together and seemed to be heading to the Bear River Canyon.

"Won't that add around 150 miles on their trek to the Salt Lake Valley?" asked his companion.

"Yes, maybe they got tired of sitting around and being harassed by our militia?" quipped James. They had already burnt the grass in front of the army, and due to their stock's weakened condition, they only managed to travel three miles a day. There were six inches of snow on the ground when the group suddenly turned and seemed to be heading back to Black's Fork.

On November 17, a deserter from Johnston's army came stumbling into James' scout camp. They gave him some dry clothes and warm soup. The next night he was able to join them around the bonfire. He explained that he was a teamster on one of the supply wagons and had never intended to fight anyone. He explained that most of the companies rendezvoused on November third at Black's Fork, where their commanding officer, Colonel Johnston, finally joined them.

"We had the Uintah mountains to the west and the blasted endless prairie to the east," he explained. According to the teamster, Colonel Johnston vowed to march to Fort Bridger and said, "Come the spring, we will have our revenge upon these heathen, who refuse to fight like men. Their kind of fanaticism will not be tolerated!"

"We started our march to Fort Bridger just as the temperature plunged to zero. The next night, five-hundred animals perished in the cold. The men began to refer to Black's Fork as the 'Camp of Death,'" he said. The snow was blowing around them, and the living animals and men were crowded together practically on top of one another in the camp.

"March On!" were their orders, he said. "As we moved from camp, we were suddenly surrounded by a dense cloud of frosty air. It took all our effort to put one foot ahead of the other as we traveled up a small hill. We could not force the mules from their shelter behind the scattered bushes of the valley." As James listened to the story, he could not help but remember the wondrous miracle that saved the Waldensians in 1487. The dense cloud had come down and engulfed the soldiers in the canyon at Pra del Tor. It sounded like, once again, the providence of God had protected his people.

"We tried to pull the wagon through under a tree, but it dang froze to the tree," explained the teamster, "eight mules weren't able to move it. Tent pins broke when we tried to drive them into the ground, and many horses were left frozen on the road."

"Couldn't you just stop and make camp," asked James.

"There was no stopping. We could only hope to reach the shelter of the fort. Unfortunately, we lost fifty mules the next day, and the thermometer read sixteen degrees below zero. I left the next morning when there was a break in the weather. I never signed up for any of that."

News reached them later that the company had reached Camp Scott, two miles from Fort Bridger and one-hundred fifteen from Salt Lake City. The army had retreated to Winter Quarters.

JAMES

Cache Cave, Near Echo Canyon,
November 1857

The lanterns made their shadows tall across the cavern walls. The boys spoke in quiet tones among themselves until Lot came to the cave.

"Well, boys, that's a job well done!" he enthused as he stood at the entrance. "General Wells believes we have done all in our power to slow the army's progress. Now we are sure that they have camped for the winter. So we can rest a bit," James smiled and joined in the cheers as the men congratulated one another.

"Some of you with families will return with me to the valley tomorrow. They have asked the rest of you to make camp at the head of Echo canyon. We have located several lookout sites so we can make sure to see any surprise movement toward the valley or any spies trying to access the canyon. I hope by next Spring, saner minds will prevail, and we will see an end to this wrongful attack upon us."

Lot asked James to go to the Weber campsite at the mouth of Echo Canyon and continue their ongoing mission to keep the valley safe. As he prepared his bedroll for the night, he looked up at the cave's walls, which ran about fifteen feet deep and twelve feet high. He noticed names etched into the walls, including *Joseph*

Toronto-1847 and many others he did not recognize. He pulled out his pocket knife and scratched his name into the rough surface. When he finished, he touched his warm fingers to the cold rock, and he remembered another cave with the names of his ancestors carved into the wall. He said a quick prayer, "may my children be as proud of me, and may our family continue to live with the freedom to worship." With these thoughts, he climbed into his blankets and fell asleep.

In his dreams, he was back in the Angrogne valley of Piedmont. His father was there waiting for him. It was Sunday, and they walked together to their church service at the temple. But instead of going to the temple, James suddenly found himself walking towards the cave, the secret meeting place of his people centuries before. He was surprised that there was light emanating from the cavern. Someone must already be there. He was alone as he stepped into the glowing light inside the cave. He glanced at the wall, there were no torches or lanterns, but all was bright. A man approached him. He was taller than James and had curly brown hair. He was wearing an ancient-looking tunic and a packet of arrows at his waist.

"Hello, James," said the man as he looked deeply into his eyes. And suddenly, James knew who he was. His great grandfather, whose name was carved on that same wall, Daniel Reynaud.

"It is wonderful to meet you!" exclaimed James

"It is wonderful to meet you again," exclaimed Daniel.

"I hope you are proud of me," he found himself saying, tears coming to his eyes, "I wanted to make you proud."

"You have made me very proud," said Daniel. "You have been courageous in battle and your spiritual journey, perhaps the bravest of all in that."

"Now it is time for you to let go of your fear and anger. Love is the way forward; loving your fellowmen is the way forward. You can put down your weapon. Now you have the armor of God." When he realized he was holding his rifle, he reached out and gave it to Daniel.

"Go forward, my son. We will always be with you," at that moment, James felt a great love and peace flow over him. And he slept on until morning.

KANE

Philadelphia, December 1857

Thomas Kane used all his verbal ability to make President Buchanan see that perhaps he had been misled by reports concerning the activities of the "Mormons."

In November, Buchanan planned to increase the army's size if needed "to convince those deluded people that resistance would be vain." But by the time Kane met with him again at the end of December, public opinion was not in his favor. So, he decided to trust Kane with a peace mission, arming him with a letter of introduction signed by the President, which granted him the right to negotiate on the government's behalf and perhaps come to a peaceful solution to the current problems. His wife, Elizabeth, was less than excited about his trip.

"Why does it have to be you?" she asked, "There must be someone equally qualified to help the 'Mormons.'"

"President Young wrote me personally as well as my friend James. They know there aren't too many of us Gentiles that understand their people's history, all the persecutions they have suffered, and their real desire for peace."

"It sounds like they want to create their own country out there?" She said, "And I'm not even sure they can be called Christians."

Elizabeth was more argumentative than usual because she worried about her husband.

"They have proved their loyalty time and again. Remember, they sent 500 of their most able-bodied men to serve in the war for the Mexican territory, while they were being driven on the prairie from their homes."

"I know, I know, I just don't see how the children and I will manage without you," she replied.

Thomas pulled his young wife into a big embrace, kissing his infant son, Elisha, on his little bald head. "I have full confidence in you to manage as beautifully as you usually do," he said. His two-year-old Harriet pulled on his trousers as she wanted to be part of the family hug. He stooped and lifted her up, "Now you be good to your mother, and don't cause her any trouble," he said.

"We shall miss you every day until you are safely home," she said quietly.

"As I shall miss you so terribly," he admitted.

"Will you do me this one favor?" she asked as she laid the baby down and ran to the desk. She took out a small empty journal and handed it to him. "Here, I will sacrifice one of my journals if you agree that we shall each keep one and then share them when you return. She knew that he was quite horrible at keeping a journal, but Thomas could see that this was important to her, so he agreed.

"Now, my parents will see that you have any help that you need," he said.

"We shall pray for you every night," she said.

"Well, that is all I will need to have a successful trip," he said, smiling, as he finished packing his bag.

"If only I could believe you actually thought that."

"Well, it can't hurt, and hopefully, you'll pray that I will have the health and wisdom to see this through," he replied.

Kane knew if there were any chance for peace, he would have to get to Utah as fast as possible. So, he decided to travel by boat from New York, across the Isthmus of Panama, up the coast to California, and then overland to Utah territory. He had also decided to avoid detection by traveling under the assumed name of "Dr. Osborne."

Kane found the journal less of a burden than he thought. With the unreliable mail, he recorded some of his journey and more of his thoughts along the way. Then, about a week into the trip, one of the young gold-seekers Kane met asked him to join them. They could always use an "experienced man," he said. So that was what he was now, he thought, although he could see himself a decade earlier in their countenances.

As he returned to his ship's quarters for the evening, his thoughts drifted to the great errand he was on. If a man could use reason and logic to their best influence, he felt he was well chosen. Because of his distance from the problem, he sensed he could see more clearly than those directly involved. Lines from his favorite poem, *On the Nature of the Universe*, by Lucretius, came unwitting into his mind:

> *"Pleasant it is when over the great sea the winds shake*
> *the waters,*
> *To gaze down from shore on the trials of others;*

Not because seeing other people struggle is sweet to us,
But because the fact that we ourselves are free from such
ills strikes us as pleasant.

Pleasant it is also to behold great armies battling on a
plain,
When we ourselves have no part in their peril.
But nothing is sweeter than to occupy a lofty sanctuary
of the mind,
Well fortified with the teachings of the wise,
Where we may look down on others as they stumble
along,
Vainly searching for the true path of life."

When he saw San Francisco on the horizon, he couldn't help but be excited along with the other passengers. All on board agreed that the voyage had been "blessed" with miraculous weather. He wrote a letter to his wife:

Dear Elizabeth,

Having never made a voyage of any length without storm or disaster. I am grateful to report that we have endured neither. We haven't had one gale, one stiff breeze even, we have not had ten minutes of rain or cloudy weather, nor one minute of haze at any hour to prevent our seeing shore or headland that we were sailing for.

He was mindful that the Mormons might have seen his passage as providence taking its part. Although thankful, Kane, the practical and non-religious man he was, decided that he would never again tempt the fates and travel by sea! After a short day-trip down the coast to San Pedro, he and a guide began the overland journey to Utah. Arriving incognito in February, he made his way to Brigham Young's house, where he revealed himself. Those present expressed excitement and joy when seeing him again.

JAMES

Camp Weber, Utah Territory, December 1857

J ames sent a letter back to the valley with Lot. He was anxious to see Louisa again. Unfortunately, they had only been able to exchange a few letters, because of the problems with the mail service.

Dear Louisa,

I hope this note finds you and your family well. It has been our job lately to watch the government army and track any movements.

It looks like they have decided to quarter for the winter near Fort Bridger. This is a great comfort to all the militia as we hoped we wouldn't have to winter on the plains. We are currently at the Weber camp and have been instructed to make all preparations to stay and have lookouts on all roads in case there is any movement of the troops. There will also be lookouts posted at Echo Canyon. I am proud to be trusted as a scout and not be just a "foreigner." I must say, I have all the war experience that I want. I sincerely hope that Mr. Kane has success in helping our people.

I would like to visit you and your family after Christmas. Please let me know if this would be acceptable.

Your sincere friend,

James Reynaud

He had finally concluded that he was better than some men and not as good as others. And he would let Louisa decide if he was good enough for her.

JAMES

Ogden, Utah Territory, January 1858

James had a lot of news to relate to the Peyronel family about what was happening at Camp Scott and Echo Canyon. Brigham Young had sent a load of salt to the camp, which Colonel Johnston had refused, ordering the messenger from his camp. Johnston had also sent Captain Macy with a group of soldiers on a perilous journey from Fort Bridger to Taos, New Mexico, to get provisions, mules, and cattle for the impoverished group.

"Why wouldn't he accept the salt," asked Sister Peyronel.

"Because it came from an 'enemy of the government,'" he said.

"It's too bad they wouldn't accept it as a peace offering," she mused.

"I don't think Johnston has any thoughts of peace. I think they can't wait for spring when they can have revenge on the Mormons," said James.

"I hope you're wrong," said Brother Peyronel, "but we will do whatever is necessary."

"Well, the army has offered rewards of one hundred and fifty dollars to any soldier who kills a Mormon and one-thousand dollars if it is Lot Smith!" James explained. "We have had quite a few teamsters and some deserters come through our camp from

Fort Bridger mighty hungry, and we have fed them and sent them on to Salt Lake City. The teamsters had no intention of fighting, nor freezing to death, but they have given us pretty good information on what is going on in the camp."

It was late afternoon when James and Louisa walked down to the pond. They wore their winter coats, mittens, and scarves. The snow drifted around the edges of the pond, which was fed by a natural underground spring.

"Does this finally feel like home," asked James

"Yes, it is nice to be close to the mountains. Although they are not as tall as Mount Cenis, we now look out into the valley like the big landowners of Piedmont!" They laughed together.

"That's right, we are just like the big landowners," he said it ruefully as he knew that even if someday they could have a bigger harvest they weren't close yet. "This spot does feel peaceful," he added. The sound of their footsteps continued crunching through the snow until they stopped at the gate to the corral. Dancer whinnied and came over to nuzzle his cheek. He had brought her a little treat from the house.

"I am glad you have Dancer to count on while you work in the canyon," said Louisa. She stroked her soft nose and thanked her in French.

"I will be back here in just a couple of months," said James. He paused, and then continued, "I want nothing more than to be with you if you will have me?" he said. "I don't think I can face mobs, oceans, buffalo, or anything else without you." Louisa laughed.

"I hope those things are behind us, but whatever this new land has in store for us," she paused and looked steadily into his brown eyes, "I want to meet all of it with you." He pulled her close and kissed her gently. She threw her arms around his neck, and they twirled around together, laughing.

KANE

Salt Lake City, February 1858

As soon as Kane arrived, Brigham Young called for a meeting of the twelve apostles. They introduced him as "Dr. Osborne," and since only a few knew his real identity, he hoped to ascertain how he would be received. Much had changed in the decade since he last assisted them.

He was so exhausted from the trip he wasn't sure he could stand. So, they brought in an oversized easy chair that enveloped his slight frame.

"Gentleman, I come as an ambassador from the President of our nation and am prepared and duly authorized to lay before you most fully the feelings and views of the citizens of our common country and of the President towards you. Specifically, as it relates to the present position of this territory and the army of the United States now upon your borders," he began. "I will give you all the pertinent information regarding the state of affairs, then call your attention and enlist your sympathies on behalf of the poor soldiers who are now suffering in the cold and snow of the mountains. I shall request you to render them aid and comfort, assist them to come here, and bid them a hearty welcome into your hospitable valley." At this, there was some murmuring among the group.

Kane continued speaking, relating all the news about the situation in Washington.

"I hear Captain Van Vliet, who traveled through here last summer, made a good report of you to the government," he said.

"I suppose," commented Governor Young, "that they are united in putting down Utah?"

"No, actually, I think not," replied Kane. "You have borne your part well in this contest, and I was pleased to see the patience of your people."

"I have been robbed several times of all that I had, and my property has gone into the hands of my enemies," said Young as he stood and walked among the seated brethren. "But as to property, I care no more about it than the dirt in the streets, only to use it as God wishes." At this point, he stopped next to Kane's easy chair, resting his right hand on Kane's shoulder.

"But I think a good deal of a friend, a true friend," he paused for a moment. He seemed overcome by his emotions. "An honest man is truly the noblest work of God," he continued. "It is not in the power of the United States to destroy this people, for they are in the hands of God. If we do right, He will preserve us." He turned and resumed his seat next to Kane.

"At this time, my afflictions are almost too much to bear," said Kane, alluding to his continued poor health. "I feel like going as soon as it is the will of God to take me!"

"My friend, the Lord sent you here, and he will not let you die. You cannot die until you finish your work. And you have a greater work still to do." With that, they adjourned the council meeting.

Kane went to stay at the home of Brother Joseph Toronto. They told Toronto that a Dr. Osborne, traveling from California, was sick and needed accommodations. Toronto was not at Winter Quarters when Kane visited there, so he would not recognize him.

After a few days, Brother Toronto learned the identity of his guest and was perplexed about the deception.

"Why did you wish to take on a new identity?" he asked.

"My friend, I have such fond memories of my kind treatment at Winter Quarters. I thought you were a good and sincere people then, but since that time there have been many negative things reported about you," he said solemnly. "I thought I would like to convince myself that my intuitive feelings were correct. I knew that if I came among you as myself, I would probably be treated well in remembrance of services rendered. I wondered how the Mormon people would treat a stranger at a time like this when I might be an enemy or a spy?"

"Oh, I see," said Toronto, "and what have you decided?"

"I have proved that the Mormons will treat the stranger in Salt Lake City as they once did Thomas L. Kane at Winter Quarters," he said, pleased with his experiment.

"I assure you, we will continue to provide you with anything we can to increase your health and comfort so that you can complete your journey," Toronto promised.

Kane hoped they could reach a compromise that would maintain the dignity of both President Buchanan and the Mormons. He knew the Mormons were willing to receive their new governor but would not allow the army to quarter in or near any of their cities. Within a week, Kane was on his way across the frozen mountains. Intent on his errand of peace on behalf of the mountain Christians.

JAMES
Camp Weber, Utah Territory, March 1858

James was at his post at Camp Weber when the news came that Thomas Kane would be there within the hour. Kane had sent a letter months ago, letting him know that he was doing everything possible to help his people. So when the call came for an escort party to accompany Kane to Camp Scott, he was one of the first to volunteer. He didn't have long to wait. Kane and his escort team from Salt Lake City arrived cold and hungry.

"I can't believe you're here!" exclaimed James, happy to see his friend.

"Well, I'm a little surprised to find myself in this place," they laughed together. Then, all sat down and hungrily ate the stew James had helped prepare.

"So, how goes the battle?" Kane asked James.

"Well, we haven't had much to do since they made their winter camp."

"No signs of aggressive activity?"

"No, we just get the occasional deserter, which keeps us abreast on what is happening there," he finished his meal and pushed his chair back from the table.

"Hopefully, you're camping days will soon be over!" said Kane.

"I would be happy to put this all behind me," agreed James.

"You and Louisa should have a great future ahead of you." James could not contain his surprise. "How did you know?"

Kane laughed. "I stayed with Brother Toronto in Salt Lake, and he filled me in." James nodded.

"Now, I think we have to find a way to get to Governor Cumming and convince him of the true nature of your people before it's too late." James couldn't agree more. The latest intelligence said that an American general was sailing for California to lead a contingent force to deal with the "rebellious inhabitants of Utah." So, they would attack them from all sides, just as they had his Waldensian people for centuries.

Laying on his cot that night, James thought of the last time he had shared a meal with Kane. He had been generous then, and now he found him just as unselfish. Hopefully, they could make a difference together, and both could return home soon.

Kane

Camp Scott Near Fort Bridger, March 10, 1858

Thirty miles from the army camp Kane asked James to come with him disguised as his servant. They left the rest of his escorts and approached Camp Scott together. A shot rang out, whizzing past James' shoulder. Kane ran forward yelling and clubbed the overzealous guard over the head with his rifle. He shouted his name to the next soldier on duty, holding out his letter of introduction from President Buchanan.

"Who do you wish to see?" he asked.

"I would like a meeting with Governor Cumming as soon as possible," he replied. "Tell him I am here at the request of President Buchanan."

Cumming sent his assistant to bring Kane and James to his tent immediately. The men shook hands and extended greetings. Kane didn't waste much time getting to the point of his long journey. Buchanan wished to avoid a costly war and had also discovered there was no support for such a venture.

"I believe President Buchanan and his advisors have been manipulated by those who had ulterior motives toward the Mormon faith," he stated. "I can assure you there will be no resistance to your appointment as Governor of the Utah territory, and no government troops will be needed. Brigham Young, having received no prior notice of his replacement and receiving news of the 1,500 troops headed to their valley, could only suppose that they were under attack. As you may know, it has happened before in the history of this people."

"I did not know there had been no communication to the officials in Salt Lake," replied Cumming.

"No, there was none, and I believe it would be most helpful to all concerned if you, and you alone, accompanied me back to the valley. You can observe the conditions of the people there, and President Young has assured me that you will be welcomed."

"I appreciate your long and tedious journey to strive to bring peace and understanding to this situation," said Cumming. At that very moment, the tent flap flew open, and two soldiers entered.

"I have orders from Colonel Johnston that you are to be arrested and held here as a spy!" said the soldier closest to Kane as he moved toward him, attempting to grab his arm. James moved to protect him.

"Now see here!" exclaimed Cumming. "This man is here as my guest and also at the request of the President of the United States!"

The soldier stopped before he grabbed Kane. Looking back at his companion, it was clear he didn't know what to do next.

"I suggest you immediately go to the Colonel and tell him the news I have just given you," said Cumming. "Please do not waste any more precious time with these false insinuations!" After the soldiers left, Cumming assured Kane and James that he would get everything sorted out and then called his orderly to have a tent made ready for them, "I hope you can get some rest from your arduous trip."

The following day, a message was brought to their tent by Colonel Johnston's assistant. Kane tore it open and read the words quickly. After his reception from the night before, he was in no mood for political pandering. The Colonel assured Kane that there had been a mistake, and he had only wished to invite him to dine with him that evening to hear the urgent news that was important to all concerned, not just Cumming.

"I'm pretty sure that Johnston was unhappy that he was not consulted first on the actions of my mission," explained Kane. "My mission is to deliver the new governor to the Utah territory without conflict."

"I'm not sure Colonel Johnston has the same goal in mind," replied James.

Kane arrived at the officer's tent at the appointed time, where they ate a meal of beef, bread, and gravy. Kane began with a message from Brigham Young.

"Young has just learned through the southern Indians that your troops need provisions, and he would be happy to send in 200 head of cattle and 20,000 pounds of flour, to which you are perfectly welcome or to pay for, as you choose," Kane assured him.

"Well, unfortunately, President Young is not correctly informed about the supply of our provisions. We have plenty to last until the government renews our stores," said Johnston. "Whatever the need of the army under my command, we would not ask nor receive from President Young, or his confederates, any supplies while they continue to be the enemies of the government."

"I fear it might greatly prejudice the public interest to refuse Mr. Young's proposal in such a manner at present," replied Kane. "I hope that perhaps you would reconsider. My goal here is peace, which is also Brigham Young's goal." Johnston retained his composure.

"I have nothing to do with the political question between the government and the Mormons. I am here in fulfillment of special instructions from the administration," he said. "I also have nothing to do with Young and his people, and when I advance, if the people stay at home and behave themselves and do not molest me, they will not be troubled," he continued. "But if my advance is opposed by force, then I shall meet it with force." Feeling that the meeting was over, Kane thanked him for the meal, and the opportunity to meet with him. There was no doubt in his mind that Johnston would fight if he had his way.

After several more days in the camp, Kane and James were getting dressed one morning when they overheard Johnston's orderly, who had been serving Kane the previous evening. He was outside Kane's tent and speaking to the soldier sent to relieve him.

"Keep an eye on the damned Mormon!" he said. Kane was incensed; he could not believe what he had just heard. He immediately pulled on his boots and headed to Cummings' tent. He was livid, and James had been unable to stop him.

"I came here at my own cost and with detriment to my own health, only to be insulted at my own tent!" Cumming couldn't imagine what had happened.

"I haven't, nor ever plan to join the Mormon faith, but I will, until my dying day, stand up for the oppressed of this world. I will

stand against slander and unjust persecution of my fellowmen!"
Kane spoke passionately. James was impressed. He had trusted
Kane, and now he knew his motives were pure.

Cumming was aghast when he heard what had transpired.

"I am so sorry. You have been nothing but honest in your
communications with me," said Cumming. "You are obviously a
man of high principle."

Cumming and Kane hastened to the Colonel's tent, scarcely
waiting for an introduction.

"I would like an official apology given to my visitor Mr. Kane,"
stated Cumming emphatically.

"Why would he need an apology from me?" asked Johnston.
The two men related the conversation,, and Kane could tell that
Johnston was annoyed he was being troubled by such a matter.

"I have nothing to do with what my orderly said or didn't say,"
he replied.

"I find that hard to believe," said Cumming.

"And I, too," interjected Kane. "From the moment I stepped
into this camp, all of my efforts have been suspect. It seems to
make no difference to you that I was assigned this mission by the
President of the United States."

Drawing himself up to his full stature, Johnston replied tersely,
"And I, sir, am fulfilling my mission as a representative of that same
government."

"Those who work for you cannot help but be influenced by your
attitude. You are their commander and, as such, should take full
responsibility for your soldier's actions," said Cumming, coming
face to face with the Colonel.

"I will not take orders from you or this self-imposed ambassador about how to handle my troops!" Johnston declared. Just as the argument was about to come to blows, the tent flap opened, and Chief Judge Nichols stepped in.

Apparently, the loud voices in the tent had drawn attention. Kane knew Nichols was traveling with the group to take his appointment as a Federal Judge in Utah.

"What is this?" he inquired as he inserted himself between them. The three men all spoke at once, but the Justice was able to get the gist of the situation. He threatened to arrest all those involved if they didn't control themselves immediately! Kane took a deep breath and stepped back. Nichols suggested to Johnston that he reprimand his orderly for his demeaning remarks. They all agreed upon the action, and Kane and Cumming returned to their tents only slightly appeased.

LOUISA

Ogden, Utah Territory, March 1858

"What do we do now?" said Louisa's mother. The family had returned from Sunday meeting to their cabin near the eastern foothills of the Ogden valley. No one knew the answer to her question. It was hard to forget about all that was happening on the borders of their territory. That night the family gathered around the fire to do their scripture reading.

"I will continue to thank God for the strength of the mountains between our enemies and us," said her mother.

"And let's not forget the large desolate prairie, which we know intimately," added her father. "I believe if we listen to the spirit and do our best to live by the principles we have been given; then we need not fear."

"The apostles have told us that if we want peace at our borders, we must have peace within our homes," observed Louisa. "I think we must each do our small part in building Zion by not quarreling amongst ourselves and being quick to forgive."

"I agree. I think if we do the best we can and always be charitable. Then, we will be able to accept God's will for us, whatever that may be," said her father.

It wasn't long before it became clear what they would do. Their leaders said they would never again leave a beautiful city made by their sweat and tears to be inhabited by military men who should take it by force or those who followed behind looking for the spoils. No, they would burn their homes and fields; if necessary, they would leave nothing left for them to take. And the people, the people they would move again, there were already plans that as soon as the storms had cleared in the spring, they would go south. They would leave only torchbearers behind to burn their towns if necessary.

"We will go south to Provo," her father announced one day. "We will take our food stores with us."

"What about Flossie and Jaque," said Suzanne, her eyes filled with concern for their cow and horse.

"They will come with us, as will the hens," he replied.

"And so, we will go forth, driven as seems to be our lot upon the earth," said her mother.

***

Louisa had helped pack up all her family's belongings, including their furniture, in the wagon. They had boarded up the windows of their cabin and piled straw and dried grass inside to make it easier to burn if necessary. Some of their neighbors had been driven from their homes before by government-sanctioned forces.

"I was just a child when I hid in the tall grasses of Missouri. I remember looking up and seeing the shadows of men on horseback galloping around us, but they could not find us," said Sister Browning, one of their neighbors. "I have faith in Mr. Kane. I helped nurse him years ago on the prairie, and I hear he is on a peace mission on our behalf."

"Yes, I met Mr. Kane as well. I am glad he is doing what he can to help us as he promised," said Louisa.

"I believe God will protect us now, as he did so many years ago in Missouri," added Sister Browning.

Louisa understood that this time was different. They would not leave their beautiful towns and hard-earned crops for others to enjoy. This time they would burn everything to the ground if threatened by the troops. Louisa helped her father remove their barn's wood siding and roof, saving each precious nail.

Now thirty-five thousand church members that lived north of Utah valley moved south, out of harm's way. Louisa walked next to the wagon, and her sisters took turns riding and walking as the family made their way south. When they got to Salt Lake City, her father led their horse along South Temple Street so they could see where the temple was being built. He pulled over for a minute and showed them what looked like a plowed field in the heart of the city.

"The construction workers have covered the foundation, so the army will not be able to destroy any of our hard work," he explained. "Teams of oxen have hauled the sandstone foundation blocks from Red Butte Canyon. But that is all underground now." So even though Louisa couldn't see any visible signs of the temple, she felt a peace in her heart as she stood on the spot where it would one day rise.

"That will be a great day when our people once again have a temple!" she exclaimed. They continued south and reached the Provo bottoms at dusk. Each ward was allocated a strip of land for temporary occupation. Louisa and her family erected a canvas tent near a small stream. Louisa picketed the cow and horse nearby on a grassy hill. She hoped there would be time to work on the new dress she was sewing. She entered the tent, set up her spinning w and started to spin some wool before helping prepare dinner.

TORONTO
Salt Lake City, Utah Territory

Toronto had moved his family south to Provo. He wasn't taking any chances. He had seen the mob mentality firsthand and was not assured that it wouldn't take over again. He returned to Salt Lake City to board up the windows of his home. He knew that if the army came, they would be hard-pressed to find any subjects to rule and face smoldering ruins. He finished his windows and was enlisted to help load up wagons with barrels of wheat. He then assisted in taking the roofs off the foundry, gun, and machine shops. They had already shipped the printing press and paper supply to Fillmore. Although nobody knew what would happen, they prepared for the worst and hoped for the best.

President Young had also asked for his help moving the pipe organ from the tabernacle. This seemed a holy task to him. Toronto and Brother Ridges carefully disassembled the pipes and loaded them into long wooden boxes.

"I built this in Australia," said Brother Ridges. "We carried it on our immigrant ship from there to California. Then overland by wagon to Utah."

"It is beautiful to look at and majestic in its sound," said Toronto remembering the accompaniment resounding through the tabernacle only last month. "It adds so much to the services."

The organ had only been in place for a year. But it had meant a great deal to the congregation, and Toronto packed each piece gently, hoping that it would be re-assembled sooner rather than later. And resume its rightful place in the tabernacle of the Lord.

JAMES
Camp Scott, Near Fort Bridger

After returning to their tent, James was hoping to calm Kane down, so he asked him about his journey to help the Latter-Day Saint people.

"You know my story, but I don't know much about yours," began James.

"Well, I got your letter but wasn't able to meet with President Buchanan until the first of November. So, as soon as I received my commission, I left my family the day after Christmas. Sailing from New York to Aspinwall, across the Isthmus of Panama, up the coast to California and then overland to Utah territory. From the moment I stepped on the ship, I was seasick and homesick. Perhaps you know something of that?"

"Yes, many were seasick on our voyage across the ocean. Luckily, I was only sick for a few days."

"Well, I have sworn to never tempt the fates again and keep myself steadily on dry land from now on."

"What was the Isthmus like?"

"Can't really recommend it, the coastal town was built on a marsh, but the newly constructed railroad across is a marvel. Unfortunately, I then had to travel by boat up the coast from

Panama to California. I have already elaborated on my aversion to sea travel."

"Why are you willing to do all this for people you barely know?"

"I decided early in life to use my talents, and I guess yes, my prosperity, to help those less fortunate. The things I learned while studying in Europe also influenced me to see humanity as an extension of myself."

"Thank you for what you have done," exclaimed James suddenly.

"I don't know that it is more than anyone would do."

"Yes, it is. You are a true Christian. You stand up for the common man who has no power, and you stand for truth. You go forward when others would go back. I have known another man like you, General Beckwith, who spent his life serving our community. Although he was never a member of our faith."

"Thank you for your kind words," said Kane, visibly touched. "You have helped me remember that fighting is not the answer here. I let my temper get the best of me. We all have to choose peace, even in the face of madness and stupidity." They laughed.

"I think I know where my path leads," James thought of the angry boy he had once been. He remembered the hostility shown to the new church members in Piedmont, Captain Austin's brutality, and Captain Eckersley's prejudice. But, most importantly, he remembered the kindness of strangers, the boatman, and Brother Walters, who had helped him and Louisa on their journey. He was thankful for Kane and others like him who stood for truth and integrity. That was who he wanted to be.

"I think your destiny lies in building something better. You will make your family proud," said Kane.

JAMES

Utah Territory, April 1858

James heard that Johnston warned Governor Cumming that he could be poisoned or disposed of in some way if he continued with his plan to accompany Kane to the city alone. Kane just laughed.

"He must be pretty desperate," was his only comment. For his part, Governor Cumming seemed convinced that Kane had in mind the best interests of all concerned.

"I do not wish to cause a war," he said, "nor any more ill feeling."

On April 5, James, Kane, Cummings, and two servants left Camp Scott with their horses, some pack mules, and a light wagon. As soon as their party entered Utah territory, they were met with an escort of Mormon militia, who welcomed Cummings as the Governor of the Territory.

The group passed through Echo Canyon at about eleven o'clock at night. James had assumed it was because the people did not want Cumming to see the breastworks and other defenses that had been erected. But instead, the entire canyon was lit by bonfires, high up on the cliffs and down below where they traveled. In addition, members of the Nauvoo Legion and some of James' militia lined their path in a salute to the new governor. The sight was quite overwhelming, with the illuminating light of the fires and the background of the snow-capped cliffs.

James passed through the radiance of the fires, his mind drawn back to other canyons, other people, and other fires lit for freedom. He was proud that he had stood with his brothers and protected their freedoms. Governor Cumming stopped his party for a moment.

"Thank you for this welcome! I am so thankful for the respect that has been shown here," he continued. "I will do all in my power to represent the territory honorably."

He turned to James, "young man, how long have you been serving with this group?"

"All winter," he said. "In camp since November."

"Well, that is a great sacrifice for you and your family," he replied. "Where are you from?"

"Salt Lake, sir," said James.

"No, where did you emigrate from?" he asked, as he had noticed the accent.

"I am a Waldensian from the northern mountains of Italy," he said proudly.

"*A votre santé le Vaudoi, vive l'emancipation,* Cheers the Waldensian, long live the emancipation," said Kane as he leaned forward in his saddle. Surprised to hear his mother language spoken in this place, James said simply.

"*Merci Frere Kane, d'avoir ecoute les cris de ce people,* Thankyou Brother Kane, for listening to the cries of this people."

As the party moved on, James looked behind him to the sheer red rock of the canyon walls. For some reason, he felt the presence of his ancestors standing forth upon the mountains, their spirits proclaiming religious liberty and tolerance for all mankind.

Toronto

Salt Lake City, May 1858

Toronto had once again been called upon to stand guard at a beloved city of his brethren. He was part of the contingent to welcome Governor Cumming to Salt Lake City. When he arrived, Brigham Young met with the Governor and gave him the records of the Supreme and District Courts for review. He had found everything in order and had given them back to Toronto to return to their proper locations.

"Mr. Toronto, can you tell me why all of these people continue to leave the city?" asked Cumming, "I can't stop them," he said in frustration. "They say it is God's will."

"They are going south," answered Toronto.

"That's what they keep saying, but where and why?"

"Well, perhaps to the Sonora valley. But as to why? They do not trust the army. They are fleeing to safety."

"How can I convince them the army will not hurt them?"

"I believe history has told them otherwise."

"I have told Johnston to wait until the peace commissioners have finished their talks."

"Well, unfortunately, we have just received word that Johnston is marching his troops toward the city."

"How could he not wait as instructed?"

"I guess you'll be able to ask him yourself, sir. Maybe he prefers the army do the negotiating."

So, Toronto found himself on a street corner of the deserted city. He had no cannon this time but had an unlit torch ready and waiting just in case. He watched as twenty-five hundred troops with their wagons and animals marched down the city's main street. From morning until night, the only signs of life were a few non-Mormons gathered on street corners. The only sound was the neigh or moo of the army's cattle and horses and the boots of the men, their drum corps keeping time.

Toronto recognized Lieutenant Colonel Philip Cook, who had commanded the Mormon Battalion in the Mexican War. He tipped his hat in front of Brigham Young's house. Johnston's personal assistant directed the band leader to play "One-Eyed Riley," a bawdy drinking song, as his group marched past Brigham Young's house.

Forty miles west of Salt Lake, they made their permanent camp at Cedar Valley, ultimately named Camp Floyd. Toronto was happy he didn't need the torch to burn down the city. This time what the people had built would last, and the temple would rise again. Blessed be the God and Rock of my salvation! He thought.

KANE

Pennsylvania, July 1858

K ane stayed long enough to be assured that the peace process was proceeding unencumbered. Then, receiving word of his father's death, he returned east with a small escort, feeling he had done all he could possibly do. A few weeks, later, he sent a letter to Brigham Young:

President Young,

I hope this letter finds you and the people in your territory experiencing renewed peace and prosperity. I thought you might be interested in this excerpt from a story published in the New York Times about the recent events in the Utah Territory:

"...Were we not guilty of a culpable oversight in confounding their persistent devotion with the insubordination of ribald license and applying to the one the same harsh treatment which the law intends for the latter alone? Was it right to send troops composed of the wildest and most rebellious men of the community, commanded by men like Harney and Johnston, to deal out fire and sword upon people whose faults even were the result of honest religious convictions? Was it right to allow Johnston to address letters to Brigham Young and, through him, to his people, couched in the tone of an implacable conqueror towards ruthless savages? Were the errors which mistaken

zeal generates ever cured by such means as these? And have bayonets ever been used against the poorest and weakest sect that ever crouched beyond a wall to pray or weep without rendering their faith more intense and investing the paltriest discomforts with the dignity of sacrifice?

...We stand on the vantage ground of higher knowledge, purer faith, and acknowledged strength. We can afford to be merciful. At all events, the world looks to us now for an example of political wisdom, such as few people nowadays are called on to display. Posterity must not have to acknowledge with shame that our indiscretion, or ignorance, or intolerance drove the population of a whole State from house and home to seek religious liberty and immunity from the presence of mercenary troops in any part of the continent to which our rule was never likely to extend."

Sincerely,
Your Friend,
Thomas L. Kane

LOUISA

Salt Lake City, Utah Territory, July
1858

Word finally came to the tent camp on the Provo bottoms, "You may return to your homes; all is well!" The United States peace commissioners had finished their meetings with the Mormon leaders, and the army was safely situated. The guards had stayed vigilant but burning their homes or fields had not been necessary.

Louisa sang and danced with others throughout the area camps. God had protected them and heard their prayers.

In August, Joseph Toronto's garden was in full bloom. Peach, plum, and apricot trees offered shade for the guests, and grapevines grew inside the walled property, grapevines filled with ripening fruit.

James and Louisa had been married in the Endowment House. Louisa loved the whispy white dress made by her mother and the delicate flowers entwined over the archway that led to the garden. Chestnuts were not available, but they had a beautifully frosted almond cake.

Many of their Waldensian friends had gathered for a reunion and a celebration. They had come through another trial of faith.

They had stood once again for freedom to worship God in this country "by the dictates of their own conscience."

Louisa looked at her countrymen with gratitude for the journey that brought her here and for all they shared.

"I can feel my parents with me today," James whispered to Louisa. She squeezed his hand. It was a blessing to know that his father and sister, Anne were on their way across the plains to join them soon. Louisa was glad to have the harsh winter and the threat of war behind them.

As the two newlyweds clasped hands and looked into each other's eyes, they saw how far they had come across not only mountains and oceans but across time and space to this moment that joined their families in a time of peace.

Their friend, Henri Chastain, stood in the midst of the garden and sang in his beautiful tenor voice:

> "O ye mountains high, where the clear blue sky
> Arches over the vales of the free.
> Where the pure breezes blow,
> And the clear streamlets flow,
> How I've longed to your bosom to flee,
> O Zion! dear Zion! land of the free,
> My own mountain home, now to thee I have come,
> All my fond hopes are centered in thee."

AUTHOR'S NOTE

Echoes on the Rock is a work of historical fiction. The religious persecutions depicted are real. In 2015, Pope Francis asked forgiveness of the Waldensians for the Roman Catholic Church's "un-Christian and even inhumane positions and actions" taken against them historically.

The Waldensians were imprisoned and killed as heretics for centuries. Some groups in Calabria, Italy to the south and other areas were annihilated. The Pope made his plea when he visited a temple in Piedmont. His father and grandfather were born in the Turin area.

In 1976, Missouri's Governor Christopher S. Bond revoked the unconstitutional extermination order issued against the Mormons by Governor Lilburn W. Boggs in 1838. This meant a great deal to the Latter-Day Saints whose ancestors experienced persecution. In 2004, the Illinois House of Representatives unanimously passed a resolution of regret for the forced expulsion of the Mormons from Nauvoo in 1846. The resolution blames "biases and prejudices of a less enlightened age."

RESEARCH SOURCES

Baird, Robert, D.D. *Sketches of Protestantism in Italy Past and Present.* London: Wm. Collins, S. Frederick Street, Glasgow; Paternoster Row, 1848. (Google books)

Beus, H. Lynn, Gunnell, Charlotte, *Whence & Whither, Origins and Descendants of Michael & Marianne Beus.* Self-published, 1984.

Cane, Robert L. Jr., *A Biography of Lot Smith (1830-1892).* Utah State University, 1970. All Graduate Theses and Dissertations. 6232. https://digitalcommons.usu.edu/etd/6232|

Faber, George Stanley. *An Inquiry into the History and Theology of the Ancient Vallenses and Albigenses.* 1838.

Foxe, John. *Foxe's Book of Martyrs, (or a History of the Lives, sufferings, and triumphant deaths of the primitive Protestant Martyrs).* John Day, 1563. (The Project Gutenberg ebook)

Gallenga, Antonio. *History of Piedmont, Vol 3.* London: Chapman and Hall, 1855. (Google books)

Gilly, William Stephen. *Narrative of an Excursion to the Mountains of the Piemont in the year 1823.* London: C. & J. Rivington, 1826.

Johnston, William Preston. *The Life of General Albert Sidney Johnston*. New York: D. Appleton & Co., 1878.

Kane, Thomas *L. The Mormons: a discourse delivered before the Historical Society of Pennsylvania, March 26, 1850*. Philadelphia: King & Baird printers, 1850.

Kane, T.L. *The private papers and diary of Thomas Leiper Kane: a friend of the Mormons*. San Francisco: Gelbert Lilienthal, 1937.

Lea, Henry Charles. *A History of the Inquisition of the Middle Ages. Vol. II*. New York: Harper & Brothers, 1888 (Google ebook)

Morland, Samuel. *The History of the Evangelical Churches of the Valleys of the Piemont. London:* 1658.

Meille, J.P. *General Beckwith his life and labours among the Waldenses of Piedmont*. London: T. Nelson & Sons, 1873.

Muston, Alexis. *The Israel of the Alps: A History of the Persecutions of the Waldenses*. W. Hazlitt, London: 1852.

Oakley, John. journal from Edmund Ellsworth handcart company-1856

Smith, Lot, *The Echo Canyon War*. The Contributor, Salt Lake City, 1882, Oct., Vol.4, pg. 27-29; Nov., pg. 47-50; 1883, Feb., Vol 4, pg. 167-169.

Snow, Lorenzo. *Voice of Joseph*. Malta: 1852.

Snow, Lorenzo. *The Italian Mission*. London: W. Aubrey, 1851.

Tullidge, Edward William. *History of Salt Lake City*. Salt Lake City, Utah: Star Printing Co., 1886.

Visconti, Joseph, Jr. *The Waldensian Way to God*. United States: Xulon Press, 2003.

Worsfold, William B. *The Valley of Light, studies with pen &* *pencil in the Vaudois Valleys.* New York: The Macmillan Co., 1899.

Wylie, James Aitken. *Wanderings and Musings in the Valleys of the Waldenses.* London: James Nisbet & Co., 1858.

Various pioneer journals

ACKNOWLEDGMENTS

Thanks to my early readers, Hayley Takeuchi, Tom Dearden, Natalie Delano, Lavinia Anderl, and Emily Abel. Your input was so helpful and necessary to improve the story. Thanks also to my editors, Courtney Stevenson and Jackie Cangro. You pushed me in sometimes uncomfortable ways, which improved the manuscript and my writing.

Thanks to my parents, Jerry and Carma Jacobs, who gave me strong roots to help me spread my wings. Special thanks to my husband, Tom, who never let me give up on this story. And read many, many rewrites. I couldn't have finished without you.

Thanks to Ruta Sepetys, who first inspired me to write the story of my ancestors. And finally, to my Waldensian ancestors who have been with me throughout my life and through this writing process. I am so happy to have the opportunity to tell your stories.

JANA J. DEARDEN

Jana Dearden received her BS in Journalism from Weber State University. *Echoes on the Rock* is her debut YA historical fiction novel. Before shifting to writing full-time, Jana was a high school teacher, community theater director, executive secretary, dance teacher, and journalist.

As a reporter, she covered subjects from government meetings to a series on historic homes. Throughout her life, she has been inspired by her Waldensian ancestors. She is passionate about family history and telling forgotten stories that inform the present.

Jana lives in the Mountain West, where she writes, reads, and dances around the house. Visit her online at www.janajdearden.com and sign up to receive emails on her new projects.